It Won't Go Away

It Won't Go Away
The Feeling

Samina Najmah

authorHOUSE

AuthorHouse™ LLC
1663 Liberty Drive
Bloomington, IN 47403
www.authorhouse.com
Phone: 1-800-839-8640

The Feeling, IT Won't Go Away is a work of fiction. Names, characters, places, and incidents either are the product of the author's imagination or are used factiously. Any resemblance to actual persons, living or dead, events, or locales are entirely coincidental.

© 2013 Najmah Al-Ameen Publishing. All rights reserved.

No part of this book may be reproduced, stored in a retrieval system, or transmitted by any means without the written permission of the author.

Published by AuthorHouse 11/23/2013

ISBN: 978-1-4918-3066-6 (sc)
ISBN: 978-1-4918-3067-3 (hc)
ISBN: 978-1-4918-3068-0 (e)

Library of Congress Control Number: 2013919584

Any people depicted in stock imagery provided by Thinkstock are models, and such images are being used for illustrative purposes only. Certain stock imagery © Thinkstock.

This book is printed on acid-free paper.

Because of the dynamic nature of the Internet, any web addresses or links contained in this book may have changed since publication and may no longer be valid. The views expressed in this work are solely those of the author and do not necessarily reflect the views of the publisher, and the publisher hereby disclaims any responsibility for them.

Contents

Acknowledgements ix
Prologue xi

My Heart

Chapter One 3
Chapter Two 12
Chapter Three 18
Chapter Four 26
Chapter Five 34
Chapter Six 43
Chapter Seven 51
Chapter Eight 60

Heart Murmur

Chapter Nine 71
Chapter Ten 79
Chapter Eleven 88
Chapter Twelve 98
Chapter Thirteen 109

Heart Spasm

Chapter Fourteen...121
Chapter Fifteen..129
Chapter Sixteen...137
Chapter Seventeen..148
Chapter Eighteen...156
Chapter Nineteen..166

Heart Attack

Chapter Twenty...177
Chapter Twenty-One..187
Chapter Twenty-Two..194
Chapter Twenty-Three...203
Chapter Twenty-Four...212

Heart Failure

Chapter Twenty-Five..229
Chapter Twenty-Six..238
Chapter Twenty-Seven...247
Chapter Twenty-Eight..256
Chapter Twenty-Nine...266
Chapter Thirty...275
Chapter Thirty-One..284

Qalbee..293
Epilogue..297
Qalbee, The Feeling..299

Dedication

To the memory of my beloved grandmother Irene Narzella Nichols-Hamilton; and to the memory of Eleanor Valencia.

Acknowledgements

To my hearts and soul, my children Ilyaas and Safiyyah, you give me air to breath—it is because of you that I live. Thank you for loving me no matter what—you are the loves of my life.

To another heart of mine, my mother Safiyyah Shabazz, thank you for your cherished ideas and the many hours you spent striving with me. Your self-sacrificing acts are the epitome of an unconditional love only a mother of your stature possess. I am grateful to be your daughter.

To my CraigyPoo, Mr. Jackson, thank you for your support in my many endeavors. I am forever grateful for all that you contribute to my success.

To Ilyasah thank you, for you gave me the sense of buoyancy to believe.

To Klassy Karyn, thank you for being a reliable friend by taking out the time to read and critique my literature in spite of your laborious schedule—I appreciate you.

To Nakitha, thank you for being an ear for hours when I needed encouraging; and for being my positive cheerleader.

To TaRhonda White, a fellow author, thank you for all of your wonderful advice; and for being zealous to assist.

To Beth A. Carpenter, my editor, thank you for your expertise, patience, and humor. You made this an informative experience for me.

To Thomas Mosley of Art of Mind Productions, I'm honored to have been captured by such an amazing creative eye. Thank you so very much for taking out the time to shoot in short notice.

To my Father, Saheeb, You are by far one of the brainiest people I know; and you being a writer inspire me. Thank you for endowing your knowledge, input, and positivity.

. . . And to my sweet, smart, and serene husband, Samuel—I fell in love with your patience and it paid off for the both of us during this process! Your tolerance is greatly appreciated—you've assisted me tremendously. Thank you for loving me—I love you . . . nice guy!☺

Prologue

Ever since I pulled out of my parents driveway twelve hours ago I have been in such a dream state, thinking about how much time has passed since my heart murmur; and the first heart spasm . . . then there was the heart attack, and how I have overcame them all . . . and now, here again on the break of tears, due to an additional heart failure. I refuse to let a tear conquer Chanelle's encouraging words about how proud she is of me for, after all these years, finally standing up to *my heart* and using my brain—seeing that if my heart stops I may still have a chance to live but if my brain stops, I'm dead for sure.

My fingers twitch as I grip the steering wheel and my body trembles with anxiety as I cruise down US Interstate-20 East headed to Atlanta, Georgia in search of *a new heart*. I glance at the gas gauge remembering that I decided not to exit 49 Fulton Industrial Blvd 10 miles back, and now I am on empty. To my right I see EXIT 56A McDaniel St, *my* exit.

As I pump gas into my tank, I hear my phone vibrate through the crack in the back seat window. My focus changes when I hear the number one question on the toddler charts, "Are we there yet?" I search through the window to find his big brown beautiful eyes and I respond with, "Just 29 more miles to our destination," and then I smile! Just as his frown mirrors my smile, reflecting an obliging smirk, I glance away from his impatient eyes. Through my peripheral I witness what caused the beat of my heart to stop—I refuse to believe what my eyes just witnessed. My smile now reflects the innocents of the little boy's initial frown, and in this very instance, I wished that I had never complained that . . . "*It won't go away.*"

My Heart

Chapter One

From my bedroom window, I instinctively watch the leaves of the flourished tree in my neighbor's back yard waltz softly in the balmy wind. My dustless blinds are pulled up as far as they can as my sheer Mickey Mouse curtain hangs in a tied loose knot. From up here the maple tree appears the size of the jade grapes I am eating when I raise them at eye level.

It is such a pleasant evening here in Edmond, Oklahoma. The sun shines through my bedroom window for not too much longer—the day is half gone and night will soon be present. I lie here comfy, wearing my undersize white t-shirt that rises to my abdomen, my stomach pressed into the warmth of my fluffy Mickey Mouse comforter heated by the sun's gleam. I barely make an imprint into my twin size mattress I'm so thin. My knees are bent, body in a ninety degree angle, bare feet dangling in the air causing the bottoms of my yellow nylon sweat pants to fall to my knees revealing my long thin calves. I lay propped up on one boney elbow that's buried into Mickey's black nose with the other pressed into his black ears; and my house phone to mine.

Through my peripheral, the screensaver of my Hewlett-Packard computer flashes to life. It sits diagonally to the right corner of my bed, across from me on my spotless mahogany computer desk. I see a picture of my mother standing in my father's arms and my neck in my brother Sebastian's arms in a headlock. We are standing in my grandfather's icy, wet yard on my 18th birthday a few months ago.

My brother and I are two peas in a pod! It was his fame at school that got me through freshman year. He is known all over East Academy High by the faculty and staff for being a prodigy child—popular with the jocks for tutoring them regularly; notorious with the girls for his easy going and gentleman like character; and he's exceptionally attractive, although he is a social loner—opposite of me. My parents look so happy together in that picture! I'm happy to have been able to snap it because it's uncertain when I'd get another opportunity to take another one. My father is always out of town on business—like he is right now. Since my mother retired from her acting career a few years ago, she does her own share of autonomous traveling as well. Though my mother is physically distant from us the majority of the time, she and I are incredibly close emotionally. She raised my brother and me strictly in morality, so I listen closely and behave accordingly; and because she utilizes an authoritative parenting style by exhibiting trust in my brother and me, I practice what she teaches. I am cautious not to defy her trust, and hold on to every word she says about the real world . . . *I have a vast amount of respect for my mother.*

Every day that I live, since I can remember, my approach to life has been to plan ahead. I'm such a perfectionist that decision making is a laborious process for me. Currently, I have been preparing for my future by studying hard, determined to get into college. I am a junior in high school and *do not want any* financial assistance from my parents when I leave home to attend college. I plan to be a huge success *all on my own*! Although I am undecided, I have a year to settle on attending Spellman University in Hot 'Lanta, Black Mecca, the Big Peach—also known as Atlanta, Georgia—or another historically black college that dwells in Sugarland, Texas, Texas View University. TVU is known for their sensational band, exceptional law school, and prestigious pharmacy school, though I'd attend their psychology program and there's nothing significant to say about *that* program.

I do much writing, typing, and listening to music, therefore, my Hallmark journal, Sony CD and cassette player, and HP computer are my best friends. And since they are all housed in my room, I love being in here! My room is my safe haven, my refuge! It's the one place I know for sure will remain clean, smell fresh, and be serene. The only other place that over thralls me is being up on the roof of my parent's house—my cloud nine!

Through the polished black corded Panasonic phone placed against my earlobe, I hear a familiar beep echo in my ear, redirecting my attention to the conversation at hand. I glance down to view the caller ID but instead I see my reflection in the base of my land line phone. One eye stares back at me, through the smooth surface as my other eye subsists under my long swooped bangs. They fall to my bra strap along with the rest of my straight lengthy black hair. My giddy face carries a bright smile, matching my complexion, as my vivacious individuality seeps through the phone while I talk "boys" with my best friend, Chanelle!

About a week ago I was leaving a study group to prepare for finals when I ran into this dude, Bill, who I had a crush on my entire freshman year. At that time he was a junior, played varsity, and was a popular jock—and I was the last female he'd take a second glance at. By my sophomore year I met Caleb, and after talking to him every day for two weeks, I was his girlfriend. Bill was no longer a thought in my mind. Caleb and I were great together that whole school year up until the week of his prom. Short story is both Bill and Caleb took girls other than me to their senior prom, leaving me all alone, by myself, sad at home and embarrassed. I never expected Bill to invite me because I never existed in his world anyway. That's why I was so shocked when he gave me his pager number last week and told me, "Don't be a stranger." I paged him yesterday and we agreed that he and a friend would come here on this Friday and accompany me and one on my friends.

As for Caleb, he initially told me he did not think he was going to his senior prom, but Chanelle came to me with a picture of him and his ex-girlfriend, Sheila, dressed *really nice* sitting at a fancy table eating their fine finger foods. I was devastated. Sheila was so desperately happy to have been there with Caleb that she was cheesing like she was marketing for Kool-Aid packages; and Caleb, well . . . he looked rather constipated, seemingly depressed.

Sheila and Caleb began dating their freshman year at Marshall High School. When Caleb turned sixteen he attended the Texas Ranger's major league tryout camp to get signed for their minor league team but was not successful. Marshall High's baseball team sucked so Caleb transferred to East Academy High his junior year to get more exposure and had hopes on getting a scholarship, which he did. Caleb attended another major league tryout camp and was signed the summer after he graduated high school. Now he plays on a minor league team. Well, before he transferred from Marshall High, he and Sheila agreed that they'd take each other to their senior prom. But with Caleb, being known for his "fast pitch", smooth talking girls, Sheila grew possessive over him and did not trust him at a different school. That led to their breakup—two months before he and I met my sophomore year. After Chanelle presented me with the photo of them at the prom together, I confronted him and his explanation was, "I promised her"—that led to *our* initial break up.

Chanelle was able to snap the picture because she was at the prom, invited by senior football hunk Trecy, a total jerk. Freshman year, Chanelle was a tom boy like me, only I was identified as "Sebastian's little sister" and she was recognized as, "*her* friend". By sophomore year, Chanelle completely transformed to a glamour girl, wearing adult clothing with daily accessories and a face full of makeup. Chanelle is medium thick framed with coco brown skin and long thick hair to the middle of her back—and that's no weave. I, on the other hand, am a straight tomboy. My favorite sport is baseball. At school I play on the softball team, am the only girl on the baseball team, and am a color guard in the band. Chanelle and I are both water girls for the football team, but, of course, for different reasons. She likes watching the sweaty boys in their tight gear as we throw the footballs on the field. She enjoys being close enough to smell their stench when squirting water in their craving mouths. I actually just enjoy football—I love the Buffalo Bills and the Miami Dolphins!

I snap out of my reverie when I hear Chanelle interrogating me about what Bill's friend looks like. She goes on telling me how she is having reservations since she does not do the whole "blind date" thing and is having qualms because the date is tomorrow. She assures me that she is only doing it because I'm her best friend and she is looking forward to me owing her a huge favor.

CHANELLE AND I are in the crowded school cafeteria at the round table alone. She gathers the last bit of her burger into her mouth when she points with her head and eyes at Caleb walking through the room.

Dang, why is he here, I think to myself. I have forgiven him after the whole prom incident, began dating him again, and was back in a relationship with him before I knew it. But these last few months have been complicated. He and I have not stopped complete communication and we *have* seen each other a couple of times since Sheila pulled those vengeful stunts after being informed that we were back together, but I'm done with all of these off-and-on breakups. This relationship has slowed down abundantly. *Why does he think he can just pop up here, at my school, unannounced?* He *is* always telling me how much "I'm the one" and "how great we are together" and I *would* dismiss those comments passively, *but only* because I do not want to hurt his feelings. It's not because I still have some self fulfilling thought that we will marry, have children, and live happily ever after. I am past that.

I slowly put my head down and raise my hand up to my temple to resist eye contact. I reach for a French fry trying to blend in with the rest of the glutinous teens when Caleb spots Chanelle's glamour and heads our way. He is about 5'11", with a medium build, baseball player physique, and dark skin with strong facial features. He has perfectly shaped lips that compels images of all the things those lips could do to you every time you gaze at them. He wears a nerdy preppie boy style similar to Mase, the rapper, bearing dark blue jeans, a plaid button up, dark blue tie and tan blazer—a very handsome fellow.

"You coming with me out to eat?" Caleb yells over the crowd with all confidence as if his question was rhetorical and with not so much as a "Hi" or an acknowledgment of Chanelle sitting right next to me.

I say to him as composed as possible not to display exasperation, "Sorry I can't. I have three more finals." *And your attempt of quixotic surprise is a stalkerish gesture—not romantic at all, and is a bit annoying.*

Caleb leans in so close that I can smell his Curve cologne and he rests his left hand on the table then murmurs in my ear, "Can we talk tonight?" There is more shock in his tone than I had at his poor endeavor to surprise me.

I am usually so bubbly and agreeable, but I have a mission tonight that my thoughts are absorbed in, and my mind needs *NO* extra clout.

I inhale a whiff of Curve, grilled beef, and condiments as I gasp, "About what?" I sigh.

"What's been going on with us."

"We can talk, but I really don't see what more there is to talk about on that subject." I stand up from the table. "We broke up a couple of months ago, we have not spoken in nearly two weeks, and you show up here with this?" I walk off astonished by his unwarranted actions almost bumping into another student carrying a tray.

"Excuse me!"

Caleb follows close behind as I walk to dump my tray. I approach the sloppy overflow of garbage in the bins noticing that the cafeteria has cleared out incredibly fast leaving only a few insubordinate students gossiping.

"The way we are now, as friends, is cool . . . right?" I pat his shoulder. "Later!" I walk towards Chanelle as she waits at the exit door.

He stands there damaged. As I walk towards the door I see girls run up to him recognizing that he is minor league player "Caleb, pitch a dick" and hear others whisper about how "fine" he is.

I SIT IN CLASS staring at my watch, anxious for the bell to ring. After lunch I had two finals, both advanced placement classes, and both I finished before the bell rang. I am so happy that it is the last day of school! Tonight I plan to celebrate like the singer Prince, and party 'cause it's 1999. I have one more year until I graduate! Chanelle and I made plans to meet up in the parking lot after school to discuss tonight's arrangement. All week it has been nice outdoors and today seems especially beautiful. The school grass is emerald, the wind blows softly, and the sun shines bright—synergistically rising my adrenaline—combined with thoughts of tonight. My plans are to ask Sebastian to use his car to pick up Chanelle around six. That gives me time to straighten up the rest of the house since my brother is a typical bachelor like dude, and I'm Cinderella. I am a borderline obsessive compulsive personality so I am engorged with anxiety when he leaves the place a mess.

I'll ask Chanelle if she wants to slumber over for the weekend. It won't be the first. During summer breaks we practically live together. Sometimes she slumbers at my house for months at a time and vice versa. Chanelle and I met in the fifth grade when our science teacher partnered us up for a science project—Which Detergent Cleans the Best. I remember having to get dropped off at her house because her father did not have a car at the time. I'd get there, barge past Mr. Evans, run through their house, straight to their back yard, and Chanelle would be back there waiting on me with her besmirched t-shirt covered in locust shells! I thought that was the coolest thing because my brother and I would do the same thing to gross our mother out. Chanelle and I would be knee deep in the mud dirtying up old shirts we cut up to test our hypothesis. We'd be so dirty that we could have actually used the clothes we had on as variables. We had so much fun doing that project that I don't think either of us cared that we didn't get the first place ribbon. As we worked on that science project together we learned we had so much in common that it was like looking in the mirror. I knew she'd grow to be like a sister to me and we've been partnered up since. Every time I smell the fresh scent of Tide I go back to those days.

Chapter Two

I BLASTED THE COMPLETE *Art of War* double disk CD by Bone Thugs & Harmony as I dusted, polished, and Pin-Soled the entire house clean enough to cause a hoarder to regress. Sebastian gets a kick out of me when I listen to raw and ratchet music like Too Short and Brother Lynch Hung since I do not curse, get high, or drink alcoholic beverages. Rap and Hip Hop is he and his crew's genre of choice and since we are so close and I am always around them I've been influenced to like some of it even though I'm more into jazz, pop, and rock.

Now Chanelle and I listen to Snoop Dogg's *Dogg Pound* cassette preparing for our company. Chanelle is bare foot in her tight boot cut blue jeans and grey lace camisole. She is standing in the double doors of my walk in closet trying to decide if she should change out of her size medium top into my size small tank top to give her breasts the impression of an enhancement. I wear a long white Indian skirt and my black and white fitted MLB Yankee fan t-shirt. In my bronze antique oval wall mirror hanging on the wall between the entry door to my room and the double doors of my closet I stare at my bright yellow tone, inarched eye brows, and two evenly parted ponytails placed above my ears hanging a little past my shoulders. The air is muddled with the smell of tart coconut, bitter avocado, and sweet tea tree oil as it invades the aroma of my freshly wiped down clean lemon scent. It took me a half hour to get them even. I was going for Da'Brat's afro puffs, only hers are curly balls of shine and mine are long pony-tails that fall like rabbit ears. I was hoping to get my hair braided up before tonight but had already made a previous appointment last week preparing myself for the summer and when I called to reschedule a few days ago after talking to Bill, it was too late to change it. Since I do not get perms, wearing my hair down in my regular Aaliyah swoop has wore out for the month in this humid weather. So ponytails it is. My jaws are red and my face is numb from having the same smile resting on my face since I made it home from school.

"So, what am I lookin like?" I turn away from the mirror looking at Chanelle.

"You look cute, Libiya . . . like yourself!"

She answers with a smile and nods, basically meaning I look like the bohemian tomboy that I am.

IT IS TEN IN THE EVENING. Chanelle and I hear car doors slam outside. We rush down. Bill paged me letting me know he'd be an hour late, so Chanelle and I have been accentuating our hearing for the past hour.

Chanelle stands behind me as I open the door before our company could knock on it. Bill wears a Bulls jersey and is laughing as he walks in.

"What's up?" he mutters as he looks down and continues to laugh. A fellow wearing a Pistons jersey follows in after him.

"This Craig."

Both Bill and Craig are basketball player tall, brown complexioned, acceptable looking fellows. They are both chortling. Chanelle begins to escort the two guys to my room. As I attempt to close the door, a third fellow appears.

"Oh, and this Qalbee . . . Q," Bill adds attempting to suppress his laughter.

I stand planted in front of the door. The sound of my music seemed to decrease, Bill and Craig's awful laughter seemed to cease, and I no longer smell my recently scrubbed down Pine-Sol smelling home. My senses grew selective to the smell of freshly clean epidermis and musk deodorant. Standing a little above average height he wears brown Timberland boots, loose sweats, and a brown pullover. My eyes are planted as he pulls off the hood of his pullover, uncovering perfectly Photo Shopped groomed hair waves, and creamy brown skin. His clean, alluring face carries a chromatic smile, displaying a slight crook in his front right tooth. His east coast style depicts serious swagger causing an erupting feeling in my vulva that I have never in my life felt before . . . *orgasmic?*

I vaguely hear Bill state something, though I'm in trance, enchanted by Qalbee's presents.

"Libi . . . Bill's asking for something to drink," Chanelle vigorously mutters.

"No. YES! No! I'm fine, thanks," I finally respond not needing any more fluid than what I already have flowing from my mouth and pouring from my vulva lubricating my panties—aroused by beauty. Inadvertently preventing Qalbee from entering, I stand here immovable, dazed, smiling at him while wiping the drool from my chin; and abstractedly embarrassed that I'm salivating like a puppy in heat.

"Come in . . . sorry!"

A FEW HOURS HAS PASSED and we are all in my room being young, laughing a great deal, talking about sports, *The Martin Show, Living Single* and multiple movies. Bill and I are sitting on the edge of my bed and his arm is placed around my shoulders. All night he has been making jokes and I have been surprisingly annoyed by him. All I can do is think about how and why I'm having these aroused feelings of lust for this guy I'm not even married to . . . or don't even know . . . and have never even seen before *in my life*. I glance at Chanelle and she seems to be enjoying herself and her box of Cheese Its. She is sitting at my single pedestal computer desk, with her back turned to the computer facing the rest of us and tickled by Bill and Craig's humor. The entire night Craig constantly gets up rambling through my things—in my walk-in closet, messing around in three of the six drawers of my cherry oak double dresser, and disorganizing books on my four shelf mahogany wood bookcase that my CD and cassette player rests on. Lord knows my nerves are bad with all the rearranging he's doing to my things, provoking my obsessive compulsive personality. He has no consciousness of boundaries *and* he cannot seem to keep still like he's some attention deficit hyperactivity disorder patient. *HUH!*

Then there is Qalbee! He is sitting, back against the other three drawers of my dresser across from my cherry oak wood bed frame with his legs stretched out, ankles crossed, Timberlands moving along with the beat of "Regulators" by Warren G, looking through my book of music selections . . . so captivating! . . . *AND COMPOSED!*

IT WAS GETTING LATE and Bill finally seemed to get the hint that I felt no connection between us. I believe I hid my interest in Qalbee well enough. Bill never questioned me and Qalbee never pursued. Maybe he's just not that into me? Well, they left about an hour ago and as soon as they walked out the door, Chanelle jumped in the shower and got into her pajamas. I showered after her and I am now trying to manage this hair into one descent looking ponytail. Chanelle lays flat on her back in my bed with one hand resting on her stomach and the other available to eat the Cheese Its she's been snacking on all night.

"That was the worst! I had a terrible time with Bill."

"Really? I had a good time! They were funny but neither were my type," Chanelle proclaims disenchanted.

"Qalbee!" I squeal than glance over at Chanelle. "That Qalbee dude was incredibly cute!" I say excitedly.

Chanelle turns her head towards me flaunting an inquiring expression.

"How am I going to pull off seeing him again?" my mind races. "I need his number," I say looking directly into Chanelle's eyes probing for her encouragement.

She has a solemn look on her face, "I don't think you can do that. You are talking to his . . ."

"I can just ask Bill," I interrupt.

Chanelle sits up "Ah, uhm uhm, no you can't."

IN MY ROOM I lay across my bed on my stomach, knees bent with my bare feet dangling in the air writing in my journal. It was a couple of days ago when Bill and his friends were over and I cannot seem to get that Qalbee guy out of my head. Chanelle convinced me that it is inappropriate to ask a dude you attempted to date for his friend's number to *attempt* to date him. She also attempted to convince me to accompany her and Trecy to the summer carnival tonight but I declined so that I can catch up on my writing. Besides she knows I don't do Trecy.

I write plays, children stories, and poems when I'm not talking on the phone, being Cinderella, or doing some extracurricular activity at school. Now that school is out I have lots of spare time. Writing is a therapy for me and lying here listening to music sooths me. I can lay here for hours at a time writing only today I'm stumped; so I finish reading the book *Beloved* by Toni Morrison.

I FEEL SORENESS in my side and I hear a faint ringing that wakes me. My room is dark but I see the faded light coming from under my door that attempts to lighten my room. It must be about ten or eleven at night. I look up at my book, journal and pen in front of me. I realize that I'm lying on my land line phone and it's where the soreness and ringing comes from.

"Yes?" I grumble answering the phone.

"Come pick me up."

"What? Man you know how my brother is about his car," I rollover straight on my back, place my thumb and index finger over my left eye brow, and massage my thoughts.

"Well, Craig and Q will be at your house tonight real soon. Have fun entertaining them on your own!" Chanelle laughs nonchalantly.

I hear a dial tone.

Chapter Three

"Wait! What?"

I quickly sit up on the edge of my bed seeing my weak shadow in the faint-light trail after me as I anxiously dial Chanelle's number. *She knows she's wrong for that!*

"Yeah," Chanelle mutters smugly as if she is thinking *"yeah, that's what I thought."*

I nervously write Q-a-l-b-e-e, draw a heart around it, and write 'May 1999' under it, then hurriedly seal the lock on my journal.

"Start talking," I demand with bass in my voice. I rest my right arm on my right thigh and intensely lean forward like a bench rider engaged in his teammate sprinting less than five yards from crossing the touchdown line in the final seconds of the game.

I animatedly interrogate, "Okay what happened? Tell me! What did you do?" My heart pumps fast.

"Okay, so you know Trecy and I went to the carnival. I was looking *real nice* with my long burnt orange tight fitted, sleeveless, Old Navy hooded shirt that I wear as a dress. You know, the one . . . ?"

"Yes, yes, keep going!" I cut her off, rushing her to get on with the story, my heart still pounding.

"So, I'm looking hot in my Clark boots and my brown accessories to match, and girl, why Trecy was clashing with his tall yellow bones . . . dressed in some flea market plaid button down," she chuckled.

I hear discomfiture in her mirth. Not being able to resist, I take advantage and take a slur at Trecy. "Along with that bad attitude he has towards females." *Such a shame.* "But then get extra cowardly when a guy steps to him," I sigh and shake my head.

"Girl, stop!"

Chanelle resumes with her story—*hopefully to the point that is essential to my ears.* "Here I am carrying a funnel cake, hotdog, cotton candy, and lemonade when I spot out Craig from a distance."

And what was Trecy carrying? Such a loser, my bias thoughts emerge.

"I tell Trecy to go get me a caramel apple. When he walks off Craig walks up to me smiling then he pops me on my ass."

"Whuuut?" I'm flabbergasted.

"Yea!" She sounds flattered! "He goes into how he sees that I'm there with my bitch 'cause I have him buying me all this shit, than calls him a chump . . ."

I knew I liked Craig, I smile!

". . . I tell him he's a buster and to get out of my face cause he don't know me like that. So then he gets closer up on me and asks me for my number, calling me 'Chell' and telling me 'don't act like that', and runs his fingers through my hair. Then he pulled this thing where he stared real deep into my eyes like I was gonna fall for that. Girl, I gently pushed his stomach feeling his muscular abs and had to *quickly back up!*" she exclaim with nervous laughter. "So what, you like him now?" I question.

"Na," she exclaims.

"Um hum." I don't believe that one bit. The way she expressed that part of the story was like she was right back there reliving the moment.

"But, I did give up my number . . ."

Um hum, like I thought.

". . . right before Trecy walked up looking at Craig up and down. Once Craig walked off I just told Trecy that he was somebody you know."

"Really?" I say indifferent. Like I thought, she never got to the point that's most vital to my hearing. *How do Qalbee and I fit into all this?* I sit hunched over in despair. I don't even bother to question. I don't have the time to hear another drawn out story . . . *huh*! I began putting on my shoes, wondering how I'm going to pull off bumming Sebastian's car on such short notice.

"I'll call you back." I hang up and quickly toss the phone down. If I were a cartoon character, you'd see a light bulb suspended above my head my mind is thinking so critically. I pop up and stand to my feet. *I have some bribing to do*! I'll give Sebastian a few females' numbers, tell him I'll buy him that Mensa word puzzle book for the gifted that he wants, and throw in a Nacho Bell Grande from Taco Bell, and he'll be happy to let me use his car to pick up Chanelle!

CHANELLE HAS ON WHITE Daisy Duke shorts and a brown Polo baby t-shirt looking like Serena Williams sitting on my plush brick red cut pile carpet stretching like she is preparing for a tennis match. She does not realize it, but subconsciously she's toning up to look good for this Craig fellow because she likes him. I've known her for almost seven years. I know her more than she knows herself and probably vice versa.

This time I'm going for round away girl, which is my everyday wardrobe. I wear my green cropped fitted t-shirt and yellow nylon sweats that I call swishes because they whoosh as you move in them. I figure I'd go less girly and more comfortable. I sit at my desk typing a love poem onto my computer, copying it from my journal. I save everything on my hard drive to be certain it's protected. Besides, my penmanship *sucks*.

"How you think you like this dude already?" Chanelle asks perplexed while sliding my Mickey curtains over to one side. She then pulls the string causing the blinds to rise and the bright street light from the next street over, that faces my backyard, beams through.

"It just happened when I first saw him." That's all I could give because that's all I have. I cannot explain it myself.

"Ah, please don't give me that love at first sight CRAP." Chanelle raises the window and a balmy trace of wind drifts across the room. It sends a warm sensation over my exposed arms and stomach, attempting to cause my goose bumps to retreat. Chanelle plops stomach first onto my bed and I wish it was me thawing out by the window.

"No!" I turn from my computer towards her. "Now you know I'm not into all that. He was just . . ." I stress ". . . *soo funny!*" I turn back to my computer giggling, thinking of how he joked when he was here!

Qalbee did not say much, but when he did it was worth hearing. If it was not comical, it was logical. His voice alone is the sound of rapture—like God's voice in the movies. He's the type that speaks less and listen more, very intelligent, conversant, and clever. I was amazed at how quick his brain formed ripostes and how judicious he was not to offend anyone. He has poise in every action! I was so allured by his reserve mannerism. It was not impetuous to prove his point. People say that "you have to know when to choose your battles" and he definitely has that wit.

A smile stretches my face. "I can just listen to him crack funnies all night!"

"And what about Caleb? You two have been together 2 years?"

I turn away from my computer to give Chanelle eye contact. Agitated, I snap "What about him?" My face grimaces. "He's so serious all the time. Plus, he messed up by not being able to tame that ex," I say resentful.

Chanelle lowers her tone "Yeah, you right." Her tone elevates as she rambles "There's no reason why you had to endure an ex-girl friend following you and your boyfriend around to the movies, for dinner, studying, baseball games . . ."

"The official breaker," I interrupt to point *that* out and to conclude *that* subject.

Caleb's baseball team won their first game of the season and it was the first minor league game he had ever played in, so we made plans to go celebrate. Late after the game he and I where backing out of the Chickasaw Bricktown Stadium parking lot when Sheila pulled up behind us blocking us in. She jumps out of her black Nissan Maxima with smolder in her eyes and gloom on her face threatening me, calling me every name in the book and several she plainly made up on the spot like some neologist. Caleb and I sit, observing her disgraceful conduct through our side view mirrors when Caleb unexpectedly jumps out of his Blue Honda Accord to calm her down. *Or so I thought.* Chanelle was in Trecy's red Ford Mustang parked next to us witnessing the whole thing, so she jumps out threatening Sheila, taking up for me. As I sat in the car listening and observing all the pandemonium, I thought *I'm a lover not a fighter . . . but she has gone too far*. So I jump out charging at Sheila only to find my boyfriend, that I forgave and took back, sitting on the ground holding his ex-girlfriend, that he took to his only prom, followed us everywhere, and that has caused nothing but turmoil in our relationship, in his arms, consoling her. I felt like I was shrinking and they were emerging. Imaginary walls appeared, causing me to feel claustrophobic. I stood there hyperventilating and at that point I realized that I am too beautiful, smart, and young to have had to experience her stalking and threatening me, him doubting and being unsure of his emotions for me, and definitely not having my peace broken by feeling the urge to brawl with some broken girl over some boring boy. Chanelle stood behind me, reached her hands out, embraced my shoulders to comfort me, and practically drug me to Trecy's Mustang. They dropped me off at home. I cried in my mother's arms and she talked me back to reality, basically setting me straight about not crying over some boy. So for the past few months me and Caleb's relationship has been stagnant.

"I think they're here." Chanelle interrupts my bitter thoughts, her eyes bugged. Quickly she rolls to the right onto her back close to the window. She lifts her right leg over my window mantel, face weary, ducking like she's on an undercover Army exposition. She might as well have a stripe of war paint under her eyes, and then all she'd need is a gun. I stand and take a step towards the window. Her cheeks are puffed full of air and her mouth is wrinkled from strain. I hover from a distance, mystified, as she climbs down the first four steps of my ladder that I principally use to go up on Cloud Nine. I stand, eyes bulging, puzzled for a moment wondering . . . *I'm sure she did not think I was going to have them come up through the window?* I leap on my bed, lean over, and close the window. I hop off the bed and head for the door. I lightly gallop down the spiral stairs plush with pearl white carpet, past the black marble table set for eight in the dining area, through the contemporary festooned living room, between the 56' inch Panasonic HDTV and pearl white curved leather Coaster furniture, to the front door and open it just as I hear someone commencing to knock. Qalbee and Craig have Billy Bob teeth in their mouths and are hysterically laughing. *Oh no, not this again,* I internally sigh.

"Shush, my mother is in her room asleep."

"Why did you tell *him* that?" Qalbee reluctantly reason as he shamefully shakes his head as if he knows something I don't.

"I'm 'bout to go poke her just *one* time," Craig declares as he shakes his hips, flaunting his male organs, visible enough to see the outline of them dangle from side to side through his white nylon sweat pants, gesturing with a sexual thrust.

Instantaneously, I identify with Qalbee's reasoning and I'm appalled by Craig's humor. With my left hand I immediately grab the left side of Craig's dingy brown, grey, and white t-shirt that falls at his hip and grip Qalbee's zipped up hunter green hooded sweat jacket in-between my right thumb and index finger and pull them out of the living room, through the dining area, to the stairs, and guide them up to my room.

We step though my door and Craig begins acting high—*or drunk?* Again, uncontrollable. *Huh,* I sigh. I'm beginning to think he *does* take Ritalin. The thick strands of hair in Craig's eyebrows point diagonally meeting the wrinkles between his brows as the corners of his mouth fall down to his chin.

"What the fuck?" Craig shouts lifting his arms mid-way in the air. "Where's Chell? I'm tryna bone that too," Craig chuckles as his left hand hoist in the air and his right palm cups his genital area; and he swirls, and lift, and drops his hips like he's belly dancing.

I look over to my right at Qalbee. His yellow New York Yankee ball cap moves side to side under his green hood. He seems slightly embarrassed by his friend's behavior. He looks up at me. Qalbee's eyes are piercing with innocents causing reality to validate that he is truly standing here. I'm paralyzed. My eyes are hypnotized, absorbing his presence. I feel solution running rapidly within the cones of my eyes processing the surreal image that stands before me. *I never really thought I'd see him again.* Blood rushes through my veins to my heart and my hands tremble, producing moisture in the palms of my hands. Unconsciously my right index finger quickly rises to my mouth to caress across my lips. My teeth clinch into my fingernail, biting in attempt to cease the quivering vibration. My jaw is frozen, though I feel a grin behind my mouth aiming to pass my lips. My brain signals are completely and utterly enthralled at the reality of him truly standing here *in my room—revitalizing!* My daze is interrupted by a tap on the window. It's Chanelle!

I firmly push Craig out of my way—*huh*. I roll my eyes and sigh at the sight of him. I walk over to the window, raise it, grab Chanelle by her underarms and help her in. I shut the window, lock it, pull the strings of the blinds down and once they touch the mantel I slide the curtains to the left. Chanelle dusts off her white Daisies, then her shirt; and scopes the three of us. She looks perplexed.

"What happen? How'd they get in?"

"The front door," I respond as non-sardonic as possible. "You know my mother is knocked out." I walk over to my cherry wood door, close it, and lock it. "Plus, she doesn't care that they're here anyway." I turn and look at Craig and Qalbee and steadfastly I declare, "As long as y'all are out of here at a decent time."

Chapter Four

DAYLIGHT DIMLY BURNISHES through my curtain. Qalbee and Craig have been here for approximately eight hours. After six hours of laughing, playing, play fighting and doing much roasting with these guys, Chanelle was fast asleep. Craig has given the impression that he is bored with only Qalbee and me with his continued complaints and rummaging through my things trying to deliberately annoy me. Without Chanelle awake for him to pester, his animated humor has subsided. Craig has been in my bathroom for that past half hour, and Qalbee and I have been in our own little world.

First it was all of us getting to know each other, conversing about school. Qalbee and Craig just graduated class of '99. Then we talked about sports. Apparently, Craig is some Kobe Bryant with his basketball skills, scoring 30 points a game and hitting 100% in free throws and rebounds each game. He could have gone pro straight out of high school, but he wasn't taking ball serious and fouled out just about every game.

Qalbee, on the other hand, is also very good at basketball, but he missed so many games that he quit the team the latter half of the season. He seemed uneasy when I inquired why he missed so many games and then evaded answering the question. So I did not push. I just modified the topic to how I play sports; and how Chanelle and I are football girls and run water bottles out to players when they need hydrating. Qalbee and Craig *both* found so much amusement in that, that they would not stop sliding in jokes about it. Although, when Chanelle voiced that she's not into all the school activities I'm in because she has an 'image to keep up', Craig immensely found humor in that and ragged on her every open chance he got. I was just happy to get out of dodge!

Now, Chanelle lays flat on her back with her right hand on her stomach and her left arm placed flat to her side. She is passed out. Craig is still in my bathroom doing I don't know what with the door closed. I hear the stool flush giving assumption to my wonder. The facet come on, then goes off; and the knob of the door turns and Craig walks out. He climbs in my bed and scoots next to Chanelle lying opposite of her body. Careful not to crush her left arm he lifts his big toe, clothed in a sweaty white Nike sock, and rubs it from her neck to her nose, being a nuisance. Chanelle turns her face towards the window in retreat and waves her right hand in the air shooing him and protecting her face, still asleep. Qalbee and I ignore them.

Qalbee and I have been talking and laughing for the past two hours without interference from Chanelle or Craig. Thoughts of why Qalbee was guarded about missing games occasionally arise as we sit here comfy and content with each others' company. He sits against my cherry oak dresser across from my bed—same as last time—and I'm leaned slightly forward on account of my adrenalin rushing so high that I'm too restless to sit back. My knees are propped up, my arms embrace my ankles, and my chin rests between my knees. I sit an inch apart from Qalbee smelling his scent and feeling his warmth.

"I can't believe you like that mutha fuckin' rapper. He's the worse rapper Nigga out there." Qalbee clutch deep within his throat, "BITCH," he mocks along with the song. "Nigga, shut the fuck up," he says with a vengeance as if he is talking to the rapper himself.

My mouth and eyes widen in shock. I inhale profoundly feeling the involuntary pull deep within my abdominal region, than unnervingly chuckle.

"Stop all that cursing!" I demand, baffled.

He looks up at me. His smile is so bright it is as if it's a reflection from my complexion. "Shiiit . . . fuck, that's what he said. What's the difference?" he explains jokingly, desperately struggling to control his amusement.

"Aah!" Again my mouth and eyes widen, taken aback.

"BITCH," he says in a low pitch tone, laughing still.

"Don't call me one of those." I raise my fingers covering my unlocked lips as if I am surprised and offended. I smile.

His eyes link with mine, then his smile matches mine. We softly giggle.

"One of those?" He asks then looks away as if he is ashamed of me. "Aah man, don't tell me you *DO NOT* CURSE," he emphasizes, shaking his head. Qalbee antagonistically slams my junior year book on his lap, hops up, and stands above me.

I gawk his stout body shielding me as I close my eyes, proudly lifting my chin to the ceiling as if I am Queen Berenib of Egypt. Pretentiously I declare, "No." I gracefully raise my dainty fingers to my chest still acting as royalty. "No, I—do—not—curse!" I emphasize proudly.

"Aah mother fucker shit no!" He turns to Craig, "Nigga let's get out of this shit hole," he utters, disgracefully laughing.

I quickly hop up. Feeling tall, I face him. Adjacent to my body, I feel the temperature of his body only an inch apart. I instantaneously flirt. With my open palm and fingers I gently push into his chest venturing a 'love tap'. "Stop that," I coax then bat my lashes.

He deliberately creates a bug-eyed face, playing, unknowingly constructing an adorable child like expression.

I stare into his eyes. "Quit all that cursing," I whine softly. I can't seem to control the laughter he ignites within me. "You are funny," I giggle.

He grins mischievously; yet so innocent it's alluring. I yearn for his lips. My eyelashes bat rapidly, spontaneously taking mental pictures.

"You know you not right," I say as parenthesis' sandwich my curved lips, crafting a tender grin on my face, hoping that he believes I'm referring to all the playful profanity and animation he's bestowed even though I'm actually alluding to the enchanting gaze he just granted me.

Out of the corner of my eye I see Chanelle sprout up. Her right arm hoists and she fist her fingers into an American Sign Language "S", than swings at Craig. Qalbee and I jump. I feel my heart flutter as I catch the side of Qalbee's smooth face when our necks simultaneously turn, facing Craig and Chanelle. Craig quickly bobs and Chanelle misses him. *Huh,* I exhale! *Thank goodness,* I thought as I picture myself as an umpire making a judgment call. *SAFE!* I signal in my head. All this involuntary eyelash batting madness that my nervous system keeps signaling to my brain . . . like I'm some Chicago showgirl . . . but saved by Chanelle's freshly manicured fist!

"Shiiiit," Qalbee stresses through a husky laugh.

I turn my face back toward Qalbee, with my open palms and fingers I push into his chest a bit firmer this time. My cheeks droop, disappointed that he is ready to leave me, hoping he will think I'm upset about his continued poor choice of words.

Craig stands. "You right bruh, it's time to go!" he agrees as he walks out the door of my room.

I step over to Chanelle. Gently clutching her shoulder, "Chanelle, come on, get up. Come with me to walk them out."

She does not budge.

CRAIG CLIMBS INTO HIS dingy pickup truck. Qalbee is alongside me as we walk out the main door of the house. I turn to slowly and softly close it. We walk towards the truck and I smile at the thought of being with him at dawn—too early to hear the birds chirp but early enough to hear the sound of stridulation! My heart pounds loudly, drowning out all other sounds. Nervously I stand close, facing Qalbee as he leans back against the dingy truck.

"Well Comedy, you cool with me. Call me sometime," I manage to get out without my lips trembling like the rest of my body.

"I'll think about it," he states expressionless.

"Huh!" I sigh with hurt feelings and for a third time, hoping it came across as playful frustration. Instantaneously my right arm hoist and I punch him in his chest. I raise the same hand to my mouth. My index finger caresses across my bottom lip and my teeth clinch my nail in attempt to cease my nervousness. *I do not know what has come over me . . .* but I don't have time to figure it out. I feel Qalbee's right hand press against my lower back causing me to jerk into him, and his left hand quickly grabs my right hand and rubs my index finger across his bottom lip. I gaze deep into his eyes through to his retina. I'm hypnotized. I quickly push up on my toes and suddenly plant my lips on his cheek. I take a step back and hastily retreat towards my parent's five bedroom, four half bathroom, two story, white limestone house, never looking back.

"Bye Comedy!" I say hearing him climb into Craig's matching truck as I approach the classic fiberglass canvas entry door to the house.

I OPEN THE DOOR to my bedroom. My brows frown in thought and my lips furrow from bewilder. I've been bamboozled. Chanelle is awake, sitting on my bed eating cold pizza!

"Wait?" I'm thrown. "I thought you were knocked out?" My frown deepens as I watch Chanelle feed her face in disgust. "Cold pizza? Really? Right this second? At 7:00 in the morning?" I reach for my music bookcase. ". . . but you couldn't walk them out with me." I say rhetorically, giving her a hard time!

Chanelle holds up her pizza in one hand. "What?" and rises a napkin up in the other as she chews with an affronted look on her face. "I was hungry".

I redirect the conversation. "I sooo like him." Feeling jovial, I put in Tony Braxton and play I Love Me Some Him as I begin wrapping my hair in my yellow do-rag.

"Well his friend is annoying." She lays her head on the pillow.

"We have chemistry," I replay the image of him placing my finger across his lips. I then pull one of my long t-shirts that I wear as pajamas out of my dresser drawer. I hear loud breathing. Chanelle is fast asleep. I cannot help to smile and shake my head at her. I slightly lift my mattress—slightly lifting Chanelle as well. I reach for my journal then climb in over Chanelle's feet. I grab my pillow, prop up on it, pull the pen that attaches to the penguin's nose on my journal and begin writing.

CALEB CALLED ME YESTERDAY, asking me if I would go out to eat with him to Bennigan's Restaurant, but I told him no. Going out to eat implies "date"—it's too personal and I no longer want any type of intimate commerce with him. I agreed to him meeting me at the mall because I've wanted to purchase Sigmund Freud's *Interpretation of Dreams* to learn more about the unconscious and to get a different spin on cognition and REM sleep. Here I am in my green Indian skirt that falls to my ankles with a loose pink cropped t-shirt reveling skin an inch above my naval; and I have freshly done, extremely thin micro braids. I'm carrying a Barnes and Noble's Bookstore sack with another book to add to my personal library. I ride up the escalator with a massive migraine the size of earth and my temple pulsates to an imaginary beat of a rock song. Caleb stands beside me looking like he's scorching hot, wearing a crimson cotton button down and cream blazer. *Doesn't he know its mid June? Who does that? This whole image obsession thing, like he's some baseball star is out of control. He's not even in the pros,* I huff. I agreed to come here to talk and finalize this, and he came to spill his guts—*as if my actions and attitude has not voiced this break up enough, huh.*

We reach the top of the escalator, Caleb gestures for me to step off first, and I comply.

"You've been . . ." Caleb begins as I simultaneously utter, "Caleb I just . . ."

We stop and face one another.

"Go ahead." Again, simultaneously.

"No really, go," I insist. I begin walking.

"You've been acting different lately." He walks alongside me.

"Yes I know, that's what I was about to say. I'm just not into this."

"Sweetheart I know you don't like coming to the mall. I just wanted to spend some time with you."

"No. Not that. Us, I'm not into *us* anymore . . ."

Caleb faces me in disbelief. We stop. I take his hand.

". . . look Caleb, I'm sorry"

He pauses, I'm quiet. I turn around and head back towards the escalators.

I hear Caleb call out my name over the shoppers, workers, white noise, and classical music played over the mall speakers. I turn back around to face him, searching for him through the crowd of superficial consumers. He holds a small grey suede box in the palm of his right hand. While he bends to one knee, I see a guy I was infatuated with for two years. He's really sweet towards me and has catered to my needs. He took me on my first date to dinner and a movie, and helped with my surprise sweet sixteen party. And most importantly, he understands my love for baseball! My left hand rise to my mouth masking my lips, and I lay my right hand across my chest. As I stand here Caleb's considerate personality comes to mind. His protective manner is in position. And the site of those perfectly shaped lips compels images of all the things they can do to me as he speak the words. "Libi, I'm in love with you. Marry me?"

Chapter Five

I HAD NO WORRIES my freshman or sophomore year like other teens do as they transition between juggling assignments, school activities, and home circumstances while dealing with peer pressure, puberty, and social appearance. My sense of self was already developed by the age of nine which prepared me not to be a follower and has kept me focused on my ultimate agenda. Plus being "Sebastian's lil sister" didn't hurt!

But now, lately, being a teenager has been difficult for me because I feel caught between the innocence of being a child and the decisions and responsibilities of an adult. I am no longer a child needing regulation from my parents, but then again, I'm frightened by the unexpected phenomenon of the future.

Huh, I gasp, daunted that just in this past year alone I've had to adjust to all the many problems that teenagers face throughout their entire high school experience. Even with all the things Caleb and I endured my junior year, I was still able to keep my independence. I didn't even change for him. Besides, Caleb liked me for me. He accepted my liberal sovereign ways and me being the aloof tom boy who only dresses in sweats and hippie clothes rather than pre Madonna fashion. Or maybe our common love for baseball kept us together, who knows?

It has been a couple of days since Caleb asked me to marry him and I had not been able to tell Chanelle the news because she left for Chicago, Illinois for a family reunion that morning. She invited me, but I decided to stay here and work out a few things—not knowing Caleb was going to add on to my list of impediments by popping the big question.

"He what?" Chanelle exclaims swept away. Her voice trembles and is more amped than usual from the vibration of the cycling red Whirlpool dryer she sits on and the echoing walls of my parent's full-size laundry room.

I sit alongside her on top of the matching washer folding spring lavender scented clothes. Chanelle masticates her baked potato, with no fork or knife, sandwiched in a folded white paper plate shaped as a taco, eating it like a hotdog.

"And you said what?" she grumbles.

"I'm just not in love, well, infatuated, with him anymore. When I wanted to run off with him after he graduated," . . . *and after we worked through his poor choice in taking Sheila to the prom*, ". . . he didn't want to. Now all of a sudden he proposes and I'm supposed to be Miss. Desperate?" My face scrunches in repulsion. "No!" I slam my folded orange nylon sweats on top of a full stack of assorted colored sweats I've already folded.

"This is about Quincy," Chanelle probes, barely comprehendible through the mouth full of carbohydrates.

"Who?" *What?* My face frowns, confused—but it doesn't take me long.

"Qalbee?" I put my head down shaking it from side to side. On my face is obscurity as I furrow my brows. *Why would she think that?* But, I know it's because she knows me better than I know myself. I continue folding in hope that she drops the subject, but I know she won't. My eyes slowly peeks up to see why nothing has come out of her thirsty mouth, hoping that I don't catch her catch me peeking. Chanelle's eyes are small, focused, looking directly into mine; her mouth is closed leaving a thin line between her lips, her qualm expression says 'yeah right'.

"Okay, yes." I redden.

Within this year I have fallen in then out of infatuation, got dismissed as a prom date, harassed and stalked by a wounded ex-girlfriend, and have fallen, well plummeted, into a deep unexplainable love affair with some new, secretive, mysterious guy . . . and all while having to make a choice on which university to attend. *Huh*, I gasp. This is what I mean when I say 'daunting'. And now, now I'm going through some type of identity, role confusion phase—well according to Eric Erickson, a developmental psychologist, I read about the other day. He poses that we as humans go through psychosocial stages of development and that as a teen I will have to reconcile with who I am and who I'm expected to be. My self-identity has taken on a whole new orientation. I never really looked at boys like I look at Qalbee! Ever since I gazed at his Photo Shopped hair waves I've been compelled to look in the mirror more. I catch myself spraying on my mother's expensive perfumes. I change clothes multiple times before I end up finally just wearing what I originally set out to wear in the first place. And lately, I've been even contemplating on arching my eyebrows. I totally thirst his presence and just want to be his gift of quench.

"They're coming over again tonight," I admit tilting my head down to shield against Chanelle's eye contact.

"They?" Her face is displeased. Chanelle hops off the dryer. "Have fun!" she throws up her right index and middle finger, gesturing the urban sign for peace.

She attempts to walk out but I hop off the matching washer.

"Noooo," I grip her right wrist and plead "I told Qalbee that you'd be here to keep Craig company." I'm desperate.

"Na cuz," she says gangster like, yanking her arm from my grip. "Not happenin." She walks out.

CRAIG'S FEET DANGLES off the edge of my bed as his stomach lies flat across my freshly washed Mickey comforter. He has five dominos in his hand. In front of him is a domino game in process between him and Chanelle. She sits upright across from him, her butt smothering Mickey's face, and legs Indian Style. She places her fifth domino down.

"25!" Chanelle exclaims.

Qalbee sits on the floor, back against my dresser with his legs stretched out, ankles locked, and Timberlands crossed. I sit against my mahogany bookcase, adjacent to him, with a half headache and half nauseated from inhaling the lemon fresh smell of my mother's perfume and my mint mouthwash. After brushing my teeth three-times longer than the American Dental Association expected length of three minutes, I gargle the cool mint Listerine; and then saturated my neck, behind my ear, under my arms, on my chest, and even between my legs in Dolce & Gabbana Light Blue. I've wanted to ask Qalbee why the faithful wearing of pullovers since I first laid eyes on his perfectly solid, gym equipped physique, but every time the words touched my tongue I figured getting a taste of his intellect and laughing at his humorous character would be more entertaining than the endless possibilities to that explanation—though, while Craig and Chenelle are into their dominos and Qalbee and I have one on one time to get to know each other, I figure now is a better time than ever.

I look away from the book that I fold and massage in my hand in which I'm conveniently using as a stress reliever and I gaze up at Qalbee.

"What's up with the pullovers in the summer? Are you always cold?"

"No." He stares at me impassively. "Hell, no. Fuck no. Shit no," he dramatizes, possibly trying to irritate me off that subject, but I stare back at him impassively, giving him nothing.

"I'm always HOT," he emphasizes in a derisive manner as if I asked him a dumb question. He flips through a few pockets in my case of CD's. Just when I think he maneuvered off the subject, he continues.

"It's the summer. The air conditioner is on everywhere you go. Like in here," His eyes move up, than around.

Qalbee doesn't say *Duh*, but the expression on his face does.

"There's a nice chill," he persists.

Who wears thick, 100 percent cotton pullovers in the hot summer to keep from being cold inside? I KNOW he just said that he's always hot.

"And that's why the hoodies." . . . *cause it's cold in here . . . You just knew I'd have the air blasting in my home?* Now I carry the "yeah right" expression on my face.

"I'm from Detroit and it's always cold there."

What does that have to do with anything? "You don't live there now," I say sardonically, rolling my eyes out of frustration.

"I know I don't live in Detroit," he responds sardonically, looking at me as if I'm stupid, and am wearing a big red nose and a pink afro. "I—am—from—Detroit," he accentuates this time, as if I am two years old. He then leans in so close that with one shift, by either one of us, our noses will battle.

"That's why I have a lot of hoodies." His eyes hub into my mine making sure I hear his words and again, as if am two years old.

Why not just say that? Why take me through all this? And again, what in the world does that have to do with anything? Huh, he's frustrating.

"I wear them as a symbolic gesture in remembrance of my father," he continues to hub directly into my eyes. "HE DIED when I was TWO." Saliva sprinkles my face as he loudly emphasizes in a matter-of-fact manner.

My chin falls to the floor. His eyes lose mine as mine follows my chin. I feel as small as a mustard seed making him answer me that way. *Aw, dang*, I feel extremely bad for being sarcastic.

I decide not to wipe his hot saliva off my face because I feel too ashamed and the least I can do is not offend him again.

The room is quiet. I hear Chanelle turn towards me and Qalbee, eavesdropping. In my peripheral I see Craig's head tilt back and forth propositioning Chanelle's attention. She does not comply, so he then taps one of his dominos against one already played causing a distracting sound. She then turns back to their game.

I'm compelled, but hesitate, to place my hand on his left quadriceps, so I pull back and place it on my thigh, continuing to look down in regret.

"Oh, I never knew." *Well duh Libiya, how would you?* "How long have you been doing that?" I attempt eye contact, ignoring my sarcastic thoughts.

Chanelle turns back towards us losing focus from her domino game again. Craig hits her knee with his domino. She jumps by reflex. To my surprise, Qalbee begins chuckling. I'm confused.

"I'm kidding," he says through his continued chuckle, looking down at me with that enigmatic grin.

"What? What are you kidding about? The death of your father?" *He's so wrong for that, lying about something like that.* "Karma is a . . ."

"No, I'm serious about my father, it just doesn't bother me as much anymore like I led on," he slightly chuckles, knowing he had me fooled.

Now I'm even more confused. So his father did die, but all the extra, mean, sarcastic, emotional drama he just took me through *is his way of a joke?*

"Not for too long," he softly speaks.

I look up at him, again lost.

"I have not been wearing the pullovers . . ." Qalbee ogles my eyes ". . . in the hot sun, for too long." His tone reduces, voice vulnerable, he expresses, "Something personal came up recently resonating aspiration in me to feel close to him."

"Do you wish to elaborate?" I softly push, subconsciously biting my nails.

This time, I hear Craig turn away from the domino game as if he has been wondering the same question.

"DOMINO MUTHA!" Chanelle yells, slamming her last domino on the bed as if it's a glass table. She wins the game, getting Craig's attention, and him out of our conversation. I take it as a sign that I'm pushing too far with the questions.

Just as I decide to recoil, Qalbee looks up to the ceiling like a light bulb appeared in the air, his face glares in opposition. He slaps my CD case closed creating a loud thud. I reach for my CD case and snatch it out of his lap realizing that his act of aversion pertains to my music.

"I'm not going to take you clownin' my music again." I stand to my feet.

"Bone, Bone, Bone tell me what the fuck is that . . . when judgment comes, when judgment come . . . my uncle Charlie y'all!" he mocks Bone Thugs & Harmony's the "Crossroad" song intentionally teasing and messing up the lyrics.

"Stop it. I love Bone Thugs!" I firmly declare.

"And Michael . . ."

Qalbee ceases his comment when he sees my head vigorously jerk down at him and my expression is of serious offence.

Michael Jackson is my all time favorite singer and I love his compassion for people. I do not take too kindly to people talking about him just because they have not taken time to understand him. I'm very sensitive to his upbringing and I wish others were too. If people would just take in to consideration of the times he grew up in. Being black, having a big nose and big lips was considered an imperfection. His environment and self esteem was jolted. Being a cute child superstar in the spotlight, then puberty producing an even bigger nose, new pimples, and extra bumps everywhere on your face while being aired on multiple television screens with thousands of viewers, how would you react? I cannot help to go on a tangent on this topic. I can only imagine MJ wanting, wishing, begging to look like that cute child superstar again before his initial nose surgery. And all the while, little does he know, he has always been cute in his fans' eyes—*well in mine at least,* I'm proud to say!

"Don't go there," I warn. "Michael Jackson is a great humanitarian."

"Na," Qalbee retreats. "I can do some Michael." He smiles!

"Yea, that's what I thought," I affirm confidently.

"NA . . . I can't *do* him," he teases.

My eyes scold. I feel bigger than him as I stand hovering over him.

"No really, I like Mike. He go hard."

I slide my *Thriller* CD from a slot in the case, put it into my Sony, and play "Human Nature."

Chapter Six

I AM IN MY SAFE HAVEN, alone, peaceful. No Chanelle eating up everything, no Craig pestering Chanelle, and last but definitely not least—actually saving the best for last—Qalbee! No Qalbee here stimulating apprehension throughout my body. It is now November and I have enjoyed them being here pretty much every day the entire summer and these past two months of fall. Ever since school started I have not been able to see him every day. My parents are serious about good grades and since I am not some prodigy child like Sebastian, with all my extracurricular activities, I have to work hard to keep up my straight A's. But Qalbee and I *do* find a great deal of time to spend with each other.

Chanelle and I have been over Craig's house a few times, though only in his front yard. I have never been inside. I think Chanelle has once or twice but it has been too cold this month to stand around out there. Plus Craig has a new job as a coach assistant for the YMCA, so when we all cannot meet over there and when I cannot bribe or convince Chanelle to hang with Craig over here, Qalbee sometimes sneaks me in his house through his bedroom window. I have not made sense of why he sneaks me in when he has already introduced me to his mother a few times before. She is really sweet and kind and beautiful! Qalbee inherited her clean, smooth brown skin, and breathtaking sparkling white, captivating smile. She is an inch or two shorter than me.

Mrs. Davis has been a widow for seventeen years and never remarried. Qalbee said that she relocated them to Edmond shortly after his father's death. She found a job at the airport and has worked there for the past sixteen years until she took a leave of absence this past year and never returned. He never said why; however, he did tell me that she dated from time to time except that her love for his father was so perpetual that she never found herself giving her all in other relationships. Come to find out I have known his sister, Katina, all this time, having no idea they were siblings, or related, or even knew each other for that matter.

Here I am laying in the comfort of my bed, preserved under the covers keeping warm. I'm reminiscing and flipping through pages of my journal, reading over the ambience of my times with "the Crew" instead of deciphering which university is the better choice.

JUNE 1999

Today I made breakfast for everyone: mother, Sebastian, Chanelle, and me. I cleaned up the kitchen real good and folded clothes before Chanelle and I caught the city bus to the mall. Chanelle wanted earrings. We walked around the mall the whole day until Craig came to pick us up, and then we went by

Blockbuster's to pick up Qalbee. He doesn't have a car. We all came back to my place. I baked chocolate chip cookies for us since it is a favorite of Qalbee's. Qalbee and I cuddled on my floor sharing ice cream while we watched a few movies and of course Chanelle and Craig bickered throughout each movie. They started a pillow fight and the next thing I knew, Qalbee whopped me with a pillow! That began war! We were all battling each other; jumping on and off my bed and running in and out of my bathroom. I slipped off the corner of my bed and fell hard on my butt and they all laughed at me. But then Qalbee still whopped me up side my head. He showed no mercy! I retreated by balling up in the fetal position. Oh, I must have hyperventilated a hundred times tonight we laughed and played so hard! At least until finally Chanelle and I decided to run and hide in my closet!

I snort at the joy we had that night!

JULY 1999

This summer is going by so fast. It is already the Fourth of July and school starts back next month. I am actually writing in you on the 5th because Qalbee had me up all night watching fireworks. I love Independence Day because it is tradition every year for my family to get together and have a mini Olympics in my uncle's back yard. We have softball throw, relay race, 3 on 3 basketball tournament and volleyball matches and so many more activities. Qalbee accompanied

It Won't Go Away   Samina Najmah

me this year and he participated in all of the sports and games! There were four teams: red, blue, gold, and green. Qalbee ended up on the red team and me on green. Neither of our teams won, but it was so festive to watch him interact with my family! It was so funny beating him in the sack race—but his team won tug-of-war. He was shocked at my arm power in the softball throw though he threw sufficiently further then me. Each team of ten had to choose 3 people to play in 3 on 3 basketball, so I sat out. I cheered for him while he competed. My team protested against me for rooting for him but I didn't care! His horse like calves stampeded the court and his team won that ribbon! After the gold team won their trophy Qalbee drove my uncle's two seated 200cc Go Kart—with no doors, no windows, and no roof—with me as passenger. He pressed his Nike's to the metal full speed and our bodies bounced, our heads bobbled around, and we thumped and banged as we hit the bumps in the ground. We hooted and chuckled extensively! We both loved the rush. It seems that we are both thrill seekers. Afterwards, Chanelle and Craig met us, and we all popped fireworks. Later, Qalbee and I went back to my place and he came up to Cloud Nine for his first time. We camped out in silence watching all the beautiful colors of the explosives. We woke up on the roof lying in each other's arms!

AUGUST 1999

I did not do much today but sign up to volunteer at a retirement center caring for elderly residents. Afterwards I came home and read How to Eat to Live by Elijah Muhammad. He was a Black Muslim prophet from the 1930's and apparently was a God that advocated for Black people for years for their independence. I came across the book while looking for health books on vitamins, minerals, and nutrition. I have always wanted to become a vegetarian however my mother said 'you are going to eat what I cook or find your own meals', so that's what I am preparing to do now. After I read How to Eat to Live in full, I went over to Qalbee's. First I stopped by the corner store close by his place and bought him a pint of cookies and cream— another favorite of his though not very nutritious! I felt uncomfortable when his mother answered the door, but she was so kind and welcoming that I relaxed without effort. She chatted with us about school and our aspirations, but for only a moment. She was careful not to take up our time together, which I thought showed how much reverence she has for her son. He and I went to his room and listened to Marvin Gaye, Stevie Wonder, and a few other back-in-the-day rhythm & blues artists. We learned more about one another, and compared some of our views of the world. He told me how he made an airbrush machine out of his asthma machine which enlightened me that he has asthma and that he can draw. He actually loves to draw! He wants to go to school for computer animation to create cartoon characters. I shared with him what I read today about nutrition and about Elijah Muhammad being God in the flesh. Qalbee and I expressed our views on religion and politics as we talked from dusk to dawn. Very stimulating!

SEPTEMBER 1999

I had a great weekend! My mother, brother, Chanelle and I spent the weekend in Atlanta, Georgia. We visited Spellman and Clark University, and Lenox Mall Friday; the Undergrad Mall and Coca Cola Company and tasted the many flavors on Saturday; and Dr. Martin Luther King's Memorial, and his house and church Sunday. We returned this morning and I was worn out. Today is Qalbee's mother's birthday and since Qalbee loves freshly prepared blue berry pancakes I decided to cater a dozen to him, his mother and his sister as a happy birthday gesture. He thanked me with a soft kiss on my right cheek and I flushed! I was so paralyzed, it took me by surprise! It was the first time his lips touched me. We hug, but nothing more. Later he met me back at my parent's home. Coincidentally, none of the crew has to work tomorrow so they came over as well. Chanelle feel asleep after eating pizza and watching The Matrix. Craig being "Craig" put toothpaste in Chanelle's nose while she was asleep. He and Qalbee thought it was hilarious. When I attempted to stop him, Qalbee grabbed me by my waist, lifted me, and drug me away preventing me from ceasing Craig's mischievousness. Qalbee covered my mouth so I couldn't yell out her name, and I tried to bite him but was unsuccessful! Chanelle never budged throughout all the action. That's funny! It is always fun and games with these two!

I chuckle!

OCTOBER 1999

I had a long but pleasurable volunteer day, today. I stayed over time because one of my fellow volunteers had an emergency and I agreed to work his full shift. Qalbee picked me up around nine. He had just gotten off work so we had to stop by his house for him to shower and change. I thought he looked and smelled breathtaking, yet he is so hygienic that he just had to shower and change. While I waited in his room for him to finish I was compelled to take a risk lying in his bed hoping his mother or sister did not come home and catch me in it. I tossed and twisted, and rolled, circling and hugging his pillows, then sniffed his sheets, inhaling the fragrance of heaven! I laid there basking in the ambiance when I looked up to see him gaping at me. Guess I should have been watching for him, I thought, embarrassed. He stood in the entrance of his room with that emerald towel drying his undulating torso, his grey jogging pants hanging off his hips, exposing a glimpse of his pelvis. He smiled his alluring smile and I melted. I could not help but laugh—he caught me sniffing, and enjoying his musk. If he was not sure before he definitely knows now that I *am undeniably into him. After he completed dressing, we came back to my parent's home. I taught him how to play the card game Spoons and either he knew how to play, or he had beginners luck because I lost just about every time. We played chess once but it did not get very far, either we both suck, or we're equally good. He and I lay in my bed together talking and laughing all night, as usual! He is my best friend!*

My hands sandwich my spiral journal and I pull the tablet to my chest. My mouth curves up and my heart flutters. *Huh!* I'm so in love with him. I cannot wait to see him tonight. I cannot believe I am always so nervous around him. I was never nervous around Caleb, not even when we first began dating—whom I have not heard from since I told him "no" to spending the rest of my life bored with him. I hear he and Sheila are back together and that he plans to go pro next year—*great for them!*

Chapter Seven

BEES SWARM THROUGH BUILDINGS and flames come out of this rapper's head as his friends follow him, all riding on motorcycles, when chills invade my spine. I sit on the floor with my back against my bed frame, in bliss that Qalbee sits to the left of me still coming around, still comical as ever, and still my best friend after six months. We sit facing the spot Qalbee usually sits when he's over, with our jawbones skewed, chin up, watching a music video on the television placed on my dresser. Craig sits on the edge of my bed to the left side of Qalbee, and Chanelle is to the right of me standing as if she is anxious to use the restroom. Qalbee has been keeping my senior yearbook hostage from the others waiting to write in it, but between MTV and BET it has been one interesting video after another preventing him from signing away. I do not watch much TV *at all*. If it is not something interesting on the History or Discovery Channel educating me—or All My Children, I'll admit—the futile TV is off. I do not know any of these dudes' names but from what Sebastian tells me, Wu Tang is a knowledgeable group of guys. I like open minded and intellectual people, so I don't mind listening to them rap about "Triumph."

As soon as Wu Tang's video goes off, I stand up, and take a few steps towards my dresser that my television rest on. Chanelle's shoulder brush mine as she heads in the same direction, but exits the room. I press the red button powering off the television and drop one of my mixed tapes filled with favorites into the cassette deck of my radio sitting on top of my bookcase.

"I like Wu Tang, I'm just more of a Mos Def fan" I clarify.

"Ahww," Qalbee and Craig grimace in sequence.

Qalbee stands. "That mother fuckin . . ." he laughs. "I mean, that blank'n nigga!" he mocks me by using my substitute word since I don't curse.

"Just sign the book," I order, with an intense look, reprimanding Qalbee's pupils.

Qalbee leans on the right corner of my desk, places the yearbook down, opens it, and puts the pen to the paper. Craig places his hand on the left corner of the desk, leans against it, and hoists. Chanelle walks back into the room eating a bowl of cereal.

"Chell you still need me to take you home?" Craig asks as he and Qalbee stare at my computer key board, positioned between them.

I notice the looks on their faces are of amusement, like maybe they are holding in some inside joke. I look at my computer key board to see what the big joke is and there is a roach crawling across the Z, X, and F keys.

"I don't NEED anything from you," Chanelle emphasizes, and then sits back down on the corner of my bed closer to the double doors of my walk in closet where she was previously sitting.

Qalbee and Craig laughs.

"Y'all seen Libi's apartment?" Craig taunts, looking at Chanelle.

"What?" I inquire, slightly embarrassed, but more disgusted—I pride myself on living in a clean environment.

"Joe's apartment," Qalbee clarifies as he continues to write in my yearbook.

"Whatever. My visiting relatives are filthy, not my house," I elucidate, thinking, *Chanelle and her appetite.*

Qalbee passes Craig the senior book. Craig opens it but stops and extends his hand reaching out to mine.

"Na, Libi . . ." His hand is clenched in a fist, positioned in the air, attempting to give me proper respect. "You cool with me," Craig utters.

Waiting for me to strike his dapp, I quickly pull my hand away still a little embarrassed, but more hurt that he would tease me about that and hoping that the wounded expression on my face is not transparent.

"Whatever," I say nonchalantly. *It doesn't matter. I know I'm not a filthy person,* I chant to myself to feel better about their insensitive joke about me.

". . . and all your cousins," Craig continues to rag in response to my rejection. He bursts out laughing and begins writing in my senior book. Qalbee points at another roach crawling on the monitor screen.

"And he means all of them," Qalbee snorts, his laugh is so rigid.

These guys are so immature. No wonder they are almost twenty without girlfriends and neither are in college. They're not smart . . . they spend their time goofing off.

But yet, they are . . . both of them *are* smart. Craig has been looking into opening his own business selling movies, music, and video games, and is training to be a personal trainer. Qalbee applied to Eastern Oklahoma Technology Center for computer animation at the beginning of this month to be a candidate for fall of next year. When he received a letter from them in the mail last week, he came over here to have me open it and read it out loud, but all I got out was "Congratulations, Qalbee Xavier Davis" and he hugged me tightly, picked me up, and spun me around. I felt like I was in one of those black and white 1930s movies they air on AMC! I know he is happy about getting accepted, but something seemed to bother him. His spirit was melancholy when he put me down. Of course when I ask him what was troubling him, he changed the subject. My concerns about his worries were shoved to the back of my thoughts when he enlightened me that he and I will start college the same month and year. All I could do was smile . . . and have been since. I'm in bliss!

Huh, how can I be upset? I know they make jokes about any and everything they can. Taking note of that, my embarrassment diminishes. I slightly huff at the humor, and shake my head.

"Whatever!"

"Y'all some jerks. Let's go Craig," Chanelle demands.

Craig tosses the senior book on my bed and heads for the door. "I thought you didn't *need* anything from me," he asks with sarcasm.

Chanelle walks towards the door. She ignores Craig, and looks at me. "I'll call you tomorrow." Chanelle looks at Qalbee. "Take good care of her."

Chanelle throws up the urban sign for peace as Craig gesture's an urban farewell by chucking his chin up and head back quickly. As they walk out Qalbee bumps his genitals against mine.

"Oh, I will," Qalbee says enthusiastically, smiling his charismatic smile and displaying his slightly crooked tooth. He is standing so close that his cool breath chills me.

Caught by surprise, I smile nervously. I shake my head and roll my eyes, timid. Carrying a coy smirk, I look deep into his innocent eyes, and whisper, "Comedy." I gently place my right palm to his chest and push. I gasp. Before I can ease my index finger to loop a lock of my hair, his left hand clasps mine. Parallel to his lips, his fingers cuddle mine. Just as I think he is going to rub my index finger across his bottom lip, he guides it down to his hardened nature. I stiffen. With his right hand placed at my lower back he pulls me closer leaving no space between us—chest to breast, nose to nose, and his tongue muscles through my nervous, clinched lips. The gentle muscle of his wet tongue causes my mouth to tingle and the tiny hairs throughout my body to stand down to my vaginal area. Heat spreads throughout my swishy pants as moisture submerges my granny panties. My body feels like a tropic precipitation region.

We've kissed before, but not like this—not soft, wet, tongue; only pure, quick pecks saying "bye", "I'll see you later". Not soft, wet, tongue causing my mouth to tingle, chills throughout my body, heat and moisture from my vagina or the desire for him to capture my virtue.

Holding me close, tight, and in his arms, he steps back and eases us up onto my bed.

We're making out and I'm on top, I panic!

With the touch of his charm neglecting not a single fraction of my being, adrenalin races throughout my glands, warming each chill in my body.

I chant to myself to *think, think, think,* of something to ease my panic. I stroke my three middle fingers across his left nipple, it stiffens.

The thought that Mickey is watching us plagues my thoughts.

Noooo, what?

Imagining that a fictional character is a voyeur, spying on me and my boyfriend—well friend—best friend—making out, heightens my panic. It only has me feel like a patient with psychosis.

FOCUS!

I rub his chest and massage his shoulder, peck the corners of his mouth, then down to his neck, nibbling.

My mother is home. She can walk in any second, I fret!

Qalbee palms a hand full of my butt and squeezes.

Who am I kidding, my mother is out cold, I chill.

Qalbee turns me over onto my back.

Thank you! I'm too nervous to be on top; besides, I have no idea what I'm doing.

Qalbee effortlessly slips his hand into my swishes, then under my granny panties. His index finger rubs around my vagina as if it has eyes searching for something.

"*Oh!*" I gasp fervently, as my back spasms.

He conquers his exploration. I close my eyes as his index and middle finger entice my clitoris. He gently . . . and slowly, massages . . . then slips them in. My eyes involuntarily open. I catch a glimpse of the back of his tapered waves as he massages my neck with his lips and tongue, harmonizing with his two fingers inside me. I quickly shut my eyes embarrassed of the joyful expression that undoubtedly conquers my face. He relieves his fingers, positions himself upright on his knees, and slides off his shirt. I figure this is the time I undress as well so I prop up on my boney elbows and nervously slide off my sweats. He smiles, making me more nervous. I scurry upright, invading his personal space so that I am too close to look him in his gorgeous face. Our cheeks touch. He takes the bottom of my shirt and raises it. The fabric grazes my nipples and they harden instantly under my golden yellow bra.

I want him, dearly!

I place my hands between his on my crumbled shirt, and lift it over my shoulders, trying to rush him, but he doesn't let me. He slowly eases it over my head and along my arms, exposing imprints of my stiff nipples through my bra. I struggle, but successfully pull Mickey from under my butt and from under his knees. I right angle off the bed, lay the comforter on the floor, and then lay on my back. My eyes look into his, begging him to lay with me. One foot after the other, and both knees and hands on the comforter, he complies. I smell a hint of musk fuming from his husky body as he hovers over me on all fours. His eyes are piercing.

"You sure you ready to do this?"

"Yes," I say partially annoyed that he asks me that. "Yes," I repeat, redeeming my annoyance. I profess zealously, "I'm in love with you, Qalbee," and the words are no longer in bondage to my poetry, shackled in my spiral tablet. They are free from my mouth for the first time in his presence. On impulse, my warm, moist, anxious hand reaches and tugs the bottom of his ear lobe, sending him a sign of passion. I then caress his jaw line down to his chin and stroke along his neck. In the palm of his right hand he embraces the back of my neck and passionately kisses me. I close my eyes tasting paradise! Just as I feel goose bumps chill my body, he stops. The tips of our noses touch.

"Yo mom's here."

"I know." *But I don't care!*

I bravely rise to unsnap my bra. Qalbee rubs his nose against mine, Eskimo kissing me, making me smile! I lay flat on my back and he follows. Self-consciously I slide my bra down my arm and drop it onto the floor. I tilt my head and slide my tongue into his mouth and he gladly receives it. Immediately I lift my hips, slide off my granny panties, and drop them onto the floor, happy that he has not made some joke on how uninvitingly repugnant they are. I feel him reach into his pants pocket, and then hear him wrestle with a condom packet so I peek. I peer at his smooth brown husky body shielding my yellow thin body. He then slides the rubber onto the tip of what is soon to grant my saturated virginity a desired wish. He instantly pushes inside of me.

"*Um*!" I tighten my jaws to counter the pain of him plunging through my threshold. "Huh," I breathe, letting out a gasp of pleasure, heart pounding. I open my eyes. His eyes robustly lock with mine. As we gaze at each other, I hoped that he, I, we both, cannot help but to be spellbound—that he, like I, longed for this moment.

As his hips thrust, his penis penetrates in and out. As I receive him, his mushroom tip provides me with the feeling of ecstasy.

"Oh!" Feeling a slight, tight pain I moan. My hymen tore. No longer am I a virgin and I assume that Qalbee knows it because he has slowed down, probably feeling the extra fluid. He stops thrusting and looks at me with concern. To assure him that I want him, desire him, crave him, I cup both of his butt cheeks into the palms of my hands and propel his hips encouraging him to continue. He acquiesces. The feeling of euphoria takes precedence over the pain. As he rotates his hips, he props himself up on his left elbow and fondles my left nipple, then bends forward and sucks my right breast. I quiver from the touch of his lips and tongue massaging from breast to breast then around my collarbone to my neck. I hear him breathing in rhythm with my heartbeat. The scent of musk and sweat perfumes the air.

After a lifetime of pleasurable wet pumps in and out, tension releases as discharge explodes. I feel his warm release unite with mine.

We exhale in unison. We lay stationary—his smooth brown sweaty body rests on me. He gently rubs his thumb up my forehead to my hairline and massages his fingernails gently into my scalp. Before long, he rushes to trash the condom and quickly clothes himself. I slowly follow suit and weakly get dressed.

Chapter Eight

I CONVINCED QALBEE to stay and shower the sweat off, and to give his pores some time to close. And though I didn't want him to get sick, my ploy was primarily so that he would stay longer so that I could spend more time with him. I want no breaths apart but I also don't want to smother him or cling too much either. Even though I wanted to, I didn't suggest that we shower together. Plus I didn't know how uncomfortable it would be for either of us, being that we're 18 and 19 and aren't grown enough to shower together-*well, in my parents' house*- or adult enough to have our own place. I gave him a wash cloth and dry-off towel and pointed him to my varied body scrubs behind my gold shower curtain, on the second row of the three stainless steel shelves in the shower. He chose peach lime, *my favorite!* While Qalbee was showering, I grabbed a wash cloth and dry-off towel for myself, locked the brass push button lock to the bathroom, used my skeleton key to lock my bronze antique bedroom door—locking Qalbee in—and showered in Sebastian's bathroom.

PARKED AT THE CURB in my parent's driveway, I sit on the hood of Qalbee's blue Cutlass in between his legs, with my back to his chest, and his arms around my waist. The cool winter air aims to chill me, but I feel so vibrant, it fails. I'm always happy when I'm in Qalbee's presence, but I feel especially euphoric after what we shared *tonight!* The smell of his sweet natural musk still lingers on his body after a twenty minute shower! I can taste his aroma as the chilly brisk air blows in my direction. I feel his wintry breath when he speaks and the bass in his voice is calm, it sooths me! He's the center of my senses—and *tonight*, I seem to be his! He constantly stares at me to make sure that I'm listening, and each time, his gaze touches deep within my sole causing me to blush. He knows I listen to every word he speaks, but he's being a bit more sensitive *tonight*. Tonight his topics have been more serious, rather than joke after joke.

Usually I'm the one thin-skinned when we talk deep. Sometimes our conversations can get controversial and when they do, I get a little scared that if I don't agree with him he won't like me, or if we don't see eye to eye on everything that he may overlook my worth and may not consider me as something of value in his future. However, I am compelled to be true to myself. I'm most comfortable when I am me which sometimes frightens me, especially when it comes to him because of my "your loss" attitude. I want no feeling like that between us. We have talked about so many things in the past, but he never really goes into details about his upbringing or life. He's very private. But *tonight,* he shared with me that ever since his mother has not returned to work he's been helping out with some of the bills at home—utilities, the landline phone, and he keeps up the lawn on a monthly basis. It bothers him that she's not working. It bothers him that he barely passed his senior year when he had a history of A's and B's, and that he missed a lot of practices and basketball games causing him to lose out on a possible scholarship. It bothers him that he's starting college a year late. Tonight's conversation enlightened me that he's an adult *and even more responsible than I knew!*

Though, thinking back, I gather that I should have realized his maturity after the Sunday he came over excited, rushing me to come outside to show me his prized possession. He was so proud and wanted to share his moment with me! I walked outside and there it was. A huge grin was on his face, the same grin every time he lays eyes on it. Here, parked in this very spot, his prized possession: his fourth generation 1988 blue Cutlass Supreme with mirror tint, chrome trimmed Oldsmobile, with white wall tires that he had just paid for in full with the help of no one. Fresh off the lot, he independently purchased it by saving the majority of his checks from working at Blockbusters since he was seventeen. Which is why he calls it his prized possession—I respect that! He took me to school the next day, my first day of senior year.

I giggle because earlier in our conversation he went on and on, grinning and on his own natural high, talking about his prized possession so much that I actually had to cut him off. I had never done that to him before! It's really flattering because I think he's apprehensive about claiming my virginity or maybe uncomfortable with *that* thought. What we did was huge! He knows that my favorite subject is physics so he changed the topic to sciences. We touched on many sectors of science though, anatomy and chemistry wasn't up for discussion. We got on nature then insects. I posed that grasshoppers jump higher than humans but Qalbee isn't confident of my knowledge in entomology, so we've been debating.

"Can't no grasshopper jump higher than no human," Qalbee says loud and laughs real hard in my ear.

"I'm telling you . . . comparing the size and height of a grass hopper to a human, the average person jumps 45-55 cm high and grasshoppers can jump 20 times itself. We can't do that," I attempt to convince.

"Ha!" he huffs. He tilts his chin, gazing at me. "You so weird." He absorbs me. Under the hood of his pullover, his yellow ball cap moves from side to side as he shakes his head. A coy smile hugs his face as I stare up at him. "Who thinks of that?" He swiftly pecks my cheek then slowly scoots us off the hood.

I turn facing him in his arms as we stand against the car.

"Who knows things like that?" He steadily shakes his head and carries that coy smile. Qalbee takes my left hand then nods, signaling for me to get in the passenger's seat of his prized possession, and then walks towards his car door. I follow suite and head towards the passenger door. He lowers into his seat then reaches over the console to unlock my door. As I lower in, I can smell his musk—it's the smell of his room, his clothes, his body; *and now my body*! I smile at the thought!

I look at Qalbee reaching to catch his eyes. He looks at me.

"Comedy, I know you are not in love with me like I am with you and that's okay," I quickly appease, lifting my right hand signaling "wait" to let me finish. "I don't regret what we shar . . . what happened tonight," I begin explaining. I want him to understand the veracity of my love for him. The words slide off my tongue "I was with Caleb for two years and we never made love," I say in a pragmatic manner, still trying to get to my point.

Qalbee's expression is concentrated. I turn away rotating my entire body facing the dashboard. I'm so nervous that my body grows tense and my mouth dries.

Being able to only produce a whisper, I profess, "That was amazing and I just . . . you are my . . ." I stammer. I look up to catch his eyes again. "Um, no pressure but would you come with me to my senior prom?" I exhaled with agony, though I'm hopeful. "I mean, you don't have to answer right now. Just let me know," I continue to appease.

"Yaya, you are real cool—and I enjoy spending time with you," he stares, "Every time I'm over here, we spent no less than four hours together; and being here just about every day straight this past summer was far from what I expected." He places his right hand on my shoulder. "I ain't eva spent that much time with a broad," he enthusiastically emphasizes.

I continue to stare, and though I'm sure my face displays offense, I take no true offense because it's him.

"I mean, you know what I mean," he disrupts my thoughts attempting to explain. He then leans back in his seat. He now faces the steering wheel. "You not just some broad . . ." he stammers, "what I am saying is . . ." he pauses.

Qalbee then leans back over towards me, reaches over the console and palms my right hand as it lies between my legs in my lap. His gaze penetrates mine and I know that he's genuine. It's so serious.

"If I can handle something I'm dealing with at home I'll go . . ." he appeases, ". . . but I'll let you know," he quickly stipulates.

Qalbee leans in closer to me. His right palm hugs my left cheek, he rubs his thumb across my lips, and then strokes his finger tips down my neck, gently resting his palm on the side of my face next to my ear. His thumb joint is positioned on the corner of my mouth. There is so much passion in his actions. I feel so much adoration for him—so intense this moment is—I lean tilt into his palm like a puppy would do his owner. My inner animal urges to bite his thumb and my reflex urges to suck his thumb for psychosexual gratification. I crave him. I'm like a puppy in heat.

I place my left hand over his, cuddle his hand to my cheek, lean towards him, and then kiss his left cheek. I hastily open the door to his prized possession because I can't be in his presence right now. If I linger too much longer irrepressible feelings of lust will emerge or the thought that he may not escort me to my prom will settle in, and neither of those feelings are healthy for me at the moment.

"'Kay." I scramble out, though before I slam the door, I assure him, "I will wait patiently for you." . . . *for you are My Heart.*

My Heart

More than anything we are friends.
Just as I talk to you with no resistance
I want you to be comfortable confiding in me.

Before anything our friendship will ascend.
Just as I display with you, all of me that exist,
around me, the same, I desire for you to present.

Sometimes I want to say I love you,
... but do I want to because I love you ...
or because I love the idea of wanting someone to love?

But then I realize ...

I crave to be more than just your confidant.
I want to be preeminent,
Emotionally intimate,
... the person you feel most ardent with.

Trust in you comes so easy for me:
I want you to trust the words that flow from my mouth with your ears,
like I trust the thoughts in my mind with the feelings your eyes express
I want you to trust your secrets with my inborn moral strength,
like I trust my fears with the security your protective demeanor possess

It Won't Go Away
Samina Najmah

I crave for you to trust your emotions, centered profoundly in my heart,
like I trust my physical essence deep within your soul
I crave for you to trust your heart in my chest,
like I trust my life in your hands.
Within my being, your aura is embedded.
Sometimes you look at me... joy. Sometimes you look at me... mysterious.
The way you adore me, I adore thee.
The way you gaze into my eyes, I stare into your heart.

Sometimes you say things... heavenly.
Sometimes you do things... genuinely.
You make me feel beautiful... you make me feel happy
You make me feel important... you make me feel worth it.

... what is that IT?...
... breathing, living, smiling, believing, and all that IT entails.

You are my hero...
... how...
... well...
... you are admired for your achievements and qualities-
you possess all aspects.
... My heart beats for you...
When I hear your name...
my heart drops, upon my face a smile arise.
My heart is blissful, my face is luminous.

It Won't Go Away
Samina Najmah

You are not my dream or the friend I prayed for
every night... You are real life...
You are more of a companion than I could have ever asked for
...and even more than I knew was possible.
You are not that missing piece...
you were just that lost part of me...
and now...
my essence is complete...
Sometimes I want to say I love you...
...because I do.

LA Nov 1999

Heart Murmur

Chapter Nine

THICK WHITE COTTON MOVES rapidly through the beautiful blue ocean creating figures of anything that my imagination will allow. Tonight there will be much glitter sparkling up there for us to admire down here and for the many camping children to make wishes on. The beautiful blue sky is a creation of dark, eternal nothingness. My thoughts will stretch no further into the clouds. My imagination has gone poignant, along with my heart.

It seems a life time ago since I have been up here on Cloud Nine. Thank goodness it is spring! It had been so cold this past winter that I was unwilling to come up here like I do in the spring, summer, and fall. At least four to five days out of the week I come up here to do my homework, write stories and poems, and bask, just as I do—well did—in my safe heaven. I enjoy talking on the phone up here whenever the cordless is charged enough to have good reception. I chuckle at the thought of how Chanelle and I sometimes press channel and listen to other people's conversations when the reception statics! One time we heard a lady fussing at her son for coming in late; and another time some man was trying to ask a woman out on a date and when he finally got the courage and asked her, she told him she was already seeing someone else. I actually felt bad for him. But, if I can hear their conversations sometimes, I think about how they can probably hear mine too. Surprisingly, I was able to convince Chanelle to come up on the roof with me today.

The night after Qalbee and I made love, I came up here that morning to hold on to my cherished memory. Qalbee called me when he made it home making sure that I was fine and not freaking out.

He makes me smile!

The odd thing is that I did not have the urge to call him like I thought I would after giving him the key to my purity. I had the idea that I would be pathogenic and prey on his every move. Plus, I wanted to give him some time to think about escorting me to my prom. But then, I did not hear from him for a few more days and I began to worry. I called and paged him several times. When I had not heard from him after the second week, to keep my mind busy, I filled out an application at the retirement center that I used to volunteer at and they hired me on the spot. I have been serving meals to residents with Alzheimer's for a little over a month now. He finally responded right after that but had no coherent answer to make sense of it all. And since then, we have only talked over the phone. I've struggled to repress the ache I feel throughout my body from not being able to see him . . . touch him . . . smell him. He has not, or will not come over, nor has he invited me over. I just strive to be satisfied with our derisory conversations about our day. I talk about how school is going for me, and he's vague like usual. I ask him what is going on with him but he circumvents and crafts jokes. I reassure him that I am here for him and am waiting patiently for him to inaugurate, but he shuns. Sometimes he'll act as if he's some big time comedian, like D.L. Hughley or someone, doing stand up.

I smile and blush at the memory, causing me flutters—*he's really good*. Sometimes he has me laughing so hard that a storm of tears flow from my eyes and I have to consciously catch my breath. Only, our conversations are brief and unpredictable; and some are uncomfortable and dull—not his usual comical self.

It perturbs me that I have not seen him since that day. It crossed my mind, but I did not have the heart to ask Chanelle to ease it out of Craig. Yet, she felt my pain and pryed on her own, but didn't find out much—only that he is going through "personal things." Chanelle thinks his distant behavior is related to another girl, and I shamefully agree with her. But, Chanelle says she does not believe he only wanted sex from me. I don't believe her. She thinks I would not be able to get over giving up my virginity to someone I'm not married to, who's not even my boyfriend, who only used me for sex, and who has *a-whole-nother* girlfriend. And she's partially correct. *I don't* have the strength to consider that he only wanted sex from me. My heart could not take it. If that were the truth then all the days and time we spent together—him eager to share the news with me about his new car; and wanting me to read his college acceptance letter to him, which was his way of letting me in; all the deep conversations about our dreams and goals for our future; him wanting to go into computer graphics, making cartoons and video games, and me wanting to own a personal care home for people with mental illness; my lost virginity—*would all* be in vain.

The hysterical thing is that we never discussed being in a relationship. I guess I took all the personal time we spent together for granted and deemed it unnecessary to bring that topic up. I haven't cried which is not a surprise. I'm not a crier; however, the beat of my heart has been murmuring so loud, and with much palpable thrill, that a doctor wouldn't need a stethoscope to locate the quality of my love for Qalbee. I have been listening to all four of Brian McKnight's CDs—primarily *Brian McKnight* and *I Remember You*. I especially relate to "Still in Love" and "After the Love". The intensity of the turbulent blood flowing through my veins is so sufficient it produces its own radiant musical rambling as I ache. I also listen to Kenny Lattimore and Carl Thomas . . . and writing Qalbee poems.

Then there is Chad. He is new to East Academy, a transfer from Putman Metropolitan way on the other side of town. He is in all my classes, excluding sixth period—weight lifting, which I got in to gain weight. Chad takes home economics. We laugh. Well, I laugh about that. He doesn't think it's all that funny. He wants to be a chef and works part-time at his brother's restaurant in the country. Chad and I clicked almost instantly. We are a lot alike, starting with our complexion and lean physique. He's fun to be around. He's quirky and compassionate, and very much unique. And also like me, he wants to make the world a better place.

We share many commonalties as well. We both like to fish, love the outdoors and nature, and enjoy amusement parks! He's been over to the house a few times to do homework, science papers, and work on group presentations. He's even met my mother. She doesn't seem to like him much though. One day after Chad and I worked on an assignment, he and his friend Terrence were play fighting in my parents' living room and were hurling out every curse word in the heathen book. The fact that my mother caught Chad tossing up his middle finger a few too many times didn't help. Since then just from the mention of his name her face pulsates in fury like she wants to swat his yellow butt until it turns black and blue like she's his mother. It's difficult because Chad and I have grown to be real close friends and we talk about so much except he has no idea about "My Heart" condition.

Now, I sit here on this beautiful spring day perspiring from humility instead of humidity and without brisk frosty air to chill me, like the last time I was up here. I am numb to happiness.

"Just call em," Chanelle prompts as she sits beside me in her dark orange baby polo shirt and khaki Daisy Dukes.

"I did."

"Well call Chad and we can chill with him and Terrance," she says with an impatient tone. "Come on, get back to the old you, the nonchalant, detached, on your own agenda you," she cheers me on.

"I know. But what about prom? It's in a few weeks? He still has not mentioned it."

"Caleb?" Chanelle blurts.

Overflowing with loathing, I stare up at her for having the audacity to utter that name in my presence. She feels my revulsion as she stares back at me lurking the resentful grimace on my face. I know she only said it to lighten me up. It's not working.

"Take Chad!" she says surprisingly, feeling my frustration.

Hum, I thought. "I could!" I say. I never thought about Chad as an option. Actually, I've thought of no one but Qalbee.

"It's just so short notice." I'm sure Chad's suburban veneer and yellow tone already gained him a date. "But we are growing to being pretty close. He's like . . . almost like . . . a best friend!"

"Yea, a best friend that's in love with you and wanna hit that," Chanelle brushes my shoulder with hers, grinning and giving me googly eyes, teasing me.

I chuckle. Playfully I boast, "Yea." A skewed smirk crosses my face. "He'd do anything for me!"

Chanelle sticks her tongue out, moves her head all around, and licks an imaginary lollypop. "Yea, anything," she laughs. Shocked by her vulgarity, my hand immediately covers my smiling mouth. I push the same shoulder she used to shove me with, and from the press of my hand she tilts to the right. Chanelle chortles, giving out a snort, then scoots to the edge of the roof preparing to climb down. Her back faces me, her knees face my back yard, and her feet touch the top step of my ladder.

"You and this damn roof," she complains like always about being on my roof.

I partially grin. "Tonight with Bert and Ernie?" I ask loudly to reach her as she moves away from me, mocking Chad and Terrence for always being together and never apart. Chanelle uses the term "*butty partners*"!

She turns her neck to look back at me. "That's good!" She applauds through the slight smirk on her face. "I see your comedian is rubbing off on you!" She turns forward chuckling, and then heads down the ladder.

I hear a car pull up so I turn towards the front yard to see who it may be. It's a black Chevrolet with black tinted windows, black rims and red-wall tires—Terrence's Camaro. I'm unable to see who's all in the car, but I aimlessly wave anyway to be polite.

"Hey? You never told me what happened with Trecy?" I bellow looking down at the top of Chanelle's ponytail. It's brushed to one shoulder as she walks along the side of the house headed towards the front yard.

"You and that damn roof!" she repeats while struggling to walk as she dusts dead wet leaves off her brown low-top Chuck Tyler tennis shoes. "He's just another victim!" she answers while approaching Terrence's vehicle. She mounts into Dark Vader—I believe it fits

Terrence's car along with his personality—they scamper off. I cannot help but smile, happy that Chanelle actually, somewhat, likes someone; and even happier that Trecy's out the picture.

I hear ringing . . .

"Yea," I speak into the cordless.

"I got all your many messages . . ." the voice pauses.

I sit here quiet, frozen.

". . . I was calling to tell you I can't go with you to the prom," Qalbee says sounding frustrated.

I sit here quiet, holding back a sob. I manage to speak, "It's fine . . . I understand . . . I said no pressure, right?" My voice fractures. Timid to ask, but I do anyway, "Why?" I ask, needing an explanation, though simultaneously he comments.

"Ok, but I'll call you soon." he rushes me.

Wait . . . soon? Wow? Why soon? I try harder to hold back my sob. I regret even asking.

"Because I'm busy right now," he sounds irritated.

"No, not *"why call me back"* . . ." I say mirroring his agitation. Terrified to ask, and apprehensive of rejection, I timidly whisper ". . . why can't you come with me to my prom?" I grumble, though am successful in not weeping.

"Because I can't. I have to go. You said no pressure. Just leave it alone," he roars, again frustrated.

"OKAY!" I wail. *I'm sorry.* I weep, but low enough that he can't hear me. *What did I do? Why is he so angry with me?* I sob.

I hear white noise, loud breathing, beeps in intervals like an electrocardiogram or electroencephalogram would make, and a quiet Qalbee on the other end of the phone; then, a dial tone.

FRUSTRATED

I'm frustrated because I can't tell if it's real
Frustrated because I don't know how to feel

I'm frustrated because we didn't talk last night
Frustrated because we can't make things right

I'm frustrated because there is no trust
Frustrated because I know it's a must

I'm frustrated because I need you night and day
Frustrated because I can't have things my way

I'm frustrated because you won't let me take your hand
Frustrated because I can't get you to understand

I'm frustrated because I can't feel your gentle touch
Frustrated because I miss you so much

I'm frustrated because we can't be together
Frustrated because I know I'll love you forever

LA 2000

Chapter Ten

I STAND IN MY sparkling white crystal stiletto pumps—reflecting the stars in the sky. I'm five feet from the proxy painted ceramic dance floor. They made it by placing four wood border lines in the shape of a box in front of a created stage draped in table cloth in the school's gym. My loose spiraled Shirley Temple hair flows under my sterling silver crystal tiara band. I specifically chose it thinking I'd wear it to look dazzling for Qalbee. I wear a long fitted turquoise nylon tube top dress, trimmed in sheer lace. It exposes my stomach around to my back stopping two inches from revealing my buttocks.

Chad stands in front of me, facing me, in his white gaiters and cuffed denim jeans. He is wearing a white notch lapel, single breasted, one button tux jacket that he left unfastened, exposing his white button down shirt and rolled sleeves. He wears a turquoise blue hank and a long thin turquoise blue tie. Looking at his slim 6 feet 2 inch build, it's a wonder I never noticed the muscular abs and bulging chest before on this fine specimen that stands before me. I can see his even skin, straight white teeth, and dimples under his newly trimmed mustache and goatee, and his long eyelashes through the thin lenses of his plastic square shaped frames. He is doing a great job at keeping my attention. Although we have not been here long I'm actually having a good time. Chad is being really sweet and catering, bringing me hors d'oeuvres and punch, walking me to the restroom, and holding my clutch.

The school gym is drenched with silver and white décor, loud music, and nonstop chatter. Keeping his eyes on mine, Chad steps a couple of feet back onto the dance floor, lifts his right gaiter behind his back, grabs it in his right hand and places his left palm to the back of his bald fade. He then begins moving his left elbow and right knee back and forth. My chin tilts as a bashful smile crosses my face, and out comes a chuckle at this goofy dance. He is being so comfortable and easy going! I glace to my left and see Chanelle approaching us in her two piece teak brown tube top and long sequenced skirt—*with no Terrence in sight?*

Originally Trecy were to escort Chanelle to the prom. He had been pursuing her "goods" for so long that he had his own agenda to go to a hotel afterwards. But since Chanelle is so resolute about not giving up her virginity to anyone until she knows it's real, she ditched him. And even though Chanelle and Craig spent loads of time together she never really liked his overly extraverted conduct. She only did it for me. After Qalbee and I fell off and Chad and I became cool—and since Terrence and Chad are best friends, and "butty partners"—Chanelle and Terrence ended up spending more time together. Chanelle gravitated to Terrence like I gravitated to Qalbee. The day Chanelle first laid eyes on Terrence's curly Afro, she knew she would ask him to her prom. Though, to avoid appearing desperate, she waited for them to spend more days together before she asked him. In retrospect, I'm thinking that Terence might have only agreed to be her escort because he knew Chad would be here.

With my head I point at Chad as he stands in front of me and I whisper loudly in Chanelle's ear, "He's not so bad." I continue to chuckle at Chad's dancing. "What happened to Ernie . . . I mean Terence?" I yell over Maroon 5 and the multitude of chatter.

Three boys in tuxedos and two girls in short fitted prom dresses walk up interrupting us. Each of them reeks of burnt grass, and looks really happy. They are loud, excited, and are constantly giggling, but they act tranquil, like they're in slow motion. One of the boys reaches into the inside pocket of his navy blue tuxedo jacket carefully pulling out three small clear plastic cups. He offers us what appears to be Jell-O. Chad took two—one he quickly gulps into his mouth and the other he tucks into the flap of his tuxedo pocket. I see Chanelle quickly scoff the third one into her mouth, when Chad grabs my hand and pulls me to the dance floor. He takes both of my hands into his and places them around his neck; and then rests his on my waist slowly leading my hips to the tune. We met one another's eyes and I know he is most likely feeling more than I am. I rest my head on his chest as we dance to the "Love We Had Stays on My Mind", remade by Dru Hill. And for the first time since I walked into my senior prom I think about Qalbee. *Where is he? What is he doing? Is he thinking about me at this very moment? No, cause if so, he'd be here.*

I feel a tap on my shoulder bringing me out of my funk. With my eyes still closed, I slowing turn around in excitement knowing that it is Qalbee! When I open them I find, to my disappointment, it's Chanelle.

"Come on girl. We have to catch up." She grabs my wrist, looks at Chad then back at me. "We haven't had a chance to talk since I walked in." She pulls me off the dance floor.

"He stood me up," Chanelle conveys.

Bewilderment envelops my face. Without pretense, I brazenly point with my head "And so . . ."

"So, I had to bring Jerk here," Chanelle thwacks her escort in the stomach with her brown clutch.

I smirk knowing that she likes him—and at the fact that he likes her enough to let her call him names and smack him in public. I think he is oddly turned on by her playing hard to get.

"Hey Craig!"

"What's up?"

"How's Qalbee?"

"He's one-hun'ed."

"Yea, that's what I thought," I grumble under my breath. I feel Chanelle clinch my wrist then pull me.

"Let's go see what's left to eat."

I CAN STILL SMELL the smoked turkey and chicken breast from earlier. The three all white tables with clear plastic-ware were set up as self serve buffets. The appetizer table was decorated with finger foods and vegetable trays, the entrée table held turkey, chicken and sides, and the dessert table displayed fruit, pastries, and beverages. Chanelle stands against the appetizer table picking through what is left of the tortilla chips and salsa, cold spinach dip and pita chips, and little deli sandwiches on fresh rolls and mini croissants. I stand beside her with my clear square shaped plastic plate full of grapes in one hand, and a clear plastic champagne cup filled with pink punch in the other.

"So, Chad is *really* my best friend. I'm having fun with him!"

"No more Q?" Chanelle instigates.

"Out of sight, but not out of mind," I blubber as I raise a grape to my mouth.

With a mouthful Chanelle attempts to convince me. "Well I hate Craig. I just needed someone to walk me in." She steadily puts scrapings on her plate.

"You are just wrong." I shake my head.

"You givin' him some tonight?"

"HECKS NO. He's my friend. I'm in love with Qalbee!" I indignantly declare.

"Well I'm givin it up to Craig."

"What? No! You have to save it for the guy you love . . . definitely not the one you hate."

"Well, look how that's goin for you!" she inadvertently declares not realizing the effect of her words.

Chanelle's words pierced like a dart. Though, I must submit to her truth. I cannot deny that at this point, I feel "what does love gotta do with virginity."

"Well, you have a point there. Forget Qalbee," I whimper again. I feel my lips form into an upside down "u" as I frown. My heart burns—and not from the spicy chicken breast served earlier tonight.

"I'm 'bout to get drunk and have a good time!" Chanelle declares.

I SIT STARING THROUGH the window shield from the passenger seat of the white Mustang rented by Chad's parents and mine. I watch the dark air travel through the water causing a rise and fall friction in the lake producing waves that reflect my inner sentiments. Just as I anticipate a bathymetric chart to my emotions, unexpectedly Chad reaches his pursed lips across the console. This is not the support I anticipated, the answer to my deep waves of emotions. This is the opposite. I hesitate then purse my lips and lean across the console. Our lips touch. His hand touches my lower back, massaging it. I am uncomfortable. I then tense up.

He stops. "Are you okay?"

"Yes," I mislead.

"Look, I know you have feelings for Q . . ."

Wait? What? How does he know? I listen.

". . . and I know you not the type of girl that messes around."

Right, right, correct!

"I'm willing to wait for however long you need."

Wait, hold up. Wait for what?

"Thank you, Chad. It's not like Qalbee and I are together." *I only would like to be.* I look away realizing what I'm saying. "He's not even my boyfriend," I utter. I pause as I hurt. I look back up at Chad. "I really appreciate your patience. I did think about *being with* you tonight . . ." I emphasize *being with*, hoping he'd understand that I mean sexually, so I wouldn't have to say it. ". . . but we are just friends. I love you . . . like a best friend. You are my best friend! Plus, I have news that I haven't told anyone yet. Not even Chanelle."

"You pregnant," he asserts loudly, and with conviction.

"Nooo! I was accepted to Texas View University. I'm moving to Texas in a few weeks."

"Wow." He looks away. "Dude, I had it all worked out in my head that you were gonna be my girl."

There is silence between us. I feel bad to hurt him like this.

"I guess now I'll have to find another one," he says with enthusiasm.

My face is dumbfounded. I had no idea that I'd care one way or the other if he'd had a girlfriend.

Chad bursts out laughing!

My ego stings just for a quick millisecond, but then I chuckle, realizing that he is only kidding. I push his shoulder with my left hand and he shifts.

No longer laughing, but with a smile to his lips, he reaches over and embraces me. "Congratulations! I'm proud of you." He releases me, and then gently pulls on my left earlobe. Giving full eye contact he states, "Just don't forget about the little people."

I reach over the console and my lips peck the left corner of his lips.

Chad's cell phone rings. He answers.

"What . . . who? Slow down." Chad looks over at me. "She's right here. What, who?" He stares at me with concern. "Car accident? Q too?"

CHAD AND I PULL UP to Baptist Hospital. I reach over and embrace Chad, then open the car door.

"Thank you."

"Hold on, I'll walk you up."

"No, it's fine," I smile at his gentleness. "Thank you Chad. Have a good night." I secure his car door and head up the stairs.

I speed walk through the entry doors of the hospital, holding back tears. The cold, empty lobby feels too huge. The walls around me are stretched. I'm a small helpless being. My eyes fill with tears. Chad said that it was Chanelle on the other end of the phone and that she, Craig, and Qalbee were all in the hospital. Chad said that she was so hysterical that he was unable to make everything out. I wondered how Chanelle had gotten Chad's number, but he was almost definite that she got it from Qalbee. It was staggering to hear Chad bring up Qalbee's name for a second time tonight. I learned that Terrence and Qalbee are cousins and that there is a group of them in some clique called Juvenile. I'm so flabbergasted that Qalbee, Chad, Craig and Terrence have known each other all this time and all have been hanging out. What I wanted to ask, though didn't, is when, how, and why was my name even brought up in their juvenile discussions.

I press the "arrow up" button. It lights up red and then the elevator dings. The doors open and I step in. My thoughts race—my best friend, my sister, both of my best friends—in a wreck, and Craig. I let out a loud gasp and begin wailing. *When did they all get together? What happened?* I wail so loud that the bell of the elevator appears vague, but the reverberation of it opening is amplified. It startles me. The wait felt like a lifetime. I rush off. I head for the information desk directly in front of me. There are two nurses in white uniforms sitting behind it. I hear white noise and peeps in intervals. It takes me back to the day Qalbee declined my offer as my escort to the prom.

"Libi!"

I hear my name being called when a quick and brief thought enters the back of my head, *could Qalbee have been in the hospital that day?*

I turn to my left. "Chanelle!"

I run to her, and then embrace her. She's trembling. I cleave to her.

"Why aren't you lying down? Where's your room? Where's Uncle David?"

Chanelle lets me go. "What? Why would my dad be here?" she holds me at arm's length.

She looks just as confused as I am.

"Cause, you were in a wreck and he should know about this," I say senselessly. "What did you do? You've been drinking." I put my neck under her arm to assist her in walking. I'm looking for her room. "So what . . . he won't be upset . . . just as long as you're okay," I attempt to convince her.

She stops us. "Libi," she says with a firm tone, and then looks at me. "I was not in a wreck. Craig was."

I associate Craig with Qalbee so for the first time since I saw my sister standing here in this hospital, I thought about Qalbee again. "What? What about Qalbee?" I begin feeling worried all over again. "Chad said . . ."

"Yea, I told Chad that Craig was in a motorcycle accident and that Q was in the hospital."

"In or at?"

"Both."

"Like he's checked in . . . without being in the accident?" I'm confused.

"Yes. He was already here when I checked Craig in."

"Oh, here for Craig." I'm relieved.

"No, here for himself. I hadn't phoned anyone so Q couldn't have known that we were here."

I'm anxious . . . scared . . . and still confused.

"When the nurse checked Craig into his room, we passed by a room with Q's last name on the door."

"But there are so many Davis' in the world."

"Craig verified it. Apparently, Q has been checked in for days . . ."

"Wait, Craig verified it? How? How is he? Is he okay?" I feel my heart pounding. "Can someone tell me what happened . . . what is going on?" I say, frustrated.

Chapter Eleven

SHORTLY AFTER CHAD and I left the prom, Chanelle and Craig found the five students that had the jell-o shots. Chanelle had four more and Craig had two. The five kids also had marijuana brownies that Chanelle ate two of but Craig had none. Chanelle was determined to make her point that love had nothing to do with sex so her plan was to fulfill her word by giving up her virginity to Craig. Well, Craig dropped Chanelle off at home to change her clothes while he also went to change. Chanelle said that she was standing outside waiting on Craig when he rolled up on her street on a motorcycle. She was so baffled. She thought that it would be exciting, but couldn't fathom why he'd think she'd really ride on a motorcycle knowing that it would blow out her bangs and the few curls from her pinned up bun roll. Having mixed feelings about riding, and with a mixture of being high, with nonstop laughter she was screaming *"I'm not getting on that"* and for Craig to *"get off of it."*

She says they were both laughing and being playful; and that he decided to show her that he could ride with no hands. A car came out of nowhere and when he attempted to catch the handle bars he panicked causing the bike to jerk and the handles turned the front tire. He flipped off, body landing in the street and head landing on the curb, hitting it so hard that when Chanelle ran to him, he was unconscious with blood oozing out of a split in his forehead from his hairline to his eyebrow. Seeing the blood, Chanelle took off her white tank top and applied pressure to it as the driver of the car called 911.

AFTER CHANELLE FILLS ME IN, we go in to see Craig. He is out cold, either from the meperidine or the hydrocodone. This is the first time I've ever seen, well heard, nothing come from his mouth. I wish for a second that he was awake being his usual obnoxious self. I walk over to the hospital bed and take Craig's hand in mine. There is white gauze bandaged to his forehead covering his wound. He had to have 21 stitches because the skin avulsion exposed yellowish fatty subcutaneous tissue though the open cut. I close my eyes and say a quick prayer. I walk over to Chanelle, place my hand on her shoulder, and squeeze.

"I have to call home," I say looking into her worried eyes.

Though I do plan to call home, I also wanted to find Qalbee's room to see if it is true that he is checked into the hospital.

Why? What would he be in the hospital for? He's too young for prostate cancer and doesn't smoke to have lung cancer. It *could* be a family inherited disease. He wouldn't be hospitalized for a sexual transmitted disease, though definitely could be hospitalized for HIV or AIDS. The CDC estimated that last year between 800,000 to 900,000 people had HIV or AIDS; and estimates that by 2010, 31.6 to 35.2

will live with it. *Qalbee surely wouldn't have made love to me if that were the case?*

FAMILY MEMBERS OF PATIENTS were using the visitor's phones that hang on the wall, and I could not find a payphone in the halls. I came outside in the warm air to use the payphone. I called Uncle David and my mother letting them know that Chanelle and I are at the hospital visiting Craig and that I'd be here as a support for Chanelle until Craig wakes up.

The dark air feels great to my skin, warming me up. I dread going back through those hospital doors for many reasons. As I gallop up the stairs I exhale to prepare myself for the cold air inside, the sight of Craig laying in a hospital bed vulnerable, and watching Chanelle feel helpless. I approach the entry door and it swiftly pulls open, blowing a gust of wind on me. I hear tires loudly track the parking lot. Then I hear a car door slam. I turn around.

"Wow." He stares "You're so beautiful Yaya!"

"What are you doing here? Were you following me?" I am shocked, confused, furious. I don't know what to say. Actually, I have a lot to say. I just don't know where to start. Maybe with, *why does he have on those blue see-through hospital scrubs?*

"No, Craig told me he saw you at the prom," Qalbee explains.

"Yea, so?" I dictate, offended. "Craig? When?" I'm happy that it's a possibility that he is awake. Impatiently I continue, "How did you know I was here?" *Wait.* "I thought you were here . . ." I say intrusively, with sarcasm. ". . . checked in?" I'm angry. "What . . . you checked yourself out?" I continue being boorish.

"I knew you'd be here comforting your girl," he ignores my rude manner.

I fold my arms. "How you know that I didn't go back to a hotel. Or back to my prom date's place once I learned things were fine here?" I delude. I'm furious with him. My heart is pounding so hard that the rest of my body is trembling to the same rapid beat. I'm hurt, confused, scared.

"Cause I know you Libiya." He steps closer, leaving one stair between. "You not like that," he declares.

I inhale the whiff of mint from his breath-saver.

"Like what?"

"You not the type of girl to mess around. You're gonna put your family's needs before your own . . . and you love me," he says with confidence, stepping up one stair, putting us at eye level.

One more step and we'll share space. I feel my heated fast paced breath, augment from his nose back to my face. *I hope that my breath smells as fresh as his.* He steps up onto the stair that I occupy causing me to step back.

But not so fast . . . he grips my waist, cleaving to my body—and soul—and presses his lips to mine. I quiver. I am in love with him. I'm revitalized by his presence, his touch, his kiss. I am furious that the feelings I have for him won't go away. I cannot control them.

"Qalbee, come on, stop it," I utter with no confidence, not even convincing myself. I latch my fingers into his, behind my waist.

"Come in."

WHEN WE MAKE IT UP to Craig's room, he's still asleep. Chanelle sits in a chair on the side of his bed with her head laid on his chest. Qalbee walks over to them and Chanelle's head rises. She has tears in her eyes and guilt lies on her face. She stands, offers Qalbee her seat, then walks over to me standing at the door to give him some alone time with Craig. Chanelle and I step out and lean against the wall next to Craig's room door in the hallway where white noise and beeps in intervals grow apparent. I embrace Chanelle and she squeezes me back.

"He will be okay. It's not your fault. It was just as it sounds—an accident."

"I know."

We release. I hate seeing my sister like this. The last time she cried like this was at the age of ten when her mother said she'd come back for her, but never did.

It's almost three in the morning. I'm hungry and sleepy and no longer have the energy to investigative the theory that Qalbee is a patient in the hospital. Plus after seeing him, I don't have the heart. My focus tonight is to send a plethora of positive energy to Craig's recovery.

Qalbee walks up. "Hey Yaya, I can take you home."

I look at Chanelle.

"Yes, girl. Go ahead. I'm staying here, with Craig," she stammers with concern. "He'll be fine." She nods her head then looks down. "We'll be fine."

I hold Chanelle's hand, squeeze it, and lock my eyes sincerely with hers. "Okay, but call me . . . first thing . . . if you need me."

We embrace.

AS SOON AS QALBEE and I get into his prized possession he begins asking me about prom. I hadn't had much to say about prom. I figured *if he wanted to know about it, he should have escorted me.* I want to know about his stay at the hospital and what best way to get that information but from the source himself and without the labor of scrambling through hospital rooms and files.

"Are you worried about Craig?"

"I am, but what I gathered from what the doctor was saying and from reading entries on different types of biology lately, since the doctor was able to stop the bleeding within eight hours by stitching his cut, and did not have to stitch flapped over skin, Crag should be okay."

I scuff. "You? You've been reading different types of biology?" I mock him in a proper tone. "Yea, reading up on your disease," I strategize.

"What?"

"I know you've been in the hospital," I answer sharply, shaking my head. "Chanelle saw your name on the hospital door."

"Do you know how many Davis' are in the world?"

"Q. Davis?" I shout with conviction, staring up at him though knowing she only told me *Davis*.

"There are many Davis' in the world, Yaya," he softly utters.

I settle down. "But, we're talking about you," I say with sympathy, looking down, rubbing my tense hands together, and trying not to worry.

"Libiya, it's not me!" he shouts, seemingly out of frustration, possibly from worry.

Worried about whom: his self, Craig?

"I'm sorry!" I shout back on impulse. Maybe he's more worried about Craig then he's letting on. "I'll leave it alone," I whisper softly, though loud enough that he can hear me.

SUN SHINES THROUGH my sheer curtain generating an illuminated view of his precise chin line, striking nose, and perfect lips. I have not been this close to Qalbee, for this long since our "incident" six months ago. I don't want to take my eyes off of his beautiful brown, flawless face as he peacefully sleeps. Moisture ensues in my granny panties as I stare at his perfect face, and soft lips. I smell his musk linger after the passionate night we had. No sex, just fore-play and passion—getting to know each other's bodies again. He held me until I fell asleep!

My daring lips slowly descend, gently pecking his kissable lips. Qalbee's eyes quickly open and they are bug-eyed. I'm slightly startled, though my heart flutters from the enchantment in his eyes rather than from being startled. Qalbee intentionally sinks into his pillow and lifts the yellow cotton sheet over his chin, lips, and nose, parading only his peeping eyes. I bounce back to get out of his personal space and prop up on my right elbow in my own.

"You scaring me!" he says while shifting his pupils right to left, right to left. "How long you been watching me?" he asks, paranoid.

My face and body is full of alarm.

"*I always feel like, somebody's watching meeeee!*" Qalbee playfully sings a Rockwell tune. He hoists and drops the sheet uncovering his jovial smile. Childlike, and in high spirits, he cheerfully announces, "Yuh boy Mike," nodding his head and face self-assured!

My fluttering and pounding heart subsides. Relieved, I lean back propping up on both elbows, relaxing my upper body. Impetuously, I burst into laughter but attempt to maintain composure though a smile as bright as the sun's shine beams across my face. "Huh," I huff. "Don't do that!" I shout and shove his left shoulder.

He leans his bare torso in close, hovering over me.

I look down feeling bashful from his gleeful smile.

"Comedy . . ." I whisper, pleased to be in his presence, though I pause. Mixed feelings of happiness and discontent surmount as I stare into Qalbee's charming eyes. I hoist to sit upright as my body trembles with apprehension.

"I need to tell you something."

Qalbee quickly jumps back as if in attempt to avoid a slap in his face. Animatedly he proclaims, "It's not mine!" He then sings a Michael Jackson tune, *"Billie Jean was not my lover"*. He actively chuckles loudly.

I can't help but giggle, infected by his playfulness and good mood. With my right fist I push his chest. "Nooo! Stop it!" I declare, giggling, but really needing to tell him. *It's essential that I get this out now.*

"Um, I'm moving to Texas in a few weeks." I stare at him.

"I had no idea. Why?" he states impassively.

"College." I stare hoping for him to ask me to reconsider, to apply to the University of Oklahoma or to some other college around here.

"Well that's a good reason," he says senselessly with his voice in a high pitch, not adding the "duh" he obviously wanted to include.

Like I should have expected, his response is disappointing, distressing. I feel my intestines twist into a pretzel. *I'm hurt—in pain—aching. Throw me in a bed next to Craig. Give me some Vicodin. Why does he sound pleased that I'm leaving?* "That's it?"

"Na, I'm proud of you!" He says, looking down, awarding me with no type of eye contact. He rolls the sheet down his legs. "We'll keep in touch!" he has the audacity to utter—nonchalantly at that—and still granting me no eye contact.

I blankly stare at him as he scuffles through the sheets. He's searching for his sweats and shirt I assume. Empty, I want to cry. I want to punch him. I want to *hate* him.

"That's it? I'm proud of you? We'll keep in touch?" I question poignantly.

"What else is there? I'm happy for you. You deserve it," he says as he slips his left leg into his hospital scrubs.

I look down with disappointment, less at him and more at myself for continuing to put myself through this. *Why would I expect something more after all this time?*

"Q!" I roar. He stops. I never call him that, I always call him by his full name. "You barely keep in touch with me now, and we live in the same city!"

I see his eyes set on mine. Before I know it I'm at the head of my bed standing to my feet. The flight action of my nervous system has taken flight and the fight system ignites confirming that *I am* more disappointed with him, angry even, than at myself. I gasp a few deep breaths, attempting oxygen intake to calm myself down. *I'm feeling a bit hostile.* I exhale a few breaths and feel cogent. Though still, I stand here in the middle of my bed room floor feeling like an embarrassment, feeling like a dumb teenager in love crying about another boy, and this one doesn't even love me. I look down to avoid eye contact.

We are both silent.

"Maaan, Qalbee . . ." I pause. I'm filled with frustration and a galore of emotions. *I want to tell him how much I need him in my life, how much I want to be a part of his, how I want him to ask me to stay, to be his girlfriend, and to roommate together.* I hold back a sob.

Qalbee sits with his legs hanging from the bed and socks pressed into the carpet. He then holds his right hand out to me. "Come here. Sit with me."

My heart flutters to the sound of his soothing alto voice. I take two steps over to him and place my left hand into his. He pulls me and I climb in bed next to him with my knees digging into the mattress and pressed against the side of his left thigh as my buttocks rests on my heels. My shoulders hunch over and my body language is docile. He scoots over to turn towards me sliding his left leg on the bed behind me. I'm now between his legs. Qalbee releases my hand and raises his index finger to the middle of my lips, signing to keep silent. From west to east he rubs his finger across my lips slowly then embraces my chin between his thumb and index finger, and looks tensely into my eyes.

"We'll stay in touch," he soothingly declares, then pinches my chin delicately.

His piercing eyes are hypnotizing and I believe the passion in his voice. "Okay."

His hands squeeze both of mine while they lay meekly in my lap as his eyes continue to gaze into mine. I realize that he's observing my spellbound eyes, silently searching for assurance that he has comforted me. I nod. He blinks and my lashes involuntarily bat rapidly several times as if I'm no longer put under. I lean forward and kiss him on his right cheek and the tip of my nose and top lip hugs his cheekbone. I inhale his musk.

"You want any breakfast?" I invite, smiling.

"Na, I gotta get home."

Feeling a pinch to my heart from his rejection, and by the fact that he must go, I whimper inside. His buttocks spin 180 degrees, landing both socks back onto the carpet, then he bends down to put on his Airforce Ones. As he slides on his left shoe, I put on his right and then tie both shoes for him.

Chapter Twelve

IT'S ABOUT 72 DEGREES out, partly cloudy, with a 20 percent chance of rain. The wind blows at 13 miles per hour and humidity is at about 42 percent. Graduation will be over well before rainfall, if it decides to, though my straight pressed hair will be a Jackson Five Afro real soon. I stare out before me, looking at fractions of my classmates' faces concealed under their maroon caps and grey tassels. I watch them sit in their chairs whispering amongst each other as I sit up here on stage with faculty after just finishing my graduation speech. I search through the humid air to the right and left of my fellow classmates, and at the bleachers full of guests. My heart murmurs with void. No Qalbee. My body turns cold. It congeals. I brim with emptiness. *How can he miss my speech? How could he miss my graduation?* I saw him every day for a week while Craig was in the hospital, three times last week when he spent time with me at my parent's, and twice this week. He didn't promise that he'd be here, but he certainly led on with surety. And I know he's not with Craig because Chanelle was over there just before she came here. Besides, after getting scans, x-rays, and being monitored for a week, the doctor discharged Craig from the hospital and he'll probably be back to work soon. Qalbee's readings were correct. The doctor said that Craig's MRI showed a minor concussion but that he is lucky to have had Chanelle there to apply pressure on the wound before he bled out, and that Craig had fainted from shock and was only unconscious temporarily for less than an hour. Chanelle gloats, declaring that Craig had just better be glad she had on a clean bra underneath her white tank top!

"Libiya Ali."

I vaguely hear Dr. Jones, the school principal, call out my name, interrupting my stupor, and then excessive clapping begins. Dr. Jones' head gestures for me to go sit with my classmates. I stand looking into the crowd and I see Caleb standing at a distance from the bleachers. I smile, and nod letting him know that I appreciate his support. He smiles back and walks in the distance. Being so disappointed with Qalbee, a thought about how Caleb has always been here for me emerges, but just as an inkling of a thought of getting back with him *attempts* to surface, I see Trecy apathetically applauding in the bleachers. I'm not offended by his lackadaisical attitude—we never got along—but seeing him made me realize that going backwards is not the answer. I look over to Chanelle and her face is cheesing *so* brightly for me! I smile back. Next to her is Chad. A feeling of cheerfulness materializes within me. I feel my lips cheesing like Chanelle's, and I give Chad a *Forest Gump* slight wave. He blows me a kiss as I step down the last step.

Help my sadness run free

Its graduation time and I'm no longer blind.
I can see all the pain that's in store,
all the people I've grown to care for-
all the things we've shared.

I just can't bare
the feeling of them not being there.
Not here to keep me company,
not here to look after me.

Life's so unfair...

Does anyone care-
that I'm hurt?
Am I the only one-
the only one who cares that this part of my life is done?

There is no one out there-
that can compare-
to those...
whom are in my prayers.

*These feelings will not die.
It's so hard to put this behind-
to get this all,
out of my mind!*

Love and fun-

*the special times are done.
Help me run-
run from this pain
that I've gained from him leaving.*

*Help me accept this depart-
by knowing,
he'll always be in my heart.
Help my sadness run free from within me.*

LA May 2000

I SIT ON MY BED looking around my room. I look at my computer . . . my radio . . . and then, my packed luggage. It's all I'm taking, these two bags, and the rest of my 18 years of life will be left behind. Many thoughts run through my head, thoughts that have me feeling melancholy. I reflect back on the Monday that I consciously walked into the Post Office, purchased a couple of Forever stamps, and specifically made sure that the post office clerk mailed off my graduation invitation to Qalbee's address. For him to not even show up today bothers me. I expect more from him than he is willing to give. *I wonder if I'm important to him anymore.*

My thoughts stream like water invoking agonizing effects on my body. As of tomorrow, this won't be home for me anymore. My arms placate my stomach as I react to the more damaging thought of being far away from Qalbee . . . well both of my best friends, Qalbee and Chanelle. I'm wearing my yellow nylon swishy pants as a gesture of how I will miss Qalbee. I wore these the day I met him. Just as he wore pullovers for months in memory of his deceased father, I feel a similar void pending with our distance that is yet to come. I'll miss him and Chanelle, as well as Chad and even Craig too.

I feel the central air unit blow on my topless skin taking me out of my day-stream. I quickly grab my red cherry printed bra, snap it on, reach for my green cropped t-shirt, pull it over my head . . . then I hear the sound of my door knob turn.

It's my mother. I smell her Dolce & Gabbana Light Blue! I adore my mother and her daintiness. She is *all* estrogen—miss fashion Prima Donna! Everyone calls her by her epithet, "Mrs. Beauty". She only wears the best, bearing nothing but expensive clothing on her caramel complexioned skin. She stands four inches taller than me with those three inch Chanel sandals on.

My mother graduated from Marshal High with a full track scholarship by exploiting those long vigorously built legs of hers. She won medals in the 800 meter dash finals and the 4 x 400 meter relay finals in the UAA Indoor National Track & Field Championship. My mother has always loved running, and in high school she became a USA Track & Field member to gain candidacy for the National Olympics. She was successful in the NCAA high school competition her senior year meeting the "A" standard they require and was automatically invited to the US Olympic Trials.

After she graduated she met my father, got married to him four months later, and had my brother ten months after that. My father was my mother's virginity vanquisher. He's her first and her last! That's how I imagine Qalbee. Two months after my brother was born my mother began training for the USA 50-kilometer Race Walk. She missed Sebastian too much and said that family comes first, so she stopped training to care for him. Mother had done a couple of commercials for Gatorade and sports equipment after making it to the US Olympic Trials, which was an aperture to her acting career, her true passion.

Mother hasn't changed out of her white Saks Fifth Avenue slacks and burgundy Ralph Lauren blouse she picked out especially to match me for my graduation. This is where Chanelle gets most of her fashion pointers from. We all joke that Chanelle's name fits her new personality, and how Chanelle was supposed to be my mother's daughter because of their interest in fashion. My mother and I are so opposite. She says that I don't have expensive taste, which used to bother me. But I realized that I actually feel a sense of dignity and strength with my decisions on purchasing inexpensive things for myself to employing my "expensive taste" on others. I would much rather do something noble with that kind of money—like give it to the starving children around Africa or for upgrading the ghettos here in America.

My mother's diamond Chanel earrings twinkle, as do her brown eyes, as she fretfully gazes at me.

"Are you okay?" she asks as she walks up on me. "Today is one of the happiest days of your life . . . and your speech was amazing!" She sits next to me "Though you seemed distracted the entire graduation." She strokes my hair and places her right hand on my knee.

"Thank you, mother. I just have *lots* on my mind," I say returning the comfort as I take her hand into mine, and squeeze it. "I'll miss you, mother."

"Hey, hey, hey! You ready?" Chanelle shouts with excitement.

Just thinking of these two divas, I thought as Chanelle walks in. "Ready for what?"

"I called her and told her to come pick you up," my mother confesses as she stands to her feet.

"Well come on! Some folks in the car waiting," Chanelle states with a cunning tone and a guilty expression across her face. And I instantly know what, well *who,* it is!

"What!" I quickly stand, rush to slip on my New Balances, and run past the both of them. I feel my adrenalin racing as I sprint down the stairs. My nerves are filled with excitement as I force the living room door open. I see "Dingy" backed into my parent's driveway. "Dingy" is the name I gave Craig's pickup. Qalbee sits in the hatchback. Chanelle's pace picks up once she passes me as I stand in the doorway. My mother walks up. I pucker my lips and plant a kiss on her proud cheek.

"Thanks mother!" I express gratitude, valuing her sensibility.

Mother smirks then nods her head, gesturing for me to get going.

I run to the truck, place one New Balance on the back tire, lift the other, and hop real high into the hatchback. I look into Qalbee's face and he looks hopeful. He grins as if I am a sight for sore eyes. I'm not familiar with *this* particular gawk he gives me—it's relatively puzzling; however, I don't think twice about it, I simply slide between his propped knee and the other leg that lies down flat, bogarting my knees between his lap. I position my face next to his—so close that I can smell his mint fresh breath. I unfasten my lips and slide my tongue into his mouth. He jolts—possibly startled, maybe even impressed by my actions. He kisses me back like his life depended on it. I attempt to unlock our tongues, but he sucks firmer, imprisoning my tongue. He lifts his delicate hands to my face and hugs my cheeks between them. His tongue frees mine and he scrupulously stares into my eyes, not letting my face part more than a centimeter from his before he drops his hands. Qalbee clutches my hips, spins me around, pulls my butt to his groin, envelops his arms around my waist, and jostles my upper body to his right shoulder. He squeezes me tight and leans his chin into the top of my hair. I hear him take a cavernous breath, possibly inhaling my scent, though I think it's much more significant than that.

WE PULL UP IN FRONT of the movie theater. Craig backs into the first empty space he sees. Chanelle and Craig each climb out of "Dingy." Qalbee gestures to Craig to go ahead and leave us. Not saying a word, Chanelle's arms raise to her hips, though her hands and eyes ask "ya'll not coming?" I shake my head. The look of empathy displays on her face showing me that she understands clearly. She knew I wanted my intimate time alone with my Comedy, my Heart. She turns away and walks around to the front of "Dingy" with Craig and they walk off.

Qalbee and I speak simultaneously.

"I'm not going to tell you how sad I was that you weren't at my..."

"I'm so sorry to miss your..."

"Graduation," we say in concord.

I'm not even upset anymore now that he is here in my presence, and not because he apologized, but because no matter how sad or upset I am with him, I'm unable to resist his enchanting aura.

"It just seems that when I need you most, you're not there."

"Yaya, I know. I just have so much going on."

"But you know you can talk to me about anything. I mean, I'm so in love with you, and I don't know what to do." I sit up from leaning against his shoulder.

He stares. I turn towards him sliding between both his legs that now lay down flat, bogarting my bent knees between his lap and resting on the back of my calves.

"I know you don't love me, but you do care about me..."

His look is impassive.

I continue, "... and I'm cool with that. All I want from you is your trust and for you to open up to me."

He begins shaking his head. I take both his hands in mine and hold them and squeeze them.

"I'm begging you to let me be here for you."

"Yaya, Yaya, shh, shh. I know." He leans forward and comforts my cheeks with those delicate fingers again before he slides his welcomed tongue into my mouth. His right hand eases under my shirt and he strokes my left nipple with his three middle fingers. Both nipples harden then his open palm cups my areola massaging my breast. I'm in complete bliss! I close my eyes in effort not to dwell on the fact that I'm surrendering to these inapt—and oh so yearning—proceedings in full strength of daylight. Oodles of fluid extract my essence and I attempt to hide my nervousness, but I perspire at his every touch. He slides his left hand under my sweats, into my panties, and then enters his middle and index finger into my vagina, massaging deep within my core. I moan. My body is drenched with covetousness. He unleashes his tongue, works it down to my neck and sucks with passion. I then feel his nose between my breasts as he slides his right palm across to my right breast, grazing my nipple though he continues rubbing down to my stomach. I feel his breath descending further as he pulls my sweats down to my ankles. Synergic with his touch, I feel the ray of sun heat my nude thighs. His hands grip each of my knees and spread my bare legs, introducing the lips of my vagina to the pure light of day. I peek to see if anyone is around, but I only glimpse the top of Qalbee's perfect waves as he descends towards my happy place, shielding my exposed lips. I feel wet muscle enter. His tongue swirls with rhythm—gentle, hard, slow, fast . . . easy. I moan. He continues . . . swirling—gentle, hard, slow, fast . . . easy. I gush. His tongue eases out. I gasp.

He looks up instantly. By the look in his eyes I knew someone was coming. I quickly pull my sweats up. He dives beside me, ramming his back against the rear window. He wipes his mouth on my sleeve. He stares . . . then smirks . . . I glare. We chuckle under our breaths! Two Caucasian men walk up to the 3 Series Beamer parked next to "Dingy." They scramble into luxury, slam their doors and start the engine. Qalbee and I burst out chortling. My heart palpitates as my palms sweat along with the rest of my body. My cotton mouth is as dry as my juices that stick to my skin between my thighs. I look over to the right of me catching Qalbee's smile, revealing his slightly crooked tooth. Then our eyes meet. I lift my hands to his shoulders, straddle on top of him, hug his checks between my palms, and lean my pursed lips to his. I peck him with enthusiasm and desire. My arms cuddle his neck and I rest my ear on his shoulder. I inhale him. His arms envelop my waist. He squeezes me in such a way that feels as compulsory as the blood flowing through his veins and the pumping of his heart as if I'm his oxygen to breathe.

Chapter Thirteen

I STRAIGHTEN LOCKS OF hair one by one as I stand in my bathroom mirror with Chanelle on speaker phone. She and I have been planning a graduation party and going away party since after prom. I designed the invitations and Chanelle found the venue. I really used my creativity on these. I used a blueprint imitating a diploma with a real precise format and printed the invitations on high grade parchment paper. We passed them out at graduation to friends and fellow graduates and used Sebastian's car one day to pass some out to others at different schools. The outcome ought to be ostentatious. We are having it at the Renaissance in their ballroom and we even purchased a suite just for us to kick back, relax, and enjoy our first real sense of freedom as adults.

"You picking me up for the hotel?" Chanelle beleaguers.

"Right Chell, around seven," I respond with sarcasm. She knows this already.

"Is Q coming?" she inquires.

I invited Qalbee, though did not bother to ask him if he was actually going to come. I chose to avoid feeling gloomy until this day finally arrived.

"You know he never makes it to any of my events," I respond with cynicism, straightening my hair with aggression.

"But you leaving!" she voices in a high tone filled with flummox.

"Why is that any different from my birthday, prom, graduation, and now, my going away shindig?" I sulk, putting the pressing comb down on the towel that lies on the counter.

"He does like you though," she encourages.

"And I know that. It's just . . ."

"As much time he spends with you, and you being at his house, he at yours and ya'll talkin all night. Yes, he cares," she interrupts.

"You know what I've noticed . . . is that he loves talking to me and loves spending time with me, I can tell that. It's like he appreciates our time together and he feels our chemistry . . . and not even sexually, but just the smiles, and fun, and comfort . . ." I go on a tangent. "But, he's never here for me outside of that," I snap out real fast.

"How in the hell are you gonna leave, to a whole 'nother state when you in love with this boy?"

"Well, I still have my life, which I must live. You know me." I take a lock of hair and straighten it.

"Yea, you pretty resilient . . . and determined—but damn, it's gotta be hard!" she questions.

"Actually, I'll have so much more peace of mind without hoping to see him and him not appearing. It really will be out of sight out of mind."

"Hum?" she questions.

I roll my eyes and change the subject. "What's with you and Craig is the question?"

I hear a smile on the other end of the phone. "He just lusts after me. I don't take him serious *at-all,*" she noticeably emphasizes, trying to hide her guilt.

"So you gave it up!" I say with conviction. I can tell. "Why you holding out on me?" I giggle with surprise.

"Well of course it wasn't prom night—it was the night at the movies . . . in the movie theater!" I hear her voice crack.

"WHAT!" I put the pressing comb back down. "Have you no shame? Are you okay? How do you feel about it?" I solicit with concern and curiosity.

"I'm cool with it. He buys me things."

"Wow," I say boggled—*that's a shame.* "Love or lust?" I shake my head. "At least lust gets you nice things! Love only gets you disappointment." I go on a tangent again. "Well, all I can say is . . . we growing up!"

WE HAD A GREAT turn out like I expected. Of course Qalbee *did not* show up. I've learned to cope with him taking my heart on a systolic and diastolic rollercoaster, skipping and adding beats. Chanelle and I had simple but lavishly chic décor for the party. When you walk into the entry door, to the right and left are long rectangular silver dressed tables that house the food. Our dish choice remained simple—burgers, nachos, chicken wings, and meatballs, and vegetable and fruit trays with lemonade. As you pass the buffet tables, ahead of you are more silver dressed tables, though these are round and seat eight guests. Above you are gold streamers trickling down, giving the illusion of gold rain falling. After you pass the guest tables there is the dance floor. On the wall behind and up high is a projected slide show of video and pictures Chanelle and I have taken of us and friends at school activities and of teachers and faculty over the course of our friendship since she and I met in the fifth grade. It was priceless to see guests' reactions to the pictures we displayed. Some were amusing, others were intimate, and most can be used as "black mail" pictures in the future—all in fun though!

Once we said farewell to everyone and assured that the ballroom was clean, Chanelle and I began our slumber party in the suite. We did so much mingling and entertaining at the party that neither of us found much time to eat which is a first for Chanelle. We ordered room service—wings, celery and carrots. I also ate the leftover fruit wrapped from the party!

Chanelle and I did a lot of catching up. I caught her up on nearly everything about Qalbee and Chad. I had never told her that Chad tried to kiss me after prom. I guess that was because Craig's accident and Qalbee's alleged hospitalization took precedence. She wasn't surprised though she was upset at me for telling Chad my final decision about school, and moving, before telling her. I told her about me and Qalbee's last episode. Chanelle was *so* shocked that I let him taste my happy place in pure daylight! She was even more shocked that he didn't hesitate to do so! She and I both had tears pouring from our eyes and had to catch our breath several times from making back to back jokes about it.

"He enjoyed his genital slurpee."

"I did too!"

"Don't let the grapefruit squirt in your eye."

"Would you like fish in your taco?"

"Any further back, he'd have asked, "got ranch?"

Then we hysterically laughed long and hard about he and I almost being busted. My side began cramping. Chanelle told me that she believed that she loved Terrance whom I already knew, but he is a playboy. He really hurt her when he pulled that prom swindle. She went into depth about her feelings for Craig—how they have gradually developed from when she began using him to get over Terrence and since his accident. She says that he caters to her and takes action whenever she needs him to. He pretty much worships at her feet.

Chanelle and I are jumping up and down on the plush beds celebrating the success of the party and happy about our sisterly bonding time. There is a knock at the door. I jump off the bed and peak through the peep hole—it's Chad and Terrence. I tell Chanelle who it is at the door and she is initially excited; however, she acts as if she couldn't care less that the person she *just* told me she was in love with is at the door. I let them in and Chanelle instantly closes up. I call her out letting her know that this is the perfect time to express *all* that she needed to. I gather that it helped because it prompted them to take a walk to talk.

Chad and I power the television on but we do more talking and laughing than anything, and listened to the complete Snoopdogg *Dogpound* CD. We put "Ain't No Fun if the Homies Can't Have None" on repeat. It is both of our favorite song on that disc. It's always so easygoing with Chad! He confides in me, accepts my advice and he trusts me. I know he is dating someone but he won't mention *that to me*—just as I don't mention Qalbee to him. After an hour Chanelle and Terrance walks in the room, "what's up?" us as they pass the open joint doors, lay down, and are out.

I WAKE UP in bed next to Chad. We are both in the fetal position. I face him and he faces me. I try to ease out of bed, careful not to wake him. My knee abruptly bumps his and he wakes. Our eyes meet. We smile. Chad reaches his arm out, pulling my waist to him. I turn over to look at the radio clock sitting on the dresser between the two queen size beds and it reads "4:32"—we have only napped for about thirty minutes. I turn back over towards Chad and lay my head on his shoulder. As we cuddle I hear movement in Chanelle's room. Chad and I raise our heads in sequence and seconds later Terrence appears, tip toeing into my room through the joint doors. Chad and I ogle.

"Come on man," Terrence whispers.

"You're not gonna wake up Chanelle and say bye?" I instigate with my neck still raised, feeling strained.

He completely ignores my question and gages Chad.

"Nigga, come on," he demands.

"Dude!" Chad snaps.

Terrence begins walking towards the door to leave, than stops. "I . . . Look, I don't wanna wake her." He seems frustrated, as if I'm inconveniencing him by slowing him down.

I suppose his attempt is to creep out so that he won't have to deal with Chanelle's interrogations or emotions. *He's not a playboy bunny—he's a playboy Doberman pincher.*

His hand clinches the door handle. "Just let her get her beauty sleep," he says in a smug tone and with sarcasm.

"Good one." My tone mimics his: sarcastic. "CHANELLE! Get up!" I bellow.

Terrence's eyes roll. Chanelle walks through the joint doors with a blanket wrapped around her body. She moves slothfully with her eyes still closed, looking like a sleep-walking zombie.

"Huh? What ya'll doing?" she mumbles then stumbles out. I hear her plop on top of the bed . . . then loud breathing. I realize that she and Terrance must have had drinks earlier. *No wonder they passed straight out.* By now Chad and I are sitting up. I look at Terrance and shake my head in defeat.

"Peace out." I fan my two fingers in the air in submission.

Terrence throws up the deuce and walks out. Chad's hand grasps my shoulder then he squeezes. He leans in to me, furrows his lips and kisses me on my cheek. He gazes into my eyes. "I'mma call you soon to see how your transition goes."

Chad scampers up and scurries through the main room then out the door. It slams. I climb out of bed, close Chanelle's joint door, walk to the bathroom, put toothpaste on my toothbrush, and start brushing. I begin thinking about Qalbee when I hear a knock on the door. *Thank you Chad for saving me from my depressing daydream before it got out of hand.* I walk to the door.

"Sorry for taking too long," I bellow as I open the door.

"You miss me?" Qalbee smiles. "Where the party at?" He expresses joy, swinging his hips from east to west.

I can't do anything but stare impassively. I turn my back to him though invite him in by holding the door open behind me. Qalbee grabs my wrist turning me towards him.

"What's up?" he asks real innocent like, then releases my arm.

I impassively look up at him, and then walk through the main room back to the bathroom. Qalbee follows. I begin brushing my teeth—*it's not much to say.* Qalbee stands in the doorway, grips the border of the door; and contrary to the look upon his face, the tone of his voice is joy.

"I'm here," he attempts to convince—*as if I should jump up and down ecstatic.*

"Late, like always," I whisper under my breath with sarcasm. "Did you see T and Chad?" I ask in attempt to ignore Qalbee's presence.

"Yea." He sounds annoyed. "I just saw those chumps going down the stairs when I stepped off the elevator," he snickers with dominance.

I roll my eyes at his egotism. "So they didn't see you? Where's Craig?" I ask, still attempting to ignore his presence.

"Na, they didn't," he gloats. "Why does it matter . . . and why you askin me bout Craig?" he seems aggravated.

YES! I now gloat, at his agitation. *Who does he think he is to keep letting me down, then expects me to jump for joy when he's in my presence? No, not happening.*

"This is time that we can be spending doing us . . ." His voice is strained with discontent ". . . doing what we do."

I've never seen this side of him, frustrated and riled up—*serves him right*!

"And what exactly is that?" I instigate, again rolling my eyes and still brushing.

"Talk, laugh, learn from each other, have intellectual conversations . . . and just joke around. You know we have fun together," he reaches.

I put my tooth brush down feeling bad that he might be upset at me . . . *but I am too and it's because of him.* So anxious to respond, I sputter the toothpaste from my mouth, neglect rinsing, lean on the sink then stare at him through the mirror.

"No, what we do best is . . . I wait on you, I'm patient with you, I don't know where you are or what you are doing half the time, while YOU *"do as YOU do, when YOU please"* . . . and then it's, "Oh yeah, Yaya." "I mock. I feel a rapid flow of blood pumping from my heart and I know I have reached my breaking point. "Qalbee, I can't do this anymore," I utter with exhaust, feeling a burning sensation in my mouth.

"I understand where you comin from," Qalbee states impassively.

"Impossible!" I snap looking straight at him, no longer through the mirror. I feel toothpaste oozing down my lip, then tingling on my chin, but I'm in such an uproar *I don't even care*. I continue, "You just really don't understand my love for you," my tone augments. "I leave soon and you act like you can care less." I'm so angry. I'm so hurt. Rhetorically I ask, "Are you going to even miss me?" My tone's docile, fragile, broken—as too, my heart. "Huh," I sigh. I take two steps to him and raise my right palm to his left cheek. "This is the best thing for me. Just know that you'll have me forever. Please don't stop popping up in my life out the blue like you do." I free his cheek then embrace his hand that rests on the door. I feel my eyes fill with tears. I hold them back. "What I feel is unconditional. I'll wait patiently for you to pop up again and again until . . ."

"What are you talking about?" Qalbee exclaims, interrupting me. He looks down as if he feels poignant—maybe ashamed? He takes my hand, secures it in his, and lays it flat on his chest to his heart. I feel it beating. He wraps his other arm around my shoulder, then inhales deeply.

As we stand here in a huddle, I reflect, "Déjà vu." Unintentionally my thoughts surface out of exasperation.

"What?" he whispers.

"I love you." I conceal; surely I cannot tell Qalbee that Chad was in the hotel, at four in the morning, this close to me. He would think I'm a whore.

"I love you but you have to go. You have to let me let you go," I whimper.

Qalbee puts his fingers on my long straight hair. His gentle fingers caress my scalp, then he strokes through my hair.

"No Qalbee. Aren't you hearing me?" I pull away.

I hear the joint door open as Qalbee and I stand in the doorway between the bedroom and main room. Chanelle appears. Qalbee and I stare. Chanelle's eyes widen as she does a double take. Her brows wrinkle, pointing down. I frown. I'm sure she's wondering how the interchange went between Chad and Qalbee. Zombie-like, she backs out then closes the door. Qalbee looks at me pleading with his eyes. He rubs my bottom lip from right to left with his thumb, leans in, and kisses me on my sad lips. Then, he walks out.

Heart Spasm

Chapter Fourteen

I SIT ON MY bunk, reach to shut off my Creed CD, and rest while I wait on Elaina to come collect these flyers. I listen to the thunder roar, the wind whistle, and the rain pour, taking me back eight months ago to my first day here. Mother would not let me help her drive any of the way here so she drove the entire six hours on her own. It should have taken us seven hours but she drove like these Texas folks so we arrived early. Mother wanted me to have my own things and did not want me using any of my roommate's possessions so we stopped off to get some appliances for my dorm. She purchased me a mini refrigerator, microwave, and portable CD and cassette radio, and she made sure that I had at least two weeks of food. She bought boxes of noodles and soup, a galore of sandwich meat and chips, Marie Calendar TV dinners, and Miss Debbie snacks to hold me over just until my meal plan became activated. As soon as we made it to campus it began pouring raining like crazy. *I laugh at the thought of my mother that day!* She told me that she needed to go buy some comfortable tennis shoes since we were going to have to rush in all of my belongings in the rain. I'm thinking she's talking about going to the nearest store that sales shoes; however, *this lady* finds the Galleria Mall and purchases some Prada tennis shoes from Niemen Marcus. *All I can do is shake my head . . . and chuckle!*

When we made it inside my dorm room, Elaina my roommate from Denton, Texas, had already chosen her side of the room. I presume her mother and mine had read the same "Daughter off to College 101" book because Elaina had her own mini-refrigerator, microwave, and an abundance of food as well. Once my mother was sure that I was fine, we gave hugs and kisses, took a picture, and she headed back to Edmond.

I remember standing there, at the door, staring at the tan ceramic tile walls and the white dry wall ceiling and immediately turning on my new CD player. I played Nelly's *Country Grammar* album, and began rearranging my side of my new home: a 13 x 15 square foot room. Working counter-clockwise, I slid the 10 foot tall wood box closet on the right side of the entry door, which is on the north wall. I moved my four draw wood chests on the west wall between the closet and my bunk. I taped posters of Michael Jackson, Brian McKnight, Bone Thugs and Harmony, and Nelly on the wall above my bunk covering the west wall. On the south wall in the corner above the bunk's imaginary headboard—which is next to the long horizontal window that faces out to the student parking lot—I taped pictures of my family and friends. Our microwaves sit on top of our refrigerators, which are beside each other, under the window seal. Then it's Elaina's side of our abode. When you walk out of our room into the hallway, directly across from our door is the entry to the community showers and restrooms.

After showering, I sat on my bunk and reminisced over my taped pictures. I love the cheek-to-cheek close up of me and my mother's smiling faces just before she left. Elaina snapped it. There is one of me acting like I'm going to steal my brother's car the day before I left. In the picture I am sitting in the driver seat trying to close the door and Sebastian is pulling on me. *I love my brother.* There are several of me and Chanelle from over the years: at the eighth grade talent show; tenth grade military ball; and one out of many of us at the Langston University's football homecoming game that we attended with her father. I also have one of Chad and I at graduation with our cap and gowns on and us at prom. Qalbee embezzled the professional one of me by myself. One Thursday when he was over to the house he kept staring at it as it hung modestly on my wall saying how stunning I was, and how on all those nights he was over I had deprived him of my beauty by looking like a tom boy. He only loved that my hair was straight and out of those braids. *I laughed at his absurdity and told him how much I'd like to punch him in his chest!*

I called Qalbee when I made it here and again after my first full day of classes to catch him up on everything. We didn't talk long. During both winter breaks I chose to stay here instead of visiting home and wound up talking on the phone for hours to everyone that is important to me, informing them of my new life here. Of course I talked to Qalbee and he humored me, literally, listening to me ramble on like Speed taking girl on *Coming to America*. As usual, he didn't have much to say about his life, but I heard the sound of white noise and beeping in intervals in his background again. He and I talk very seldom; however, he *did* actually call me on my birthday which was a surprise, and like heaven to my dejected solitude because before he called I had cried the entire day wanting to be home. This time it wasn't my choice, it was a misunderstanding between me and my parents. They figured that I didn't care to go home for my birthday since I passed on the last two holidays; therefore they didn't bother booking me a flight. Qalbee talked to me for hours cheering me up that winter night—*my nineteenth birthday!* I'm sad to say it but he doesn't call me often. I don't hassle by any means. I talk to Chad and Chanelle often enough . . . plus school activities and Elaina keeps me eventful.

ELAINA AND I HIT it off pretty well. She is real tidy and organized like me, and she is very smart and very sociable. Elaina is an only child and comes from an aristocratic family. Mr. Williams is a scientist and Mrs. Williams is a nurse. When the months grew closer for her to go off to college, Elaina's parents had her partake in a debutant cotillion ball. Elaina is a criminal justice major with plans on becoming a police officer and working her way up to detective. She's dainty, but is also chameleon enough to pull it off. Though Elaina has the squeaky stereotype voice of prissy girl, she has a bit of a St Louis country accent to go along with her hood undertone. She plans to pledge Delta Sigma Theta sorority our sophomore year, something I never really got into, but she has me accompanying her to all of their events and now other students think that I'm interested in pledging. I think it is all legal gangs and a form of slavery with the hazing, branding, and "yes masa" stuff. It's all politics. Although, I can admit, organizations such as those *do* provide you with much exposure, fun events, and a sense of pride by rewarding you by building your status. However, I have already developed a soaring status—PRADA EXTRAVAGANZA, Prada E for short—and I'm in the Student Program Council.

I joined the SPC my first month here. It's a student organization that informs students about what's occurring on campus and in the community, and it gets them involved by putting on events on campus, which is right up my alley. I ran for chair of publicity and won 89 percent of the votes. I think students voted for the other candidate due to being content since he had been chair for the past two years. He seemed to loathe me at first, especially after a month of seeing my productivity in publicizing the events and the way other students gravitated to me. He finally ended up conforming after about three months. Then he had the nerve to try to pursue me, asking me out on dates and accompanying me at functions! *I shake my head at that thought.* Prada E is a charity that I started, with Elaina's assistance. After I advertized a few events as chair for the SPC, and them being successful, I pitched my idea about Prada E to Elaina and she was right on board.

Prada Extravaganza targets upscale individuals that have a child or family member with a mental health disorder. Prey on their sympathy, and make them aware that others in society have difficulty surviving because they not only suffer with problems of mental health, but also suffer from poverty therefore cannot afford health care, clothing, food, shelter, and other amenities. We anticipate that our targets will sympathize with these low status economic families and sponsor a family, or donate to Prada Extravaganza so that we can help the families. It sounds calculated, and a bit manipulative, but it's just the democratic way. Take from the rich and give to the poor! It has been difficult for Elaina and me to find well-off families dealing with these issues since they are more confidential, and the fact that neither of us is from here. Elaina and I went around the dorms and asked students in our classes to donate clothes that they didn't wear. I don't think we were supposed to solicit clothes from students on campus since we are faces of the Student Program Council, it being possible to affiliate the two organizations as one. But we figured it was for a good cause. We gave them to runaway teens living in shelters. This was after the Thanksgiving break so students were very giving. Prada E was only founded about six months ago and we have already put on one successful event, so I figure that we're doing pretty well!

Elaina and I have planned two other events but the bigger one is for the three holidays in December—Christmas, Kwanzaa, and Ramadan. We have three months to prepare for the Back to School fundraiser, and by August we'll only have two months to prepare for Tri-December. Even though the event is about five months away, I have designed and printed out the flyers for Tri-December so that we can inform people of our event early. Tomorrow night is going to be one of the biggest opportunities for us to get our information out and gather emails and contact information from sponsors because SPC is having a fund raiser and 97.9 The Box is hosting it. There is supposed to be big names there like, Sista Soulja, Michael Basin, Tavis Smiley, and some others.

THE DOOR EXPLODES OPEN causing me to sit up.

"Girl, you got the box of flyers?" Elaina shouts with enthusiasm and motivation. "5000 right?" She impatiently asks before I can answer her first question.

Elaina stands about 5 feet 2 inches, with firm horse legs under her tight denim jeans, a flat butt, but nice proportioned hips to make up for it, and a loose lavender blouse that fails to hide those triple D breasts. She has a real cute coffee completion and a bronzed colored layered bob, so thick and with so much body that it looks like weave.

"YES . . . yes," I stammer from being startled. "Why you burst through the door like you the police?" I ask, annoyed and still trembling from being alarmed. I stand and reach for the box of flyers on my wood chest.

She laughs. "Girl I'm sorry. I'm just excited to see them! I'm excited about tomorrow! . . . And that fuckin storm is ferocious. It had me frenzied as I was running in it all the way from the Law School building!" she explains, still hyped.

After her EOPD swat-team door bust, which startled and annoyed me, I don't have the energy to brazen out her cursing. I just simply hand over the flyers.

"Thank you for picking them up between classes in this rain," I make sure to appease.

We won't be able to walk in the entry door at the SPC event with flyers without our SPU advisors seeing that we are the organizers of Prada E, so to keep it clandestine, Elaina is going to take the flyers to my SPC office in the student center so that we are guaranteed to have them to pass out tomorrow night at the SPC event, which is also in the student center.

"Now, tomorrow night is the biggest night, and only chance to get Tri-December on the map in other Texas cities. Don't fail me!" I cheerlead with a firm tone, and it allocates objective as my eyes hub hers. "Prada E, 5'oclock sharp," I enforce with a determined but fun voice, acting as though I'm on her investigative team.

My phone rings.

"I got'chew girl!" Elaina backs up, and bounces out.

I take a step to reach for my land-line phone that sits on the window seal.

"Yes Chell!" I say with exhilaration. I have a feeling it's her!

"Libi." Her voice is soft.

Instantly, I grow concerned from the tremble in her soft voice. "Yea . . . I'm here." I sit down, grab my pillow, hug it to my stomach, and listen attentively.

"Libi girl, it's Q."

My heart spasms uncontrollably. I lift my free hand to my mouth. It's trembling "What about Q?" My voice trembles as well. I'm petrified of the words that will soon come from her lips through the phone to my auditory ossicles.

"It's not him, it's his mother. She passed."

"What?" My heart drops, I'm in disbelief. My eyes tear up. "What happened? When? How is he? When is the funeral?" I interrogate. "I have to see him." I worry.

"Tomorrow morning," she answers with no optimism, as if she knows it's too short of a notice.

"What? I can't . . ." *Yes I can. I have to.* "K, let me call you back." I hang up before she could respond. *I can't let time, or Chanelle's hopeless tone discourage me.* I pull out the prepaid card that's tucked inside the information slot on the base of my corded land-phone. I dial.

"Hello dear!"

"I need you."

"Okay?" Now there is tremble and concern in her voice. "What's going on?"

"Q's mother died." Tears plague my eyes.

"Oh." She is silent.

"I need a flight home—tonight."

"Okay baby. I'll see what I can do," She says with less concern and more aspiration in her voice.

"Thank you mother. Thank you." Though I'm hopeful, my tone is comatose. I hear my voice crack as tears flow down my cheeks. All I can do is think of Qalbee, what he must be going through.

"Of course."

Chapter Fifteen

IT WAS STILL DARK out when Cab 775 dropped me off at Southwest Airline's Terminal. The twenty minute ride from Third Ward felt more like a road trip to Hobby City, China than to Hobby Airport, Texas. Besides the anticipation I felt about what this funeral will entail and the emotions it will provoke not only in the mournful family, but in me—*the nobody, non family member, not even girlfriend, not even ex-girlfriend who just had to be captain save-a-Heart and fly to a dude that obviously did not see the importance or feel the need to tell the nobody, not even ex-girlfriend, captain save-a-Heart that his mother had been sick for no telling how long.* The smell of armpit, musty leather and sour fish seeped haphazard through my nostrils causing my stomach to feel queasy. In retrospect, after riding for 20 minutes gasping the repulsive odor that subsided between those doors, the spew of my vomit would have been perfume to the atmosphere. The navy blue three-person-seat had slits in it, and the cotton that bust through was no longer white. It was an awful feces brown—no doubts that it was drenched in bacteria. The entire passage I sat as still as a slave, cautious not to come in contact with some protozoan infection and attempting to prevent all other viral diseases.

My flight boarded at seven-ten and it was a quarter to six when we landed. Thankfully *that* was a better experience. Mother was unable to get a flight out last night because they were all booked and seven in the morning was the earliest she could find. I only have one carry-on, a change of clothes, and my toiletries. I was tempted to change out of this red long sleeve shirt and red long mermaid skirt while I was on the plane because I'm self conscious about how bright I will seem if most everyone has on black. I didn't think about that until I was already in the air. Maybe I will change in the car on the way to the funeral. Though, I bet mother won't agree to that; however, I'm sure she'd agree that I need to change. I didn't want to miss her when she pulls up or have her waiting on me therefore I didn't chance changing in the airport restroom—although, I did unwrap and comb through my hair. I wore my satin cap in the cab and on the plane because I didn't want my hair messing up as I lied back in the seats.

Now, I'm enjoying the sun's ray as I sit on this hard, wood bench outside of Will Rogers Airport. Other than the takeoff and landing, and my ears popping, I was freezing cold on that arctic plane; nonetheless, it beats the cab ride from this morning. My frigid body and frost bit fingers are *slowly* thawing out with the help of this 70 degree weather. Somehow, I think I subconsciously knew I'd be cold in the cab, on the plane, and at the funeral. That's way I wore long sleeves in the first place. I'm always cold. *It has to be 85 degrees and no shade for me to be warm! Though I'm not anemic, I chew plenty of ice like I'm iron deficient. I've been to the doctor twice to check my blood and I'm perfectly healthy in every way. I feel bad thinking about my great health while Qalbee is mourning the loss of his mother due to some ailment that the universe dealt her.*

As I wait on my mother to pick me up, I listen to music on my Sony CD walkman. I've been listening to jazz all morning. In the cab I listened to Spiro Gyro. While on the plane I listened to Kenny G. Now I'm listening to Najee, my favorite of them all. I love jazz! It soothes and sanguinities me all at the same time. I need to relax since I feel so nervous about seeing Qalbee, particularly because I'm seeing him for the first time in almost a year under such circumstances—*and that's why I need to be optimistic when I see him*—especially because it's under these circumstances. I would hate to disintegrate and crumble into tears as soon as my pupils make contact with his.

MY BODY SHUDDERS AT the sound of a car horn. I press "pause" on my walkman and I look up to a red luxury sports car. *It's my mother in a two passenger Mercedes-Benz SL convertible!* She could not wait until both my brother and I reached high school and were old enough so that she could get rid of her Volvo and get a two-seater. "Just me and my purse," she'd always dream. It is a thin line between safety and status with her. Thankfully safety prevailed for me and Sebastian's sake.

"Libiya," she yells with urgency through the passenger side window. Leaned across the console, I can barely see her face.

I scurry up my one item and speed walk to her. "Nice," I admire as I clinch the handle and open the door.

"You like?"

"Yes!"

I climb in, place my bag on the floor between my legs, and descend into the leather seat. *Bliss!*

"Hey mother," I formally speak, then sigh.

"I'm sorry," she apologizes looking straight through my eyes to my soul making sure that my spirit is peaceful. "This morning was the only available flight," she explains feeling culpable, like she did last night. She rubs her fingers softly down my face like she used to when I was a little girl when she was proud of me or when I was sad. She then strokes my Shirley Temple S curls.

"I know mother. I understand. Thank you!"

Mother faces the steering wheel, sits up straight, and eases off slowly down the exit ramp leading us out of the airport terminal.

"Mother, why didn't you try to encourage me to stay back for my big event?" I curiously ask.

"Well Libi, I know your heart . . . it's so vast. You couldn't deny a friend in pain . . . Plus, I empathize with your love for him."

Really? I feel a smile curve up my lips. *I never knew that.* I lean over the console and wrap my arms slightly around her shoulders. Mother's mom died of leukemia when my mother was only 17. I am sure she empathizes in many ways. I feel a tear trickle from my eyes to my cheek.

"Mother, that's why I called you. I knew you'd understand." I release her shoulders and I sit back in my seat.

I see a smirk curve her lips. "Now, can we speed? 'Cause the funeral starts in 20 minutes and I want to get you there on time," mother informs with a determined look on her face. She bears down on the petal and I hear her mighty V12 engine grumble as she speeds onto the highway.

I NEVER UNDERSTAND WHY people would say "It was such a beautiful service" about funerals. I always thought people should keep that type of happy thought to themselves; and maybe say things like "the sermon touched me" or "the family held up strongly". But today, I see what it means to attend a beautiful service. I am surrounded by a variety of purples, the symbolic color for glory, power, youth, and feminine beauty. The church is decorated with purple Prince Lilies, lavender Calla Lilies, and *Orchis Masculas*. There is a poster size photo of Ms. Davis posted on a board when you walk through the entry door; and another one held on an easel where the casket will rest.

The minister meets the plum casket, covered in large bright violet Hibiscus and purple Lilacs, at the door; and leads it and the family into the temple. The immediate family is identifiable by their coordination with wearing various shades of purple. After partaking in many traditional rituals, much sanctifying, countless prayers, and greatly remembering the life of Irene Valencia Davis, the minister asks if anyone had a few words.

Katina slowly and fragilely walks up to the podium with tears storming from her eyes and pouring down her face. I instantly think of Susan Kohner's performance as "Mary Jean" at the end of *The Imitation of Life*. Before Katina could speak, tears flooded my eyes. With trembling hands and puny motor activity Katina inaudibly spoke, trying to grasp her breath.

"I wished I was there more for my mother . . ." she stammers grappling her hoarse words, ostensibly feeling guilty. ". . . but I thought I'd have more TIME, with her." She releases a volatile sob. "I took our time . . ." she gasps, ". . . together for granted and . . ." Unable to continue, she stops speaking.

A loud echo resonates from her forehead bumping the microphone as she lifelessly rests it on the podium as if she's too weak to carry on— and not with the speech, but with life. Qalbee comes out of nowhere and embraces her. Then two guys embrace Katina and lead her to her seat. Qalbee patiently waited at the podium for Katina to sit, but before he began speaking, the minister had the choir sing a rendition of Kirk Franklin and "God's Property's The Storm is Over Now."

After the many tears and groans dwindled, Qalbee spoke of happy, unforgettable, and funny memories with Katina, he, and their mother, and how much they treasured her, which lightened up the atmosphere. He then spoke of how cherished his mother was in the community and by co-workers when she was working. He concluded his eulogy by saying a few reassuring words, and ended with "blessed are those who mourn, for they will be comforted, Mathews 5:4."

FAMILY AND FRIENDS gather outside as they prepared for the tailgate to the gravesite. I walk around hoping that my half smirks are coming across as empathy sentiments as I look into puffy eyes, runny noses, and heartrending faces. I feel uncomfortable wandering around lost, holding unused Kleenex in one hand, two roses in the other, and not knowing anyone. As I come to a halt with my black platforms and chunky heels planted into the grass, I spot Katina walking out of the church alone. I saunter over to her, hand her the unused Kleenex, and embrace her. Neither of us say a thing as we hug. She seemed too fragile to speak, and I had no words to express my condolences. I knew that talking would only have her cry again. We release, and I extend her at arm's length. With poise I pinch a Kleenex from her hand and wipe tears from her cheek bones. Without saying a word she had been weeping just from our hug. I hand her one of the roses.

Katina takes it and gives me a warm smile. "Thank you for coming." She grips my hand, squeezes it, and then walks off.

I deliberately inhale a deep breath in attempt to calm my nerves but to only exhale a gust of apprehension. I turn towards the parking lot in hopes to find that Chanelle is here to rescue me from my own angst just to have a body to walk with, a shoulder to lean on, a familiar face to lay eyes on, someone that isn't crying or mourning, though no Chanelle.

My wandering eyes make contact with his weary eyes. Qalbee immediately charges toward me. My emotions recoil and I draw a blank. As I search my thoughts to find words for my scarce emotions, he firmly wraps his arms around my neck barely leaving me room to breathe out apprehension. I shift my forehead from his tight grip and rest my ear on his chest to allot myself room to breathe—I feel his heartbeat thudding. I then wrap my arms around his waist and cuddle him.

"How are you?" slips through my nervous lips. *Dumb girl*, he should respond. *What do you mean "how are you"—His mother just died, dummy.*

"I'm good."

What? . . . Yea, right Libiya. That's just the noble thing to say under these circumstances. He has puffy eyes, a red nose, and a heartrending, though *beautiful* face. *What do you think?*

"I just had to come," I dramatically proclaim. *Why?* I sigh and internally shake my head at my impulsiveness.

"How did you know?"

"Chanelle," we both declare.

"Yes. She told me yesterday. My . . . well . . ." I surely do not want to say "mother". "I got the first flight out this morning."

"Thank you for coming."

"There is no place I'd rather be than here with you . . ." *again, just wish it wasn't under these circumstances.*

His embrace tightens.

". . . you are My Heart." I can't help but to announce.

He squeezes even tighter. My breathing is again constricted.

Enjoying the love, though uncomfortable and not knowing what to do or say, I whisper, "I know you have to get back to your family."

Qalbee does not let go. We say nothing.

I have never seen him so vulnerable. He never told me that his mother was ill. I had no idea. The minister said something about Leukemia, the same thing my maternal grandmother died from. *This is what he's been keeping from me—maybe he's dealing with Kubler-Ross stages of grief—he's depressed is why he had been shutting me out all this time.*

Qalbee releases me from his embrace, freeing me from my reverie. His puppy eyes stare into my concerned eyes. My apprehension augments from the discomfort of awkward silence.

"Is there anything I can do . . . do you need anything . . . from . . . me?" I stammer, hoping this is not another dumb question, and wishing I could actually be all the support he'd ever need.

His expression is impassive. He continues to stare. I worry that *his psyche has derailed. That he has lost association after today's stress and after months of depression. That maybe he can't find his way back.* I hesitate to speak.

"If so . . . you'll call me?" I ask in effort to probe the unknown and escape discomfiture as I reach for his hand and compress.

"Na," he answers, staring, seeming to unveil a fragment of hope in his eyes. "You being here . . ." he pauses, then overturns my hand into his and tightens his hold ". . . is enough!"

My eyes shift, distracted by the sight of Chanelle pulling up in her aunt's white Caprice, finally rescuing me. Qalbee undoubtedly notices my diversion and drops my hand. I stare back into his vigorous eyes and he indulges me with a smirk. I smile, and he leans in and kisses me on my cheek. He raises his thumb to the crevasses of my lips, strokes left to right, and then down my chin and pinches it. He then saunters off, leaving me taken aback.

Chapter Sixteen

WHEN I GET INSIDE of the car, Chanelle looks at me, then at the rose, then back up at me with wonder on her face. I was so tense and bowled over at the funeral that I never gave Qalbee the rose. *DANG,* I internally wail. I had mother get two red roses so that I could give them to Qalbee and Katina to represent the love and respect I have for them, their mother, and their family. I sigh in disappointment that I will never get to give him the rose. By the time I see him again it'll be another ten months. *Well at least I was able to lay the lilies and pink carnations on Ms. Davis's casket during the closing of the funeral,* I rationalize. I had mother get lilies because they signify the innocence of the soul and pink carnations because it symbolizes remembrance.

Chanelle invited me to go shopping with her to help ease my nerves. I told her that nothing has changed and that shopping *still works my nerves*. I had her bring me home and I went straight to my safe haven and slumped on Mickey. I needed time to think, time away from everyone, time to just rest my eyes. While I was napping, I heard someone come to my door a few times but he or she never came in. I am sure it was my mother checking on me. She knows me very well and she knew I needed the alone time. I'll tell her all about my afternoon later, but right now, after catching up on some REM sleep, my body and thoughts are rejuvenated.

    I climbed up to Cloud Nine to reflect, and to finish writing this poem I begin writing after hearing the news about Qalbee's mother last night. Helping mother search for a flight, packing, and this morning's awful cab ride and freezing cold plane was all too hectic for me to concentrate. Every time I began to write, it didn't happen. And since looking into the infinite Milky Way usually captures endless emotions and writings in me I'm engaged up here. Merely knowing that there are 200 to 400 billion stars in our galaxy and probably more than 170 billion galaxies in the observable universe, generates countless thoughts in me about life. I know that I must do something to help Qalbee want to go on—like the infinite stars in the sky. After his peculiar episode this morning, I know that I must encourage him and be here for him, by his side whenever he needs me. He must know, and truly understand that his life, though broken and confused at this moment, will continue, and that his world will carry on.

    Ink to paper, I completed the poem.

Bereavement

This is how it happens: this is how it is:
We smile, fuss... and just-ah-laughin;
And just don't know that tomorrow we may be in tears

People leave our lives.
While concurrently, others arrive.
People are in sight;
And others take flight

Whether it's as unfortunate as an accident,
Or a sudden misfortune like an ailment,
We believe that some things are meant

No one knows how it goes.
No one knows which beliefs are true.
Though, we each play a role,
As life continues

We must take control;
And not fall into depression mode.
Because the world is a constant flow
And life around us continuously grows.

We must not become stagnant.
We must rise above.
And, though . . . there is heart ache felt at the moment
We can treat it with remembrance, care, and love.

We say our goodbyes.
And give a moment of silence . . .
We cry . . .
As thoughts and memories are relentless.

We shall hug our friends.
We shall visit our families.
We shall console our love ones.
For together we will be strong

We will not build a fence. We will try being happy.
We will do our best to have fun.
For that lost one would want us to carry on . . .
As she has gone on.

LA May 2001

I close my journal, look away from perpetuity, lay my back on the rough brick, close my eyes, and relax. My cordless phone rings. I pull the phone to my ear, maintaining the comfort of relaxation. "Yes?"

"You at your mother's?" an anxious voice resonate.

"What? Who . . . Oh, yes, yes I am," I stammer.

"I'm coming through . . . well, *can I* come through?"

"Yes, of course!" I say, bewildered by the sound of paradise.

"K, well, I'm pullin up!"

I immediately sit up and turn 180 degrees towards the front of the house. Qalbee pulls up to the curb in his Cutlass. Elated, I scoot on my butt to the edge of the roof. Barely using the steps I jig downward, jumping off the ladder. I run through the back field to the front of the house and see Qalbee walking towards me. We meet at the single stair of the walk way.

"Some things don't change," he says as he looks at the roof, then back to me.

I cheese and he embraces me.

"Some things do . . ." I say, referring to him choosing to be in my presence without me harassing him to do so. "But then again, I guess you're right, like you popping up whenever you feel!" I say jokingly. But, afterwards, I remember that it wasn't a choice to be away from me, it was a critical cause that had him withdrawn. *I feel terrible for joking.*

He takes my hand and guides me to the passenger side of his car. He opens my door, then strides around to his side, slides in, and closes the door. I follow suit, sliding in and slamming the door.

"Yo, I appreciate you comin today. You were a surprise I needed. You were a sight for sore eyes," he divulges while intensely staring into my eyes.

"How are you really doing, Q?" *DANG*, there goes that dumb question again. *I'm just really concerned. Huh*, I sigh at my diarrhea of the mouth.

His tone is frank. "My mother is dead, how you think?"

I'm sorry, I know, dumb question—TWICE. "I'm sorry," I say with regret in my voice, tears filling my eyelids, and panic in my heart. He hates me, I know it. I'm not offended by his tone. It was sure to come out blunt like that after being asked that dumb question TWICE. I internally scold myself, envisioning a clone of myself slapping me in the face. She shakes her head at me in pity, and looks at me with disgrace.

"For what?" he answers agitated, as if he can't take hearing that statement seeing that he's probably heard it a thousand times today.

"Why say it so harshly?" I ask, pertaining to his answer to my dumb question.

"It is what it is," he says matter-of-fact like.

I build up the courage to reach for his hand. I bring it to my chest.

"I can't imagine," I stare up at him.

"I'm straight . . . my mother did a lot of suffering towards the end . . . she doesn't have to anymore. Life's great," he says nonchalantly.

"Why didn't you tell me any of this? You know I needed to be there for you. I hurt when you hurt . . ."

"I . . ." he interrupts, though pauses, and looks away.

As he hesitates, I take advantage of the opportunity and continue. "I mean, of course, not close to how much you're hurting." I look down at my entangled fingers, feeling guilty for not giving him time to process his thoughts. Compelled, I continue, "I'm just saying, I hurt when you hurt."

He's still quiet so I look up at him. "I don't mean to make things sound like it's about me . . ."

As I attempt to redeem myself, still having diarrhea of the mouth, Qalbee cuts me off again.

"No," he responds, looking down and shaking his head. "I understood what you meant. I just didn't know how to tell you." His innocent eyes reach mine verifying his words.

It is silent, but only for a second.

"Would you like to talk about it now, or should we just chill?" I lean over the console lying my head on his chest assuming he would rather chill than talk.

"No," he rejects, taking my head in his hands and sitting me up. "Neither. We're gonna talk . . . about life. How's Sugarland?"

As much as I want to assess his state of grief, I surrender to his request. "Okay." He obviously needs to take his mind off the past few days—months—maybe years.

"I actually love it! I can't believe this year is almost up." I lean my shoulder against the seat facing him, and rest my hair on the head support. "I've missed you a lot," I confess.

"Time goes by so quickly," he utters, looking afar; and I know he's reminiscing about our times together, maybe high school, and just growing up. "Craig and I are about to be roomies!" He lights up.

I sit up. "Oh, what! Really! Wow, that's great . . . my Comedy growing up on me?" I'm impressed.

"That's what it seems." He smiles, then pauses. "Really, I just have to move out that house. My uncle's gettin it."

"Oh, whut? Sorry to hear that . . . But I don't understand? You and Katina are her children . . ."

"That's actually my uncle's house," he explains.

"Oh, whuut? But still . . ." I'm upset. "What about y'all? Y'all *did* just lose your mother. How much more are y'all supposed to lose?" Feeling pressure from my arteries I stop to catch my breath.

I'm tripping—I'm upset like I'm losing my house. I realize I went on a tangent, and apologize. "Okay, I'm sorry, *that is* your uncle. It's just that . . . that news upsets me," I explain, feeling resentment towards his uncle.

"No, it angers me as well. But I figure I do need to grow up, so I'm gonna take this opportunity to do so."

I process his words and can see the logic in that. "So you and Craig, huh? How is he?"

"He's cool. Been supportive throughout this," he nonchalantly utters, yet with gratitude in his expression.

"That's real good! Yea . . . You know Chad and I stay in touch regularly." *I felt guilty holding that in. Though, I don't know why. Maybe because they used to be close and were in the same childhood clique—yet, are rivals now—and I communicate with them both.*

"That punk," he chuckles. "Why you still entertain him?"

Uh, maybe because he has always been there for me, he likes me for me. I can be myself around him without all this tension I feel when I am in your presence. "Well . . ." I retreat, not being able to say all that, "We've always been pretty cool." I clear the air.

"Yea, whatever," he dismisses my explanation.

Now that I know Qalbee hadn't been here for me because he had been caring for his mother, makes me feel contemptible, real awful.

"Comedy, please keep my number and use it. I want to be here for you. I'm long distance, but I'll do what I can do."

My monochromatic Nokia 8250 cell rings. I pull it out my purple swishy sweat pants pocket and view the screen. It's Elaina. I don't answer. I press "sound off" and drop it in my lap.

"Gone and answer it. It's your boyfriend?"

"No, it's one of my girls," I answer repugnantly.

"Aohww, I had no idea you went dike on me up in Sugarland."

"WHAT? NO!" I punch him in the chest fairly hard.

Qalbee laughs. I smile, then quietly chuckle.

"Not funny, at all." I roll my eyes.

"So you hear about your girl givin it up to Craig on the regular?"

"What, no? I mean, yea, she told me when she gave up her virginity to him almost a year ago. It was a bit of a surprise to me. But, no, I had no idea they were doing *that* on the regular." I'm appalled.

"Nigga, they be goin *hard* at it," he exclaims with amusement.

I narrow my eyes displaying a disturbed look on my face.

". . . My bad. My bad nigga, I know you don't like that word," he snorts.

I smile at his humorous cursing. It takes me back to our good old days. However, I shake my head that he sees amusement in our friends' *sexing it* every night.

"How you gone say "she gave up her virginity" . . ." he mocks in the same tone I verbalized in earlier, "and say you didn't know they did *"THAT"* on the regular," he mocks me again. He grins. "You still Miss pure Libi, not saying "sex" or having SEX," he emphasizes. "Oh, you must not be gettin any these days like yo friend is . . . on the regular," he cracks up laughing.

I'm not amused, at all, and I'm sure he knows it by the callous assault in my expression. *And, no, I-am-not getting any on the regular; as a matter of fact YOU were the last person I had SEX with,* I scold, internally.

Without warning he slides his tongue in my mouth, using all muscle. I gladly respond, sucking his tongue back and forth and in circular motion—using all muscle. It's real intense, real passionate. He seems to miss me . . . he seems to need this.

When was your last time? I shout in my head. Yet, I don't actually want to know, I want to savor this moment. I raise my violet tank top over my head tearing our kiss apart. I wrap my arms around his neck and look him in his piercing eyes.

"It's nothing dike about me," I lean in to kiss him.

"Well, I don't know. I never could find breast tissue," he chuckles.

"Dude, I don't like you!" I punch him in his chest for that remark, and then punch him a second time for the previous one about me "not getting any".

He narrows his eyes at me and grabs my wrist. He leans in and tugs my ear with his tightened lips, then rests them behind my ear, on my neck. I feel chills throughout my upper body. He grazes his lips slowly along my neck, to my collar bone, between my breasts, down at my navel, and stops.

He begins snickering. "You thought I was gonna eat you out again, huh?" He bursts out in laughter.

Embarrassed, I narrow my eyes and look at him with a vengeance. "You know I hate you. You know it, don't you?" I express in a more serious tone and with sarcasm.

Qalbee glares, then adjusts his seat, extending it as far from the petal as it goes then reclines it to its max. His hands clinch my waste and he hoists me, guiding me on top of him. My nipples rest on his chest as I lean down to lower my sweats. I stop at my ankles when he proceeds to slip his brown draw string shorts down just enough that his penis peeks out. He captures my firm breast in his incredibly soft hands, sucks them, and begins massaging. I cup his penis in my right hand, cuddle it between the lips of my wet vulva, and rub it up and down . . . up and down, and then stroke his head along my clitoris in circular motion producing extra moisture. I hoist, and then descend on his penis, though only half of his shaft slides in, so I hoist again. Never releasing his cap, I plunge his entire 8 inch 6 girth boner in, striking my cervix. I continue with the same up and down . . . up and down, round and round pace hearing the sound of juices slush around and feeling sweet agonizing adoration with every assault to my pelvic floor. I moan, enduring the overwhelming sensation, though slow my pace because he feels *so good*. I look away from the 18 inch 2000 watt DAS speakers, which occupies the top of his back panel, to glance down at him. I catch his eyes shy away from watching the explicit contact of our genitals when he stares up at me with an expression of wonder.

I commence a new rhythm in effort not to alarm him yet he sits up. I place my palm in the middle of his smooth chest and continue propelling my hips . . . up and down, then circular, then left to right. I feel the passion of pre-ejaculation run down my leg. I smell the mixture of various sexual fluids perfume the oxygen we breathe between the windows of his Cutlass. *I'm riding him, and I'm doing Awesome! Well at least I think . . . it feels really great to me!* I flex my Kegel muscles, sucking him in. I clinch tighter and tighter each time. I repeat up and down, then circular . . . and left to right, faster, hearing the seat squeak in conjunction to my tempo. As I lean in, I smell his musk—a new musk, a sweet musk, a masculine musk. I claw my nails into Qalbee's shoulders to bear the painfully majestic stimulation. I gasp. I feel myself twitch, and then he exhales. I ooze. He sighs then quickly grabs my hips. He raises me up, pulling out his 8 inches, and sits me on his lap then explodes on my stomach. He groans. His eyes stare up at me and he nervously chuckles.

"That was close."

Chapter Seventeen

I'M LAID FLAT ON my back. I can only move my head from side to side. I can't move any other appendages. I'm not paralyzed since I can wiggle my toes, and jolt my fingers, and I'm not in restraints or chained down. I'm in an empty, sterile room, like a hospital. I feel cold air touch my body but I'm warm—hot even. I derail, having an outer-body experience, seeing my immovable body lying on bleach white sheets in a propped up hospital bed as I float at the foot of the bed bewildered. My stomach is engorged? Qalbee appears out of thin air, stands beside me with blue scrubs, a blue yarmulke looking cap on his head and a blue mask around his mouth. He holds my hand, and I can feel him squeeze very tightly. "Push," I hear a voice with bass command, but it's not from Qalbee. "Push, I see the head!" the same voice shouts. A man appears. I can't see his face. His back is to me. He has on all *white, a doctor's uniform. I hear the sound of crying. The doctor holds up a baby wrapped in white cloth, and then hands it to Qalbee. I've amalgamated back with my body. The man disappears then Qalbee begins gliding slowly away from me. I see him moving further in the distance. "No," I cry. Derailed again, I see myself reaching out to him. "No, please, come back!" I shout. Qalbee is gone. I hear beeping.*

I OPEN MY EYES seeing 12:00 flicker on my digital alarm clock. I reach to shut off the beeping. I'm lying on my bunk in my dorm room. My flight arrived early this morning around six. I didn't bother having Elaina pick me up because I knew she had our big event last night, so I caught a cab. When I got in, Elaina wasn't here, but came bursting in minutes after me. She was drunk, wobbling, and slurring her words, and slinging around the "B" word way too much. Elaina filled me in on the night and said that the crowd loved the flyers. People were talking about how clever our idea was by giving a "save the date" flyer at an event like this. Now that our event is on their minds, we have to watch our competition since it's so far away. We don't want to be side swiped by someone else's event. Thankfully, Elaina was able to briefly pitch our idea to Mr. Basin, Mr. Joyner, and Mr. Cosby, and was able to get their personal email information. She was able to talk to Mr. Smiley, though less about Prada E and more about Omega Si Phi. She claims she was flirting with him, which didn't help us, because he didn't provide his personal information.

So, Prada E was a success without me, and I am content with that! Elaina is top notch and she pulled through when I needed her. I apologized for changing my 9pm flight, which would've gotten me to the event no later than midnight, to a 5am flight. I decided to spend more time with Qalbee, even though summer break is in a week. I would have just stayed in the city if it wasn't for finals this week, but now I'll have to catch the Greyhound back for summer break.

Qalbee and I had gone into my safe haven after we effectively exploited the "pull out" method. At first I was real nervous at the thought of being pregnant, but my conscience was eased after he and I touched on so many different topics. I told him about Elaina and about how we have grown so close, about Prada Extravaganza and all the ideas I have for it. I joked with him about my many love interests—*nada!* He didn't believe that there is no one pursuing me, so I told him about Kenneth. It's embarrassing because he's the only guy that has showed any type of interest in me which was only a ploy to keep me from being chair of publicity. Qalbee doesn't believe that it was only a ploy. He believes that Kenneth genuinely likes me and wasn't surprised. Qalbee also believes that there are others, declaring that he knows that there are more, but that I'm too naive to see it. It made me feel some kind of way—special and tingly inside. I was even more flattered when he seemed optimistic after I told him that I'm not interested in anyone—*as if he likes that I'm dating no one.* Qalbee finally disclosed why he was unable to make it to my prom, graduation, and going away shindig.

One day in the summer before Qalbee was a freshmen in high school he came in from playing outside and found his mother hunched over in her bed vomiting on the floor. It scared him because he had never seen his mother sick before. She had always worked *"and hard at that,"* he emphasized. Qalbee said that he didn't say anything to his mother. He just went into the bathroom medicine cabinet, reached for the Alka-Selsa-Plus and Pepto-Bismol, warmed a cup of tap water and gave it to her. He went to the kitchen, got the mop and a few towels and cleaned up her vomit. He and his mother noticed that she was always feeling fatigued, started having a loss of appetite, and weight loss in a course of a year. Following that year, Ms. Davis went to the hospital for an infection and learned that her lymph nodes and liver were enlarged. It was then that she was diagnosed with Chronic Lymphocytic Leukemia. She was thirty-seven at the time. Doctors couldn't tell them the cause, only that it's a combination of genetics and environmental factors. It took Ms. Davis two years of having anemia, fevers, night sweats, and other flu-like symptoms for her to agree to chemotherapy. By that time Qalbee was a junior in high school and on the varsity basketball team. She relapsed by the time he and I met, the year he graduated, and was given pentostatin every four weeks for six months. Her body didn't take to this method of treatment which resulted in that last relapse and led to her death.

In the midst of all that sorrow, he told me that he has been getting sex from some girl that works with him at his new job at the hospital. *I must of died*—I literally almost passed out. My body was warm, my face was flushed, and my stomach was nauseous as my mind regurgitated thoughts of their bodies touching, lips kissing, smelling each other's breath, holding . . . being intimate. He says that he entertains her because she is always buying him things and shows persistence, and that her presence is what kept him from thinking of the awful suffering his mother was enduring. I feel loathe and betrayal because all this time he has been telling me that he needed space, and was having Craig have Chanelle tell me that *"it's a family issue." I'm so hurt. I've been fighting back tears of pain all night.*

I understand that before her relapse he was with me pretty much daily. I understand him not being there for me to be there for his mother, *and* I understand that I left around the time she began relapsing again. BUT, I was unaware of all of this, until now. I feel so sad—damaged—weak. I'm angry because Qalbee deprived me of this critical information, yet, he let her in. If I would have known that his mother, family, and he was going through heartache, anguish, and disaster, there is no question that I would have been around: at the hospital being supportive; catering flowers, and showering her with gifts; and at their house cleaning and preparing meals. Doing things like running errands for her and bonding with her. I loved her just as I love him. *Why didn't he tell me . . . why doesn't he know that? I'm in distress every time I think of the decision he made to keep me in the dark.*

WARM WATER SHOWERS MY NAKED, tired body after having a full day of classes. I open wide getting a mouthful of water rinsing out my mouth. I reach for my toothbrush and tooth paste on the bath banister and begin brushing. *Back to life, back to reality.* I'm going to miss my summer job working at the retirement home again. There is so much life and wisdom in the elderly. Working is pretty much what my summer consisted of. I didn't see much of Chanelle or Chad. Chanelle spends her spare time with Craig and Chad is head chef at his brother's restaurant which didn't leave him much time to come to the city. Qalbee and I actually talked over the phone regularly, and even spend some time together almost like when we first met. It was paradise. We only had sex three times the entire two mouths of summer. I think it is that girl, but he said they no longer talk. Chanelle verified that when she's at Qalbee and Craig's apartment the girl is never there. Craig says that Qalbee never really liked her to begin with, that he was merely going through some things at the time—basically his mother being ill and dying, though no one talks about it.

On a lighter note, I didn't have to catch the Greyhound back to Sugarland. When I was loading my bags in the car to head back to school after the summer, my mother handed me a red box. When I opened it there were keys to a car, my new car, a mustard yellow Toyota Tacoma! My mother whispered in my ear, "You deserve it," and she kissed me on the cheek! Both my mother and father went on about how they are proud of me, how I've proved that I'm responsible enough to have an automobile away from home, and how I've earned their trust. Yet they still made me follow them back to campus, I guess to further augment their sense of security. Elaina and I moved out of the dormitory and moved into apartments on campus. I've been back for about two weeks and Elaina returned a couple of days before me to pay the deposit for the apartment. We still have plenty of tidying up to do given that our focus has been Prada E since we've returned.

"Back to School with Prada Extravaganza" was a sensation. We were able to raise eight hundred dollars over the summer. A few band members that I know got together and helped us raise two hundred dollars and some of the members of the football team that Elaina knows raised one hundred. Before we left for summer break we profited a hundred from a few of the students around campus, and when we returned we had a couple of cars washes that raised us four hundred dollars. With Office Max and Staples donating paper, folders, and binders, pens, pencils and markers, and other supplies, we raised approximately a thousand dollars in all. We took half of the money and gave back to Office Max and Staples by purchasing backpacks for children that fit criterion of any mental health diagnoses. Office Max ended up giving us a discount for purchasing from them after they donated to us which granted us the ability to purchase even more. We used that half to buy toiletries that we put in the backpacks. Then we distributed them.

This week was my first week of classes being a sophomore. I went to weight lifting at eight, developmental psychology at nine, telecommunications planning and networking at ten, sociology at eleven, a break at twelve, and advertising at one. I only go Mondays, Wednesdays, and Fridays. No Tuesday and Thursday classes since I'm scheduled to work at the library from eight to five those days, and Saturdays, starting next week. In my Telecommunications class a girl named Bambi invited Elaina and I out with her and her boyfriend, Jason. Bambi and I had Intro to Sociology together last year. We've done occasional projects together in my dorm room so Elaina knows her as well. I've hung out with Bambi and Jason a few times before. They're really cool. Bambi is a bit dramatic, but a pretty positive person. Her boyfriend is a thug guy with an aggressive attitude, but underneath the hard exterior he is as soft as a teddy bear and has a big heart.

I STEP OUT OF the shower, reach for my towel, and dry my face, neck, breasts, stomach . . . then hear a knock at the front door. I rush, drying off my legs then feet. I grab the Palmate Coco butter, dig in and slap it all over my body then rub it in. I rush, putting on my grannies panties, blue jeans, bra, and maroon tank top. I grab my sandals and as I run into the living room, Elaina has already gotten the door. She's gesturing for Bambi and her boyfriend to sit. As they sit, Elaina heads my way.

"Hey Bambi. Jason," I greet, standing in the door way of the living room in front of one of the entry doors to the kitchen. I take a few steps and sit at the dining table to the left which is in front of the other entry door to the kitchen. I slip on one sandal, then the other, and began taking out my hair rollers.

There is a knock at the door. Jason gets up as if he was expecting someone then opens it.

"Sup," Jason greets. "Miss ma'am, this Rubin," he introduces.

Rubin is gorgeously handsome! He is about 6 feet and a bit brighter than me. He has on milky-ways, blues jeans, a plain white T-shirt, a fresh fade, and straight white teeth—no crook.

"How you doing?" he asks with a deep, macho man voice, nodding his head downward as he raises a greeting hand.

He must be a thug if he is friends with Jason, but, he's calm, nothing like loud Jason and dramatic Bambi. Rubin follows Jason in and stands at the door presenting a reserved and polite demeanor.

"Hi!" I smile. "Y'all have a seat," I insist.

Elaina walks in from the kitchen.

"Hey hey y'all . . . Y'all ret to go? Let's get sliced and diced," Bambi articulates, completely theatrical.

"You make it sound like we dealin with Libi's patients," Elaina entertains.

"I know right."

"Wait, what?" Rubin frowns.

"Libi's in school for psychology," Bambi clarifies.

"Yea, but I'm nowhere close to having any patients yet. This is only my second year," I say modestly.

"We rollin or what?" Jason rushes.

Chapter Eighteen

ELAINE, BAMBI, JASON, RUBIN and I are all sitting in a booth at Diego's Tattoo Shop. It's been a long wait and the crew is playing cards for entertainment to keep from being ready to go. We've played two full games of spades and Elaina and Jason are getting restless. Elaina has stepped out several times to take a smoke break, which is new. She just started while she was at home this past summer. Jason has tried to bribe the tattoo parlor twice, with extra pay in addition to him already paying for Bambi's, Elaina's and my tattoo. Bambi is being herself, chattering like speed-race-car talking girl off of *Coming to America*, which makes me think of Qalbee since he's always calling me her. When I would get nervous around Qalbee I would do lots of talking and to shut me up he'd mock, "I want to be a pop singer and a rock singer and write my own songs and produce my own songs." *I chuckle at the thought!*

"What's funny?" Rubin asks.

Rubin has been eyeing me all night, but then again, I keep staring at him, trying to figure out how it is possible for him to be as visibly gorgeous as he is? I've probably been making him uncomfortable. *Na, he's a thug guy, he doesn't get uncomfortable. I'm sorry,* I don't mean to judge.

"Hellooow? Libiya . . . I asked you what is funny?" Rubin says real genuine-like.

"Oh . . . nothing!" I search for an answer. ". . . JUST AT HOW I HAVE JUST WON THE GAME!" I shout as I lay my guarantee joker down, winning the game with four books and setting them each with three.

"I'm next on the game," Elaina insists, smelling like lung cancer waiting to happen.

Rubin rakes up my joker, the ace of spades, jack of spades, and an eight of hearts then reaches out to slide my winning book over to me. I extend my hand to collect all the cards then Rubin rests his hand on mine. I look up. He is ogling me. I smile.

"I'm up to get my tat," I announce, slowly taking my hand away. I stand and walk towards the booth. Rubin follows behind me.

"You sure you ready?" he asks, with a worried smile.

"Yes." I sit in the chair. "I'm a soulja." I smile.

The tattoo artist cleans my lower back with Tincture of Green Soap, shaves it to prevent ingrown hairs, and wipes the area again with the Green Soap. He then, for a fourth time, sprays the area for moisture and then applies the stencil transfer of my illustration. He peels the stencil paper off and hands me a mirror. I hold it up to the reverse mirror in front of me . . . and I see an abundance of rising stars. I nod with satisfaction, and gesture to go ahead with a smirk. The artist begins. I feel vibration, pain, and aggravation. The trebling feeling annoys me; however, it's keeping me from dwelling on the pain.

"You cool? Rubin asks.

"Yes," I respond, holding my breath and sounding as though I'm taking a dump.

"Why you making the bitter beer face?" he chuckles.

"The what? What's that?" I have no idea what he is talking about.

"She doesn't know what that is," Elaina informs as she walks up.

"Yea . . . I don't get it." I'm lost.

"You know, when you drink some bitter beer?" he attempts to explain.

"She doesn't drink," Elaina informs.

"Oh!" I giggle. "I get it." I chuckle even more as I imagine my bitter beer face!

I look in the direction of Rubin and discover him gawking at me again. He smiles at me when my eyes meet his. The vibration stops—the pain stops—the agitation stops—and then the artist sprays and wipes my back. He hands me the mirror. I hold it up to the reverse mirror and I see *an abundance of soaring stars!* I nod with satisfaction then smile! Cautious not to injure my wound, I ineptly stand. Rubin hurriedly comes behind the booth, places his arm under my shoulders, around my upper back, and helps me get positioned. Once I proficiently stand straight up, he holds my hand and leads me outside.

AFTER ELAINA GETS HER tattoo, she is ready to get home because she is in so much pain. She got a huge elephant in the middle of her back, all shaded in. Bambi is still getting her tattoo so Jason is staying with her while I ride with Rubin to drop Elaina off. Elaina sits in the back seat complaining the whole way home, whining about how she should have gotten drunk before getting the huge tattoo. So now she plans on getting drunk when she gets home. Rubin has not said much, he's being very patient. He detours just before we hit our corner and drives up to this small decrepit looking shack, park, and runs in. Elaina moans some more about the after pain from the torture she still feels until she sees Rubin approaching the car. Rubin gets in and hands Elaina a brown bag and we pull off. Elaina opens it, reaches in, and pulls out a bottle of Crown Royal. She animatedly thanks him. I shake my head with pity thinking, *"Lord, she's been around Bambi too long tonight. Bambi's theatrics has rubbed off on her."*

We pull up to our apartment complex. Rubin gets out, walks around to Elaina's door, and opens it. She gathers her purse and staggers out though Rubin assists her to her feet. He closes the door, walks back around to the driver's door, and stands there watching her as she walks into the apartment safely.

He is real considerate. Did he really just purchase her some liquor, open her door, and wait on her to get into the apartment without me even having to suggest it? If he hadn't flirted with me at the parlor, held my hand, and invited me to ride to take Eliana home, I'd think he was interested in her. *I see he's just a wholesome gentleman! Maybe he's not a thug.*

"Thank you for getting Elaina home. She seemed to be in great pain," I giggle, looking down at my entangled fingers and pacing thumbs.

"No prob. I like the time spent with you," he cajoles.

WE PULL UP TO our destination, a bare blank metal shack with the name "DEIGO'S" airbrushed in blue graffiti font covering the front of the building. Rubin parks in front of the entrance door, lets down both windows, and shuts off the engine.

I stare up at him, and then smile. "They should probably be almost done with Bambi. I'm getting a bit tired".

"I'm sure they are. You goin with Bambi over to Jason's?"

"No?" *Why would I do that?* He's lost me. "I hadn't planned on it." I'm confounded. "I didn't know. Was I supposed to?"

I hear chattering coming from the entry door. I turn forward and it's Jason and Bambi walking out the building.

"Hey girrrrlll!! How you feelin!" Bambi articulates as she steps to the back door of the car.

"I feel goo'ood!" I sing Toni Tony Ton'e's tone out the window.

"Cool! Let's get to Jason's. You goin over to Rubin's?" Bambi asks.

She and Jason lower into the car and we pull off.

"What?" I inquire, even more lost.

"Yea man, take me and Bambi to my crib. Then y'all can do what y'all wanna do," Jason directs, referring to Rubin.

"What?" I'm a bit frustrated. "If I would have known that, I could have gotten dropped off when Elaina was dropped off," I clarify feeling discouraged and tired.

"Just chill with my boy. He a cool fella right?" Jason ventures to convince.

"It's not that. I just didn't know . . . plus I'm exhausted."

"I'll take you home," Rubin offers.

WE ENTER A PLEASANT looking neighborhood with regular size homes and a few luxurious looking houses. After turning three or four corners we pull up to a posh house. It looks as though it is two stories, but by the single window up so high by itself, it may be three, or it has an attic. The crystal in the pearl bricks sparkle, the outdoor-wall-lights ornament each window, the flower garden flourishes along the side walk and alongside the house, and the grass is freshly scythed with no mower lines.

Jason and Bambi slide out of the backseat.

"Take good care of my girl," Bambi warns with her head leaned in through the back window.

"She in good hands," Jason defends.

I gesture farewell and look intensively into Bambi's eyes inferring retribution. We pull off.

"You say your place is close by?" I ask, with consideration of going there.

"Yes!"

"How close?"

"Right here!"

We pull up to another posh home, maybe four houses down from Jason's.

"Oh! What?" I'm shocked at how close they live from one another; and even more by the size of his home. *How can he afford this? He's only twenty-two?*

"Okay," *since we are here*, I justify. "But, if you don't mind, I am a little sleepy," meaning *no funny business*.

RUBIN WALKS ME THROUGH his posh home and all I can say is "Lavish". It has four bedrooms, 3 bathrooms, a game room, and a movie room, and the common areas. As we approach his room, a clean sugar pine forest aroma touches the hairs in my nose. I inhale deeply a few times to savor the fresh pine scent. We step into his room and it is as if we were in a cottage in the woods. The bed, the dresser, and the armoire are all made of soft Northern White Cedar. I know this because I was compelled to rub my fingertips across the smooth cabin-like furniture. *He had to have gotten this custom made.* I sit in his cottage log platform bed, and he tosses me a white t-shirt from his pine dresser chest to sleep in. I come into his bathroom, I change, and as I walk out, I see that he is laid comfy on the bed. Earlier, during the tour, he told me that I can sleep in his bed, leading me to believe he would sleep somewhere else, but now, I realize he meant in addition to him. I'm pretty tired, so I make the choice to lie uncomfortably next to him. He hands me separate covers, I think to assure me that he has no plans of try anything. *Thank you!*

"You can trust me. I sense the good girl in you and have no intentions on messing you over."

As we lay in his plush bed I suddenly become talkative. I ask him fundamental questions about his parents, if he has siblings, what he enjoys doing, and what he does for a living. I was afraid to hear the answers to that one. He subdues to answering all of my many questions then politely suggests that I get some rest.

I OPEN MY EYES to find my cheek resting on Rubin's chest. *When did he take off his shirt?* I feel his arm around my waist. Careful not to wake him, I slowly slide my face to look up at him. He's gazing down at me.

"Beautiful, you are," Rubin cajoles.

"Why thank you!" I rise up to conceal my blushing cheeks then tensely grab my things, walk to the bathroom, and change into my clothes.

The conversation on the ride home is about cleaning, moisturizing, and taking care of my tattoo—*OH*, and breakfast. We pull up to my apartment and Rubin gets out—I assume it's to open my door. I open it before he has the chance and I climb out. Once I stand to my feet he's directly up on me, less then arm's length, imprisoning me to the corner of the car door—hemmed between he and the car. I can't go left and I can't go right.

"You sure you don't want some breakfast?"

"No thank you. I have so much to do. But, rain check?" I offer stepping to the left, yet, he steps in front of me.

"I wouldn't have it any other way!" he smirks.

I squat down in to his car, reach for a napkin stuffed into the cup holder, lean forward to grab a pen from the door pocket, and write my number down, never breaking eye contact and holding my breath. My look of annoyance is visible. I stand, hand him the napkin, and step to my right. He takes a step back as I exhale. He lets me by with a proud smile, never uttering a single word. *I'm guessing my digits are leverage enough,* I smile inside! He follows alongside me to the door of my apartment. With confidence, he leans his lips towards my cheek, *I guess as a "see you soon" farewell.* Nonetheless, I lurch back, frown, and shake my head as a slight smirk embrace my lips. I wave "bye". He smiles a luminous smile. His bright yellow skin tone lightens with optimism as if he enjoys the chase. I playfully roll my eyes and step into the apartment.

IT SMELLS OF BEEF bacon, pancakes, and maple syrup as I head straight for the kitchen to tell Elaina about my night. I barge in and like my nose detected there is bacon, pancakes, eggs, hash browns, and Malt-o-meal, but no Elaina. Famished—after proposing a breakfast rain check this morning—my stomach figures that purging my story to Elaina can wait until after I binge some food down. I open the cabinet next to the refrigerator, pull out a plate, help myself to each breakfast item, pour a tall glass of Simply Orange juice, and take a bite of my bacon before I exit the kitchen. I walk into the hall and see Elaina lying on the couch, asleep. I had walked right past her when I came through the door.

"Oow," Elaina taunts. "Um hum! Someone was out being fast," she teases with shut eyes.

I place my plate on the open bar counter, then gallop towards Elaina. I drop to my knees, rest my folded arms on the edge of the couch Elaina lies on, and lean in disregarding any sense of boundaries.

"I like him," I say dramatically, like Bambi.

"YOU GAVE IT UP!" Elaina shouts with conviction and with her eyes bulging from their sockets.

"NOOO!" I screech, flabbergasted by her accusations. "I just like him." I place my right hand to my chest. *Geeezsh!*

"Well, I'll be. Thank you God," she praises like her life depended on my love interest. "I was a bit worried 'bout you in that department."

"What? How?" Again, I'm flabbergasted. "I talk to guys all the time., I clarify, hearing my voice ascend with a high pitch.

"I know. That's the issue," she huffs as she sits up to attain her personal space. "You have all these male friends you talk to and hang with, and they all feelin you, but you don't give either a real time of day."

"I want someone who makes me laugh and that has some intellect. Is that so much to ask for?" I say in a no-nonsense manner on the defense.

"Ronald!" Elaina calls out as if she expects an explanation.

"Rapper," I capitulate. *Boys wanting to be rappers as a first dream choice is exasperating. Can we get a full time job, AND THEN rap part-time? I'm just saying.*

"Evan," she precedes.

"Possessive." *I'm too free spirited for that.*

"Kelvin," she persists.

"Too sensitive." *I'm pretty honest and you can't be easily offended.*

"Okay, now this guy?" she perseveres.

"He makes me laugh," like Qalbee, "and he has this innocent naïve'ness to him," like Qalbee. Only, I feel the sense to protect Qalbee, but with Rubin, I feel protected.

"And you gathered all this in one night?" she utters sarcastically, slightly rolling her eyes with a "girl, you're pitiful" expression on her face. "Ain't he an ex-gang member?" she goads then rests her head on the red pillow case, and closes her eyes.

"What?" I'm dumbfounded. "Why you say that?" I stare in denial.

"I heard them talkin 'bout it," she turns over with her back facing me.

Chapter Nineteen

"TRI-DECEMBER WITH PRADA Extravaganza" turned out great—divine—better than I could have ever envisaged! Towards the end of preparations, Texas View University actually came on board and sponsored us. There was a leak that Elaina and I were lobbying. We almost had to come up before the board for soliciting but when the provost learned that it was Elaina and I behind it all, he dropped it. Elaina and I are honor students, and have been since last year. Provost North lectured us about how 37 percent of freshmen drop out, how an even smaller percent are honor students, and how he won't be the *"negative reinforcer"* to something that is positive just because it's written in the university regulation. And I'm sure it helped us that he shared the prognosis with TVU's president, Dr. Woods, about how colossal Tri-December's turnout looked. Naturally they'd want for their university to receive some type of resignation. Nonetheless, we all shook hands like some winning politicians, and had a *splendid success!*

I DROVE TO EDMOND afterwards. Being back home for the extended four day weekend was great! It went fast, but I used most of my time parlaying with Mickey Mouse, which I needed. Between Prada E, Tri December, fundraisers, studying for finals, and trying to have a personal and social life, to say I needed sleep is an understatement. And since it snowed, I definitely parlayed! I missed out on the pleasures of sparkling white snow as it brightened the wintry air last winter given that I didn't come home. I was actually happy to be able to catch the frosty snowflakes on my warm tongue and feel the crunch of the ice under my Steve Madden boots as I sunk in making prints!

Being locked in for a few days gave me a chance to bond with Sebastian. He and I did a great deal of talking, like when we were kids. It was jovial. It meant a lot to me! He's moving to New York this spring since he has a whole heap of buyers interested in his extraordinarily divine art work! *He's such a prodigy.* I shake my head at his brilliance while internally applauding him! *I'm so proud of my big brother!*

"SITTING HERE LOOKING OUT my window," I sing a tune by Case and change words out of connivance.

"My nights are long and today have faded away," I continue as I drive down Interstate 45 back to Sugarland.

"If only I could find him," my voice cracks as I attempt to hit the note, vibrato style.

I called Qalbee's phone on my way to the city but his phone was disconnected so I drove past his house, well his uncle's house, with hopes that he would be there visiting or something. Just my luck, there were no cars parked outside and no movement inside, as far as I could see being that I was parked in the street on the curb crossways. And of course I didn't bother with harassing Chanelle about where he and Craig live. She knows all about Rubin and how much I like him. I didn't want to confuse the situation. She doesn't know that I'm still in love with Qalbee.

My relationship with Rubin has really blossomed, though, when I go back home *or* talk to someone from home, I think of Qalbee. Certain things like cookies and cream ice cream, blue berry muffins, Eddie Murphy, and standup comedy elicit thoughts of him, causing me to reflect on our times together, movies we'd watch, music we'd listen to that he'd clown most of the time, clothes I wore around him, *and just all the laughs we shared.*

I'm saddened when I look back. I must put us to rest for the New Year. I know that much. I plan to make *new* memories with Rubin! For New Year's Eve he's taking me out to the Cheese Cake Factory in the Galleria Mall, so, I figure, *what better time to start!*

EXPLOSIONS OF BEAUTIFUL SPARKLING LIGHTS of fire bursts in the darkness of the evening sky resembling multihued falling stars. Though loud and pongee, Rubin and I sit in his russet Oldsmobile Aurora in the midst of downtown watching the excitement and fireworks brighten everyone's night. We talk a little about how we were raised, our hobbies and interest, and our goals in life. I evade all discussion about past relationships and never once does he broach that he was in a gang.

After the firework show we walk profusely up and down the streets of downtown. I'm impressed that he knows his way around the city the way that he does being that he's not from here. His family's from New Orleans. He's shown me various non-profit organizations that will be of some importance to me in the future, pointing out Catholic Charities and Donate with Us. I'm falling for his considerate and gentlemen like manners. He's held my hand and has been hugging on me as we walk practically all night. We've been doing lots of flirting and complimenting each other. I'm learning that we have many similar views about life like: health, morals, and politics. We seem to understand where the other is coming from most of the time.

We walk up on Starbucks Coffee and decide to get a thirst quencher. More, so that I can rest my body—my calves are as firm as Jesse Owens' and my feet are as tender as Richard Simmons' appearance. As soon as I walk through the glass door I sit comfortably in the first vacant chair in sight. I'm tempted to take off my boots but I don't want to embarrass Rubin. He walked straight to the counter to order us two decaffeinated drinks since I don't consume caffeine.

Rubin sets the two large glasses of Tazo Ice Passion Teas on the table and I devour mine in one long gulp, leaving no back wash behind. *Refreshing!*

I lean in. "Are you in a gang?" I ask after dating him for four months.

"What? No!" he shouts, seeming genuinely offended as the bass in his voice grows hoarse and screeches.

"*Were* you in a gang?" I press, sounding reproachful.

"Why are you asking me all these questions, now?" He stares looking confused and seemingly frustrated while he rests his forehead in the palm of his left hand massaging his temple. By the weep in his eyes he seems worried. "We've been dating since August and you're asking me this, now? Why?"

I know I just asked a question . . . just 'cause you feel some type of affronted, doesn't mean refuse the question or prolong answering it. You do realize. "I have every right to know who and what I'm dealing with here. I deserve answers and the opportunity to make decisions based on precision, not on false pretense. Don't deny me that," I protest, feeling deceived, swindled . . . apprehensive, and feeling myself spasm. I'm upset. I stand to my feet and as I take a step to walk away, he stands to his feet and I hear my name spin off his tongue with condiment.

"Libiya!"

He reaches over the small round table, snatches my dangling wrist, and my body jerks towards him. *The audacity of him*, I thought. I narrow my eyes at his with full intent of aiming telepathic thoughts of disgrace at his soul. *He has his nerve putting his hands on me, manipulating my arm like I'm battling with battered woman syndrome, and making a scene like we're in some domestic violent relationship.* I look down at my imprisoned wrist, and peer back up at him feeling disappointed and deceived.

"Wait . . . I'm sorry." He expresses regret, releasing my wrist and again seeming worried. "Please sit down," he asks, holding up his five fingers for me to yield.

We sit.

"I *used* to associate with a gang . . . yes," he admits, lowering his voice.

Well I can see that. Never taking my eyes off his, I embrace my wrist with my other hand, clearly making a point, still displeased. I continue to peer.

"That was some years ago. I went to job core, got my Commercial Drivers License, will begin my undergrad next semester, because of you. I aim to pass the LSAT when I graduate, which you already know all this," he explains. "That life is my past. You—this time together—is my future, if you decide to have me," he pleads.

AFTER OUR SPAT, WHICH was long overdue, Rubin continuously apologizes for omitting pertinent information, and practically begs for me to come spend time with him at his home. I accept, but our journey home is a quiet one.

We make it to his home and I head straight for the shower. I pull off my boots one by one, slide off my granny panties along with my jeans, and then pull my sweater over my head when Rubin walks through the bathroom door. He's carrying three jumbo candles and then begins dispersing them throughout the bathroom. He knows how I feel about candles. Uncomfortable by the awkward silence, I glance over at him a few times wondering if he's going to say anything. He doesn't. However, he walks up on me, places the last candle on top of the commode, and attempts not to voyeur my body as I stand here next to the shower, between the commode and straw hamper, with just my bra on. He never looks up. And as he walks over to the sink and his ingenuous aura allures me like the first day we met, I begin yearning for his touch. I then venture welcome signals through my body language by stalling to get into the shower. I slowly fold my dirty clothes then I gradually put them on the floor in the corner next to the straw hamper.

After my parade, he walks over to me, and I'm like *finally!* He reaches his arms around my body and my nipples graze his chest. I feel his firm fingers unsnap my bra. He then leans in down low, reaching his left hand behind me and passing up my nude existence when I hear the shower jet spurt. I feel moisture between my legs though project that it's from the steam of the shower. As I stand here exposed I feel my pubic follicles sway to each inhale and exhale that he breathes as he ascends from below. My stomach flutters. *I'd anticipated that it would only be a matter of time before he gestured some form of sexual act ever since the day we began dating. What better time and place?*

To my surprise—and regret—he shovels up my clothes and head towards the door. *I don't know if I should feel really astonished or really mortified; nonetheless,* I *do know that I must have looked really desperate.* I hastily jump in the shower and let the water torrent my face. As I let the water drown my mouth, I feel a sharp pain in my stomach, and then I hear a grumble. *Being so caught up in all the tumult tonight, I hadn't realized how hungry I am. First the brawl at the coffee shop and now, here I am pretty much throwing myself at this guy and he blatantly disregards me. Huh,* I exaggerate an exhale while shaking my head with humiliation.

My thoughts stream back to a couple of weeks ago when Rubin first ran down the plan for the New Year to have cheese cake, watch fireworks and to take me home afterwards. Though, after my epiphany to start a new beginning with Rubin, I made the grand decision to just go ahead and stay the night with him and carry out my new found New Year's resolution of making personal and special memories with him instead of going home afterwards. My fantasy was to prance around with only his t-shirt and my panties on, listen to music, eat popcorn and sour patches, and initiate fore-play as we lie tempted in his bed. Now this ridiculous brawl happened. I only agreed to come here after being misled and mishandled, because I realized that my impatience during his cathartic process of explaining the secrecy of his past life caused us more conflict when all he was doing is trying to protect me in his own way. So I figured *"why not rectify my behavior?"* . . . and of course *he* had no objections prior to all this . . . *but now he disses me?*

I step out the shower and look through cabinet after cabinet searching for a towel. I remember Rubin getting one from the hall closet when I was here a time before . . . *But after what I just pulled, I'd rather not be caught butt naked in the hall.* I peak my head out the door and look left, right, and then left again. There is no Rubin in sight. I zoom from the bathroom to his room, then, realize that I have no change of clothes. And since he chose my clothes over my body, I don't even have dirty clothes to change into. I valiantly pull one of his white T-shirts out of his chest and slipped it on. I figure I can do that since I've come here at least once a week since we met back in August and he's always telling me to make myself at home. I pull the sheet and covers back, scoot under them, and lay in his bed wearing only a T-shirt but no panties or bra.

Just as I get nice and cozy Rubin walks in carrying a tray of food. He places it next to me without saying a word. It's my favorite meal: turkey bacon, scrambled eggs, crunchy hash browns, and two slices of toasted wheat bread! I order this every time we go to I-Hop . . . *but his attentiveness, mixed with care, added with him taking out the time to prepare it for me makes me appreciate its taste that much more!*

Heart Attack

Chapter Twenty

IT IS ALREADY SPRING and I just don't know where all the time went. People say that time flies when you keep yourself busy. I agree! Prada Extravaganza has gone to countless shelters throughout the city passing out food and clothing to the less fortunate. After Tri-December's success many companies donate regularly without us soliciting, and many of the university's students have been volunteering with Prada E. They make no money. It is all community service to help us and our consumers. I am sure it looks great on their resume. We have had a fundraiser every month and just had an event where the volunteers played baseball with mentally impeded children and teens.

Not only have I been laborious with Prada Extravaganza, work, UPC, and finals coming up next week has been stressful. Even spending time with Rubin takes a toll, although, he actually alleviates much of the stress. He keeps me happy! Elaina taunts me about dating an ex-thug and believes I only agreed to make it official because I received word that Qalbee is dating *some girl*. And yes, it may be some truth there . . . it hurts . . . BUT, *I do* really like Rubin. When I'm with him, I only think of Qalbee *sometimes instead of all the time*. I fold my arms and lift my head proud about that. *I believe I'm doing pretty good! Right?* The thing is I knew that when I moved from Edmond that Qalbee and I wouldn't be anything. As a matter of fact, I wouldn't have moved far-far-away if I had thought for just a second that we'd be something. I'm falling for Rubin. He's such a manly man. I need that. He takes charge. He balances my shortcomings. *That's what I need . . .* I pause, hoping that I'm not subconsciously attempting to convince myself.

The other day I was at Tom Bass Park lying on my royal yellow satin blanket surrounded by text books, when I suddenly felt a smooth, soft, furry feeling tickling my lower back, around my neck, up to my nose, and then a kiss on my cheek. It was Rubin with a bundle of picked flowers. All I could do was lean back on his chest, smell the roses, and smile! He did me the same way for Valentine's Day. Although neither of us is big on holidays, he said that he wanted to take advantage of the day and indulge me. So while I was studying at the library he walked in with one long stem red rose and begged me to leave with him. Rubin knows that I bury myself in books without eating, taking a break, or even coming up for air unless deemed necessary, so when he came in showing grave concern, passion, and enthusiasm to leave with him, I was convinced enough. I thought it was adorable! When we walked into his place, he had previously cut the stems of calendulas, coltsfoots, coreopsis, daffodils, dandelions, jasmines, and sunflowers, and had aesthetically placed them in clear vases on his living room coffee table, dining room table, kitchen bar counter, and in the bathrooms. Yellow rose petals were laid exceptionally on the bed, nearly covering it. He knows I love yellow flowers! I love yellow period! He tells me that now his favorite flower is yellow because they remind him of my yellow tone. He calls me his Black-Eyed-Susan because he says that I'm encouraging, motivational, and impartial like the Black-Eyed-Susan's representation. I brighten his darkness. *He enjoys watching me blossom being an honors student, participating in different organizations, and managing to run my own illegal nonprofit. I believe he loves me by the looks he gives me sometimes when I catch him staring. I'm reluctant to admit it out loud, and to myself, but I know it's true because it's the same look I give Qalbee.* Rubin's not used to girls like me or used to seeing productiveness so approximate and intimate—so up close and personal. I assume it's the "gang" thing. He *is* from the gutters of the ward.

Rubin's father died when he was two, which elicits thoughts of Comedy. Rubin's mother had two children to fend for: he and his younger sister. His mother was always out in the streets making money to support them and pay off debts. Rubin was real resolute that his mother was no prostitute and was doing no drugs. He tells me that he would eat out of dumpsters and sleep in back allies so that his sister wouldn't have to feel the destitution. Rubin began to sell marijuana at the age of nine, pills at twelve, and became a loan shark by fourteen, when he met Jason. Rubin's sister was shot after her boyfriend, who was in the same business they were in, shot and killed a guy for not paying him interest for a loan. That guy's 14 year old son shot Rubin's sister and her boyfriend at the grocery store, killing the boy friend and putting her in intensive care. Rubin promised his mother that he would detach himself from all of that trepidation and so he went to job core, received his Commercial Drivers License, and began the journey to a changed life. Now, he's such a gentleman—he takes me out, open doors, pays for dinner—even when I'm adamant to do so. He enjoys cooking for me. He even washes my car for me. *I do love him!*

I'VE NOTICED MY style of wardrobe has transformed over the seasons. I have not worn swishy sweats since maybe last spring. *I guess I am growing up!* Today I have on a sapphire blue spaghetti strapped pin up dress, and grey sandals that are flooded with diamonds across the buckle and toe strap. I'm matching the sky on this beautiful summer evening. My hair is parted down the middle flowing down to my bra strap with waves like a Brazilian weave. Rubin and I are having an early dinner at Princess, my favorite burger joint, before we go to Happy Hour at Elaina's job. She's a bartender at a hole-in-the-wall in third ward and has been for a few weeks.

I sit at the bistro table alone when I see a glimpse of Rubin at a distance walking through a mass of men that stands around the restroom door. My reverie is disrupted as he walks towards me. *He looks so stunning in his denim jeans and Persian blue and grey striped Polo.*

Rubin sits down adjacent to me. "Are you ready, sweetheart?" he cajoles.

"Yes love," I appeal.

WE'RE IN A SMALL white shack, maybe the size of my apartment, minus the walls of course. There is one bar, one bathroom, and one DJ—each in their respective corners. I'm sitting at the bar after dancing to six songs straight with Rubin. *The crowd has been great!* Other than being packed in these four walls like grocery stores on the first of the month, the atmosphere is nice. I like how the DJ plays a mixture of old school music and hip hop throughout the night. I chat with Elaina whenever she's not taking orders and giving drinks.

"Two Amarillo Sours," Elaina announces while handing over two mugs full of mood alteration to two substance dependent females. "So, who yo boys, home boys?" Elaina wipes her hands on her apron and points with her head.

Rubin and three guys are standing on the dance floor, though are static to the beat.

"I don't know?" I suspiciously stare.

Rubin's lips are moving ten times a second. His expression is intense. One guy, not much taller than Rubin, steps up on him, leaving him without personal space. Rubin slightly pushes the guy away from him then holds his hands up as if he is surrendering to the police. I stand to my feet. I feel Elaina's hand constrict my shoulder.

"Uh, no you don't," she commands.

Another guy even shorter swings his fist at Rubin. He misses. The crowd starts closing in. I'm unable to see Rubin. *What's going on?* My long thin neck raises like ET the Extra Terrestrial, and my expression is like a deer in head lights. I'm able to take two steps before Elaina stands in front of me.

"Hell naw!"

A fragment of the top of Rubin's tapered hair rushes through the crowd. His expression, annoyed, and he's gnashing his teeth. He reaches through the swarm of people and snatches my wrist. My body jerks towards him as he pulls me—*déjà vu,* I thought as the heels of my sandals drag while I strive to walk to keep up, though he's practically hauling me.

We make it outside of the club.

"What was that about?" I ask, upset that he was just almost in a fight, that he drug me out the club causing this huge scene, and that the night is ending like this.

"Nothing . . . they said some disrespectful shit."

"Babe!" I screech.

He pulls me in his arms. "I'm sorry babe, didn't mean to curse," he serenely apologizes. "They just pissed me off," he says with a more aggressive tone.

"Babe?" I'm poised.

"Sorry!"

We hear commotion in the building.

He releases me. "We have to go!"

"Wait! Elaina's in there. I'm not just leaving her!" I shout.

"SHIT!" he runs towards the door then looks back. "Go to the car, NOW!" He enters the club.

I continue to look over my shoulders leery that one of those guys or someone else might walk up on me, yet I walk at regular speed to prove that I'm not afraid. I see Jason speed walking towards the entrance. *Why is he here?* I'm tempted to call out his name but his demeanor is too grave. He looks like he's on a mission. I am about four yards from the car when I hear gun shots. I run, terrified for my life, and an image of Qalbee flashes through my mind. I hear loud and rapid thudding like a horse stampede along with screams resembling a horror movie. People are screaming and running every which way. I hurdle into Rubin's car, lock all the doors, and sprawl in my seat. *Oh no . . . Rubin, Elaina . . . Jason.* I am petrified for them. Not even a minute later Rubin walks out with Elaina. His left eye is puffed up, his left cheek bone is red, and his lip is busted. Elaina's in one piece. *Huh, thank goodness!* I hear police sirens.

I OPEN MY EYES to sunlight bursting through my window. My first thought is . . . *Rubin!* Last night he dropped Elaina and I off at home and then was supposed to go to the police station. I haven't the slightest clue about what happened there or at the club for that matter.

Rubin was supposed to call me after he left the police station to fill me in on everything to ease my worries. That didn't happen. *I'm sure he's going to say that I needed my rest.* I sigh at the thought and shake my head. I hoist from bed and reach for my robe. *Elaina has it freezing in here.* I head for the bathroom.

"So, you stickin with yo thug?" Elaina's voice taunts from the living room as I push open the bathroom door. "That Qalbee fella must have been a real drug . . . cuzz you done lost yo damn mind endangering yourself over some rebound. Well, I'm not gonna let you."

I turn away from the bathroom and yell across the apartment, frustrated, "Elaina, how is he a rebound when I love him?" I then lean on the hall wall and peek my head into the living room. "We've been together eight months and this is the first and only incident." I back up into the bathroom, and yell again, as politely as possible, "Please give it a rest!" However, a hint of irritation comes through the shudder in my tone. I begin brushing my teeth.

A knock is at the door.

"It's Rubin," Elaina hollers.

I gargle, rinse, and then sputter. I open the bathroom door, and there stands Rubin.

"Came to talk," he shamefully utters while looking apologetic.

I enfold my arm under his and usher him to my room.

"Please don't tell me any of that had anything to do with your past life, Rubin," I desolately hope.

"Jason got into some trouble about a week ago with those niggas and I got myself in it by tryna make peace."

"Gang?"

"Yes."

"I'm leaving for Edmond Wednesday morning."

"I thought you were gonna stay?" Now *he* sounds desolate. He sits on the corner of my bed. "What about finals?" he sighs.

I pull out my yellow, cherry print duffle. "Well, three of my tests I'm taking on Monday . . ." I pull undergarments from my two top chest drawers and shove them into the duffle. "And my biopsychology and statistics professors gave the option to take their exams on Tuesday instead of Thursday for those who are leaving the town for the summer." I stuff a few folded jeans in the bag. I know that I'm self sabotaging, but when I heard those gun shots, I thought of Qalbee. I miss him. I know I won't see him back at home, but just knowing that I will inhale the same air he exhales will suffice. It's like eating at a restaurant you know your idol ate at, and then having the chance to sit at that same table, or like squirming your toes in the ancient sands of Egypt knowing that your ancestors squirmed their toes in that same sand. It's a marvelous feeling.

"Just like that?" Rubin states disgruntled.

"I need to do some serious thinking." I stop packing then look up at him "I'll be back in three months."

"Three months," I hear him whisper as his head drops down. "Don't leave me," He stands to his feet. "You're my stability," he pleads and takes my hand. "I'm insane without you," he gapes, then rests his hand on my cheek.

I rest my hand on his. "I love you too, Rubin." I gaze at him. "We'll talk every day . . ." I pause, ". . . But Rubin," with a serious tone, "I'm NOT coming back to danger. Fix this." I fret looking intensely into his eyes. I'm scared for his life.

He purses his lips, leans towards me, and slides his tongue into my mouth. I breathe a capitulated gasp as I engage.

AFTER A SIX AND a half hour drive from Sugarland, I'm pleased to stare at my roof as I pull into my parent's driveway. Cloud Nine is a sight for sore eyes! I open the door of my car, leaving everything in it, and head straight to the backyard then climb the ladder up. *I'm so happy to be up here!* I lay flat on my stomach and hug C9. The last time I was up here, Qalbee was with me for his first time after his mother's funeral.

I hear tires treading the pavement so I lift my head to observe who is approaching. Chanelle climbs out of her new chestnut brown Volkswagen Beetle.

"You and that damn roof!" Chanelle shouts.

I sit up and stretch my arms. "Girl, it's great to be back!" I shout back

"I'm not climbing up there in my stilettos . . . or in my white capri's," she grumbles.

"Of course not!"

I scoot to the edge of the roof and leap down. I meet Chanelle at the front door of the house, and we embrace. The last two times I was in the city we saw each other maybe twice, if that.

In the kitchen I offer Chanelle a banana and orange juice. She accepts, as expected.

"It's good to have you back for awhile."

"Yea," I respond casually.

I lead us up the stairs to my room.

"Craig and I have gotten really serious!"

"Really," I say sarcastically. *I know this. That's one of the reasons we do not see each other when I'm here.* "I remember the days you could not stand him!" I chuckle. "Well as long as you feel he's the one for you," I raise my orange juice gesturing cheers.

Chanelle taps hers to mine and before she sips, she pauses as if she has something serious to say.

"What?" I ask nervously.

She sips her cup ogling me. "Qalbee runs that chick over there."

I roll my eyes not caring to hear about what My Heart and *some girl, whom is not me,* is doing.

"She cooks for him, buys him shoes, and damn as well call him massa." She forces a diminutive chuckle out, never taking her eyes off mine as if she's expecting a certain reaction.

"Wow. That's what he needs, 'cause I am not the one to do all that," I self-assuredly express.

"I just knew you were gonna tell me you were engaged! How's that goin?" She treads off that subject real fast.

Now I realize that her earlier anticipation was only from not knowing how I would react to her bringing Qalbee up in our future conversations now that I'm with Rubin and Q's serious with some girl amongst the fact that she and Craig will accompany them now and then.

"Well . . . actually, I think Rubin was going to the other night but he got into an altercation."

"Altercation?" She looks stymied. "You don't need that in your life."

"Yea, I know." *If only you knew.* I'm *too happy* about life right now to go into that episode right now. I will catch her up when it's not so fresh. "But he's good. Good to me and just a good person in general. He'll do the right thing."—*which is how he got into this mess to begin with.*

Chapter Twenty-One

I CONTINUE TO LOOK over my shoulders leery that one of those guys or someone else will walk up on me. I see Jason speed walking towards the entrance. His demeanor is grave. I am about four yards from the car when I hear gun shots. POW! POW! BANG! I run terrified for my life. An image of Qalbee flashes through my mind. I hear what sounds like roaring thunder. People are screaming and running every which way. They all stampede over me. I'm in horror.

I JUMP UP, AND open my eyes to a dark room. My body is drenched in sweat. I'm panting exceedingly hard which is causing me chest pains as if I'm having a heart attack. My stomach grumbles. I know these are symptoms of acute traumatic stress—minus the hunger pains. I should call Rubin. *But I'm not.* I roll out of bed, enter my bathroom, and start brushing my teeth. I am famished. I guess I will go to Taco Mayo and get myself two tacos and a tostada. We don't have Taco Mayo in Sugarland. Besides, there are not many options to choose from at this hour. I look into the mirror to examine how I look. *My black do-rag looks great all lop sided from night terror and lumpy from the sponge rollers I have snapped in my hair.* I'm trying to produce big full bouncy curls that will have to last me for the next two weeks. I straighten my do-rag then tighten it. *I'm just going up the street.* I slip on my thong sandals lying beside my bed post and head for the door.

I saunter up the dark streets after successfully making it to Taco Mayo before they closed. I'm listening to "Over My Head" by the Fray. My radio clock reads "2:11". I pull up to the intersection and stop at a red light. I look ahead and there is only one car on the street. It's stopped diagonal from me. My light turns green, and I press on the gas, mumbling the words to the song. As I approach the car to pass it while it waits to turn, I look inside of it. Piercing, familiar eyes gaze at me then perfect Photo Shop groomed waves tilt gesturing for me to follow. My eyes are planted. Despite his perturbed expression, the sight of that smooth brown skin and alluring face causes me to smile. He then smiles with charisma displaying his oh-so-illustrious slight crook in his front right tooth as the sound of Fray ebbs. I make an illegal u-turn in the middle of the intersection.

After driving about three blocks I realize that I still have on my do-rag and a head full of rollers. I began un-spiraling rollers from my hair as I follow him into an apartment complex. He parks then instantly climbs out. I park and hesitantly scramble out, attempting to hide my rollers and do-rag under the seat. I'm so nervous. My stomach has butterflies and my heart flutters. Qalbee walks up on me. I look up into his innocent eyes. He's so close I smell his cologne.

"My Heart." I feel so overjoyed my body trembles. I feel sensation in my eyes. I raise my hand to shovel hair behind my ear in attempt to deflect tears. "It's been . . ."

"A long time," Qalbee finishes my sentence. He smiles a boyish smile as he gawks at me.

"God, Comedy . . . how have you been?" I feel protective.

"Shiiit, I'm straight . . . Craig and I roommate here." He continues to gawk.

I'm captivated. "Oh, really! So *that* all worked out! I'm so happy for you . . . so proud of you!"

His eyes never leave mine. He wraps his right arm around my waist pulling me even closer to him. He places his left hand on my right and pulls, salvaging my nails from my teeth. *Dang, I didn't realize I was munching on my nails, now he knows that I'm nervous.* He guides my thumb across his bottom lip then barges his tongue into my mouth quenching my anticipation. I was thirsty for his kiss. If we were on the big screen, fireworks would rupture vibrantly as our passion flares.

His tongue liberates mine. "Taco Mayo, huh?"

My eyes widen in shock as my mouth does the same. *How humiliating.* I push my fist into his chest.

We laugh in sequence.

"Where were you headed?"

"My parent's."

"How long you here for?"

"The summer."

"They asleep?"

"I'm sure."

"Um . . ." he accepts ostensibly, contemplating as his chin slightly lifts.

I've never been fazed by rejection, until him, but I dare anyway. "Come over?" I ask.

He smiles as if I said what he wanted to hear. He grips the back of my neck, pulls me to him, and lays a lengthy peck on my lips.

I LAY A SHEET OUT on the floor of my room, set my MP3 to shuffle through R. Kelly's many albums, and leave Qalbee in my room in hopes that he will be undressed by the time I finish brushing my teeth.

After brushing I wash my face, under my arms, between my legs then I look at myself in the mirror and I look . . . *revived!* I feel alive! I always feel alive when I'm with him, I'm in heaven!

"Dedicated" by R. Kelly is playing on the stereo when I step out of the bathroom. I walk towards Qalbee completely nude. *I won't dare let him see me in my grannies and I don't own any lingerie so bare it is.* Qalbee stands up with only his boxers on, but soon pulls them off. When I approach him, he instantly squats down and his lips vacuum my right breast as he cups the other with his right hand. Immediately I leak. I massage his shoulders as his wet tongue spirals my stimulated nipple. He releases then swaps. He arouses my right breast with the tips of his fingers and tastes a mouthful of my left breast as it fits firmly between his jaws. He sucks with frenzy as he leads me to the bed. We stumble and when we fall to the floor, I collapse onto his stalwart body. I'm amused by the clumsiness, but to my better judgment I keep my composure. Qalbee doesn't acknowledge the awkwardness by any means. He grasps my butt, spins me over, and I roll on my back. I wrap my arms around his neck, pull him to me, and hug him tightly. *Bliss!* He mounts on his right elbow, tilts his ear towards his shoulder, and gapes at me as if he feels privileged of my actions—maybe flattered. I'm smiling tremendously because I'm in heaven and my heart is giddy! He leans in, slides his tongue between my lips, absorbing my salivation then manipulates my quivering tongue. I entangle mine with his and we contract as one. My heart rapidly pounds against his chest. *I'm so in love with him!* I take my right palm and hug his strong elongated penis and begin stroking up . . . and down . . . up . . . and down . . . slowly. I embrace tighter continuing an up and down rhythmic caress. I manipulate his colossal penis in a circular motion against my craving threshold producing more moisture. He plunges in, slipping effortlessly through my streaming fluids. I gasp. He excavates up and down . . . then up and down. My entire lower body is paralyzed. The sensation is so immensely gratifying. I've never felt it before . . . no one has. This feeling is first of its kind—*it's the only one of its kind*. There is no other sensation in this world! I'm tranquil.

I reach my peak and begin gasping for air as I endeavor to catch my breath. My body trembles. I climax, exhale . . . then gush. He continues to excavate and fluid continues to pour between my legs, flowing like a riverbed. He cries out a diminutive moan. I feel him convulse inside me . . . he pulls out. I'm tranquil . . . *and loving it*! With strife I grab his firm butt then squeeze and rub. I glide my hands upward, performing the same squeezing and rubbing motion as I massage his back. Qalbee rolls off of me laying his back on the blanket and his arms to his sides. He then sighs.

After Qalbee catches his breath he leans on his side, props his jaw bone up on his knuckles, gawks my paralyzed body, gapes into my captivated eyes, then begins fondling my nipple. I gaze into his childlike eyes and melt within.

I STARE OUT THE window at the fascinating sapphire sky and burnishing vivid sun as fragments of ashen clouds glide slowly in the heavens, resembling a three dimensional painting with all the combinations of blues, yellows, whites, greens, and browns. I love spring weather, not only the fresh air, blooming flowers, and fruitful trees but the rejuvenating customs—the representation of rebirth, renewal, and growth. Yet, it will be summer soon.

It reeks of rubbing alcohol, polish, and other perilous chemicals as I sit here taking pleasure in getting a manicure and pedicure. Chanelle talked me into meeting her here at the nail shop. She has already gotten her manicure and pedicure. Now, one Asian lady is painting her finger nails brown as another paints her toes French tip. I'm only getting the latter done, but in green. Chanelle sits in a cubicle beside me concluding her phone conversation with Craig. I have not spoken to Rubin. As a matter of fact, I had not even thought of him since I laid eyes on Qalbee on the street the other night until Chanelle asked about him. Qalbee has been keeping me occupied.

Chanelle presses "END" on her Nokia 6100 cell phone, and instantly starts charging me. "I can't believe you! You cheatin son of a dog! Ohh, I can't wait to see how you handle this summer. Woo, girl. Woo!" she says in a fretfully loud tone never taking a breath or giving me time to respond.

"Are you done?" I ask sardonically giving her an acute look.

She returns a stare, and then slurps her bottled water basically waiting on an explanation.

I continue, "I know. While you were on the phone, I figured I'll just have to tell him."

Chanelle removes her bottled water from her ginger orange lips. "Tell him what? The hell you will," she melodramatically states, and then gulps the rest of her water. "No need to volunteer information . . . that you KNOW won't leak out." She gets up from her chair. "That boy way in Sugarland." She pitches the bottle in the trash next to her cubicle.

"Yea, maybe I should just write it in my journal . . . just to get it out."

"Pitiful." Chanelle shakes her head. "Yea, stick to that. Shut ya month!"

I LAY HERE IN bed writing in my journal after just hanging up with Rubin. It was actually good to hear from him! He was telling me how he will be incognito for a few days because he and Jason are going to Dallas, Texas to get away. At first I was upset because I thought that their plan to skedaddle was with corrupt intention and illegal motive, but he assured me otherwise. I trust what he says. Other than him omitting things from his past, he has never blatantly lied to me. He's a good guy.

I realize that I do care a great deal for Rubin. It's just that I am still in love with Qalbee. I'm confused. Well not really. If I had to choose it would be Qalbee. But then again, Qalbee has *that girlfriend* that he fails to mention . . . *but then again, I've failed to mention Rubin.* But Qalbee is using that girl and I don't consent to that kind of conduct. I don't know. From what Chanelle says, he doesn't even like her. I mean, it can't be that serious if he spends time with me all hours of the night . . . *right? I am so disappointed in myself for contemplating all of this. Libiya, you are messing with someone else's boyfriend and are cheating on your own.* Huh, Qalbee has always taken me out of my character. Anyone like that cannot be healthy . . . *right?*

Chapter Twenty-Two

I AM OVER AT my aunt's house helping renovate her home. She is preparing for retirement and I promised her when she returned from Jamaica that I would help her spring clean. Well, she was there the entire spring and here it is July and she just returned yesterday. Now I will probably spend the rest of my days here helping summer-clean the 3 bedroom, 2 bathroom, den, and common areas in her two-story home. Our goal is to get all of her appliances and furniture to her garage this weekend, well, except for this old orange and brown chair and ottoman my grandfather bought my grandmother decades ago. We hope to sell her things before I go back to Sugarland next month so that I can help pull up the carpet and help with painting. I have no doubts that we'll sell it all, everything she owns is so nice. And any unwanted things will get loaded in my trunk to take back with me so that Prada E can donate it.

My aunt is upstairs boxing her things while I rest comfortably in the dining room on this old orange and brown chair after cleaning out her garage. I look out the curtains every time I hear a car pass eager that it's Qalbee. He should be here any minute. He's coming to spend some time with me during my break.

A fourth generation 1988 blue Cutlass Supreme mirror tent chrome trim Oldsmobile with white wall tires pull up to my aunt's curb. I immediately spring up, place my pen inside my journal, and run anxiously out Aunt K's front door. I see her neighbor Mrs. Pam across the street planting in her garden. I wave. She takes off what looks like an Easter hat instead of a gardening hat, wipes her forehead, smiles, and then waves back. I feel every bit of the 97 degree weather on my bare skin. I have on my denim Daisy Dukes, white v-neck t-shirt, yellow thong sandals. My hair is in a high *I Dream of Genie* ponytail that falls 2 inches past the kitchens in the back of my neck. Just as I reach Qalbee I snap a picture of him with my iPhone for keepsake.

Qalbee grasps me as I jump into his arms. I hug him tight and he cradles me in his arms as if he were carrying a baby. He then rotates 360 degrees around and sets me down in front of the passenger door of his prized possession. I laugh from the rollercoaster ride, and then wipe the hood of his car with my index finger collecting particles of dust.

"You love this funny looking car," I tease.

"Don't talk about my girl. She's gotten me through SOME SHIT!"

"She look like it." I crack up, not being able to hold my tongue. He would tease me if the shoe were on the other foot. He always does!

Qalbee swoops me up, swings me around, then over his shoulders, and my emotions jerk along with the additional rollercoaster ride. From startled, to shocked, to uncontrollable laugher—it's difficult for me to speak.

"Stop it!" I protest.

He spins us in circles.

"Put me down," I order.

He jolts me side to side, and then dips me up and down. I take my open palm and in rapid sessions I spank his butt repeatedly. *I am laughing so hard . . . I'm happy about the reality of us being so close this summer!*

"Okay, okay." I look at his car. "I'll quit talking about the *blue monsta*." I emphasize "blue monsta" with animation.

He continues packing me as he heads toward the side of my aunt's house.

I hold my two palms up in surrender acting as if I'm scared. "Don't kill me, don't kill me . . ." I carry on with the animation. "Don't kill me with those rims." *I can't stop laughing.* He won't put me down.

"Okay you are goin down!"

I see Aunt K's blue roll out garbage container reading "WE RECYCLE" in white letters filled to the brim with paper, glass, plastic bottles, and aluminum cans, and a green one reading "TRASH" in white letters that is not so full but reeks. He clinches onto my waist, stretches his arms out, and reaches over the garbage containers. I dangle in the air careful not to move too much so that he won't drop me.

"Nooo! Don't you do it . . ."

He does. Qalbee releases me into the trash as if I am disposable waste.

"Qalbee!" I yell, kicking as I fall.

Before I know it I am standing in Aunt K's trash bin. It . . . I reek of spoiled milk, bad meat, and maggot eggs. I frown then pout and then grunt. "Oh, I'mma get you, Mr. Comedy!" I threat.

"I'd like to see you try," he dares as he guffaws.

"Aahhh!" I holler raising my hands out to his neck and tilting the container over.

I scoot, struggle, and then finally crawl out. Soiled waste covers me from my knees down to my sandals and I hold trash in both hands. I quickly clamber up and immediately charge towards Qalbee. He begins running as he guffaws hysterically. I launch my right hand aiming a banana peel and noodles at his head. Both fly past his shoulders. I take the ice cream carton from my left hand into my right, leaving only a few squashed grapes in my left; and then I toss the pint of ice cream. The carton flies past him and ice-cream disperses out onto the freshly cut grass. Qalbee looks back at me though he continues to run. I throw the squashed grapes and just as he turns back around, a couple of grapes hit the back of his head! *Yes! These baseball skills are on point! Okay, SO WHAT he's not covered in garbage or reek some disgusting odor, BUT I STRUCK 'EM!* I focus my eyes, zooming inches ahead and witness Qalbee slip on the spoiled ice cream. He then slides downward abrading the side of his calve and knee. I run right into him tripping over his ankle. In sequence we both roll—literally and figuratively. He lands in the grass on his butt and I fall on him. We continue rolling with amusement in harmony. Qalbee stares at me in a way that convinces me that he loves me too. He elevates his head, and plants a quick passionate peck on my lips. He rolls over on his side, lays me on the grass, then gets up.

Qalbee scoops the scattered trash into the blue garbage container, and then lifts it. He discovers the water hose connected to the wall on the side of Aunt K's house behind the containers. I turn the valve and water pours out. He takes the hose and rinses me off. *I just knew he was going to play and spray me in my face.* But he didn't. He humanely cleans the waste off me and then rises himself.

"Comedy, I can't believe you put me in the garbage can!" I secretly cherish the ambiance.

He delicately rubs his thumb across my bottom lip. He hugs my head pressing my cheek to his chest, and then rubs my hair.

"I am having so much fun with you today," I'm compelled to convey as if I don't feel that way every time I'm with him. I love him and want this moment to last a lifetime.

I slide my cheek from his chest to his abdomen, all the while unbuckling his Marc Ecko jeans. I inhale the aroma of his sweaty testicles through the opening of his boxers. I'm lustful. Somehow he's maintained the smell of body wash—*so sexy!* I plunge my nose through the opening, and churn around with aim to mouth his glans. I engulf the head of his phallus as if it were a large noodle. My thoughts stream to Freud's psychosexual stages of development. Freud might posit that I have a maladaptive oral fixation because *I am craving* the sensation of Qalbee's elongated—massive—penis between my lips! As I massage it against my jaws and stroke it along my tongue, my saliva and his precom blends, fully gratifying my oral obsession.

Fingers grip my shoulders. My eyes stare up at Qalbee though I never depart his penis from between my jaws, thus it continues to validate my oral cavity. He halts me.

"No! Not here. Not now," he says with an apologetic smile.

A red four foot tall brick wall starting from the beginning of Aunt K's driveway to the end of her backyard is the only thing partitioning us from the freeway. We can see and hear the speeding cars and raging drivers toot their horns as we stand openly on the side of her house. I loosen then emit his penis. Just as I commence to stand, he bends and takes my hips into his arms. I secure myself wrapping my wrists together around his neck. He gently lays me on my back onto the grass. He leisurely licks my lips then kisses me, exploiting all tongue muscle and fulfills the void of his desired penis.

THE WATER SHOWERS QALBEE and I as we bathe the lingering specks of trash we cart from earlier, the smell from indecent sex we illegally commented on the side of the house this afternoon, and the bodily salts we acquired from moving furniture to Aunt K's garage this evening. Qalbee reaches for my Carols Daughter shampoo, and lather's it and my hair in his hands and begins massaging my hair and scalp—*so idyllic!* He washes and conditions my hair and even swirls it in one huge twist to let it drain. I reach for a dry towel, dab my hair with it, and spiral my hair inside the towel into a Nubian Queen wrap to let it dry.

Once we dress ourselves Qalbee excuses himself. He *says* he has to "handle business." The first thing, well person, that came to mind is *that girl* he entertains but I am so worn out that I do not even concern myself with the distress.

CHANELLE DRIVES WHILE I ride shotgun on the way to the beauty supply store. Chanelle plans to stock up on her hair products now to prepare for fall's weather and I need to do the same! After Qalbee washed my hair I let it air dry and now I cannot keep it from frizzing. It keeps puffing up into an afro so I've been wearing it up in a high bun on the crown of my head. Once we leave the beauty store, Chanelle is going to run me by CVS Pharmacy to develop the pictures from my iPhone.

"You and Qalbee been kickin it real hard this past month and you never once brought up him and that girl?" she scolds.

"Well, since you tell me that he's just not that into her, and that it just seems that he has nothing else to do, I figure since I'm here, I'm who he can do!" I amuse.

"You've always had your morals, but when it comes to THAT man, you just lose it," she shakes her head in contempt.

"I mean, are they together?" I rhetorically ask not giving her a chance to respond. "You said it yourself, he just has her around to use her."

We park and I unfasten my seatbelt.

"I figure this . . . every since his mother died he has needed someone, a female to fill the role . . . and since she plays *that* role, he keeps her around."

"You and that damn psychology prattle." She pauses. "You right though . . ." she opens her car door. ". . . cause she *does* do all the motherly duty type-stuff like cook and wash his clothes and buy em things."

Suddenly I feel nauseous. I lean on the front of her car. I feel a hot exploding sensation up my esophagus. I gag.

"Come on now girl, you not that against being submissive, huh?" she laughs.

Inexplicably I'm annoyed by that comment, and I assume her laugher comes from knowing how ridiculous that is. She knows I'd submit to the right guy. I explain anyway.

"NO! I just haven't been feeling well." I hug my stomach.

"You need to sit down somewhere and get some sleep," she commands as she hugs her arm around my shoulder. She sighs, "You and that damn Q," she smiles and shakes her head!

THIS MORNING I VOMITED once and I regurgitated like three times last night. I checked for a fever but my temperature is a perfect 97.9 degrees. I figure that it must be all the different fumes I've been inhaling this past month while renovating this place. I'm thinking about packing up my things and going back to my parents' home to get away from these fumes for awhile only it's been so convenient being able to get things done whenever I feel up to it. I'm not trying to doing all that back and forth driving. But then again, dealing with this indefinite stomach virus is not much fun either. I don't know what to do, but I do know that I haven't been able to shake this nausea.

I showered, dressed, made breakfast, *did not* eat it, came home to my mother's, and fell asleep in my safe haven. Elaina and Chanelle both called my cell phone, twice, but I was too exhausted to answer either calls. My mother has come in checking on me periodically. She brought in some soup, crackers, and orange juice, but all I could eat was the crackers, and it was an obstacle to eat that. However, I vomited it up minutes later and I'm feeling much better now and in just enough time to prepare for Qalbee's arrival!

I wear my Victoria Secret Pink collection pajamas—blue pants and pink shirt, "PINK" in yellow letters. Qalbee asked if I wanted to go out, maybe to a movie, but I preferred to stay in for the night.

I hum the lyrics to "Hanging by a Moment" by Lifehouse as Qalbee and I sit on the floor leaning against my bed like old times. He has my photo album in his lap looking through old pictures. I turn the page and there is a picture of Qalbee and Craig with Billy Bob teeth in their mouth on the second night they came over.

"We some fools!"

"Yes y'all are," I giggle. "I remember I fell in love with you so fast!" I reminisce.

As I turn to the next page a country singer begins singing.

"Uuuh . . . what the fuck is this?"

"Uuuh . . . Qalbee," I mock. "I beg your pardon?"

"My bad . . . that's that Tourette syndrome. Horrible music does that shit to me!" he says with sarcasm.

"Excuse you." I hoist. "I love rock and country music".

"I said nothing about rock music," he clarifies.

"Nickelback is my favorite rock band and I *love* Rascal Flatts, too," I broadcast while changing the song.

I play music by After 7, "One Night." I take the photo album from him, lay the back of my head in his lap, rest the album on my pelvis, and continue flipping pages. A picture of Qalbee standing in front of his decked out Cutlass, one of me climbing out the trash, and one of the both of us covered in ice cream right before our indecent exposure escapade displays.

Qalbee burst into a guffaw. "How in the hell you get these?"

"That nosey neighbor snapped them and gave them to me. I guess to notify me that she knows what I've been doing this summer," I chuckle, making reference to the Steven Spielberg movie.

Qalbee looks in shock. His eyebrows frown. "Did she . . ."

"Na, I don't think so," I interrupt with a giggle. Actually, I really don't know but it seemed to ease his mortified conscious.

"You funky." He points at the picture of me in the blue garbage container.

I hug my stomach. *Nauseated? Again?* I pop up from his lap sitting up thinking that I may have to rush to the restroom. "You stank!" I attack back and scoot closer to him, then strike him in the chest with my right fist, still hugging my stomach with my left arm. "You know you were wrong for that!"

Qalbee picks up the album and closes it. He stands to his feet then reaches for my hands, and assists me up. He ushers us to my bed and we get comfy.

Chapter Twenty-Three

I STAND IN THE bushes of Britton Memorial Park peeing on a stick. I called Chanelle early this morning to have her pick up a pregnancy test for me once she got off work. My stomach was too woozy feeling so I had her swoop me up and come here. I gagged again while Qalbee and I chatted in bed last night, and when he left, I regurgitated two more times. I have not had my menstrual cycle this mouth and this stomach flu continues to persist.

"Why in the hell didn't you want to go to my place and do this?"

"I know we grown, *but* I don't need my mother *or* your father knowing what I have going on."

"Well, why in the hell couldn't you have done this at the store?"

"I didn't feel comfortable."

"Oh, so, you do now?"

"Chanelle!"

"My bad."

"I know I'm pregnant, I just know it . . . I just need you not to heighten my anxiety."

Chanelle throws up both of her hands signaling acceptance. I ignore her gesture, and climb from behind the bushes. Chanelle and I stare and wait. After two minutes the stick shows two lines.

"Dang . . . I knew it. I can't do this. I have two more years of school."

"Ay . . . whatever happens, I'll help," Chanelle sympathetically states. "When . . . how . . . are you gonna tell him?"

"This dude wants nobodies' child. He's gonna look at me and say "you sure it's not Caleb's or Chad's?" "I deepen my voice to sound like Qalbee.

"Shut the hell up. That boy knows you don't fool with any of them. You need to just tell him," she stresses. "You can still do what you really desire to do," she consoles. "I'm here."

I DEPRECIATE MY CARPET as I pace the floor with my cell phone twiddling between my palms. My clock reads '8:37 pm.'

I text Qalbee, "Call me."

A little over forty five minutes passes. Clock now reads "9:09 pm."

I text Qalbee again. "I need to talk to you." I pace some more.

Clock reads "10:19."

I think about it . . . *why did I text that?* Guys don't do the "we need to talk" thing. I shake my head in regret. Surely he's not texting or calling me back tonight. I fretfully search for his number in contacts. I courageously press "CALL".

There is no answer. I'm hurt, anxious, disappointed. *I have no control of my life or the world around me.* I'm hopeless, helpless. I turn out my lamp and lay down with a world of racing thoughts complementing my uncertainty.

I RUSH TO GET dressed sliding on my short gray summer pinup skirt, my white sleeveless silk Ralph Lauren blouse, and a maroon vintage scarf around my neck. My hair is parted all the way down the middle of my head with hair ties under both ears bonding bone straight ponytails that drape over my breasts like a school girl. Where I'm headed, *I must look presentable!*

I rush out the door to humidity. It's a warm morning with lots of pollen in the dry air; and birds chirp to the sound of my gray pumps clapping the pavement. I jump in my Tacoma and speed up the road. I'm stopped by every light it seems, increasing my anxiety. My thoughts stream to a sermon I heard Joel Osteen teach about patience. Although I know I should take my time, I speed even faster up the highway to catch up on the lost time at all those red lights.

I pull up to St. Baptist Hospital, take 15 minutes to find a vacant parking space, and apprehensively rush through the revolving door of the hospital. My heal stumbles as I nervously approach the information desk. A Caucasian lady looks up at me. The outfit she wears almost matches mine only her clothes are loose-fitting, longer, opaque and fundamentally more appropriate than mine.

"May I assist you?" she politely asks.

My voice small, and weak, "Qalbee Davis, please?"

I'm so nervous coming up here. *It's apposite to come to his job,* I internally endeavor to convince myself. *This is a sufficient enough reason,* I justify my compulsive behavior venturing to ease some anxiety. The receptionist picks up the phone and presses a button. I hear her voice over the intercom.

"Qalbee Davis to the front lobby . . . Qalbee Davis, front lobby."

I thank her and walk over to sit in the lobby area. I chant some calming words to myself. As I wait I feel chills suffocate my arms and legs, drowning me with goose bumps. I did not realize how cold it was in here until now. At least my neck is warm, I humor myself. I realize that my adrenalin has relaxed some reducing my immunity to this frigid lobby. Qalbee walks up. I stand. Just like that, this man—or maybe this situation—perhaps both—has my heart pounding nervously all over again, just that quickly. Qalbee looks shocked; though surprisingly, he looks delighted to see me.

"What's up? Sorry I didn't get back to you last night."

"It's cool," I respond nervously and without deviating from my objective I disparage, "Will you just get back to me tonight?" I say with lots of hope, a smidge of exasperation, and with no inhalation as my left hand tightly clinches the chain of my clutch purse and my forearm strongly smashes down into the side of my rib. I feel the perspiration under my arms.

Qalbee's eyebrows frown. "Yea? Sure!" he sounds concerned but by the beam in his eyes, I know he's more pleased to see me. "I get off at 3. Wanna talk then?"

"Cool." I'm relieved—*that felt too easy.* Anxious and still with a smidgen of frustration I ask, "Can you just meet me somewhere?" My right palm now clinches down on my left hand as it still clinches the chain of my clutch. I'm uncomfortable and feel as though I'm standing awkwardly, like some timid child. I really don't mean to sound like I have a chip on my shoulder, I'm really just scared.

"Yes, where?" he anxiously asks seeming to finally realize that my subject matter must be serious, enough for me to rampage him at his job.

"Brittan Memorial Park, 4'o'clock, slide," I say precisely, like a business woman.

"Kay." He now looks with concern.

I uncomfortably smile attempting to hide my nervousness. I back up from him and walk off.

I GO TO PLANNED PARENTHOOD in Norman, Oklahoma to see an obstetrics and gynecologic medical doctor. It is a large number of women and children waiting and some men. I wait two hours, in the cold lobby, waiting for the nurse to call me back to get my vitals, height, weight, and urine sample, and another 30 minutes for the OB/GYN to see me. He does a pelvic exam and pap-smear— no ultrasound—and calculated my menstrual . . . well, lack thereof. He provided me with some papers and sent me on my merry way.

When I made it home I fell right to sleep. I woke up a little after two, texted Qalbee and asked if we could meet a little later. He had no problems with it and understandingly complied. It's too hot in the day and that wouldn't be good for me. We agreed on 7:30. Chanelle brought me over some BoBo's Chicken around five and I ate every bite. I was happy to eat, and to my surprise I kept it down. *I love BoBo's Chicken!* I set my alarm for seven o'clock and fell right back to sleep.

I PULL UP IN the parking lot of Britton Memorial Park. I spot Qalbee sitting at the swings. I clamber out my truck in orange swishes and a white t-shirt. I walk towards Qalbee. I look over to the slide and there is a women and child playing. As I approach Qalbee I nod my head pointing their way. "This is not the slide!" I slightly smirk at my ice breaker.

"Figured, no kids here," he haughty states with his hands halfway in his pocket lifting his shoulders to his ears.

"Other than the one in my stomach." *HOLY MOTHER, FATHER AND CHILD!* Dang, dang, dang, I didn't imagine it coming out like that. All that rehearsing . . . *for what?*

"What?" He says softly, and his features crook producing wrinkles everywhere possible on his face. He looks completely lost, befuddled.

I look down at the dirt with a diminutive smirk, *Yeah, um . . .* "Wow!" I'm relieved to get *that* out. "I didn't know it was gonna come out that easily." I ponder . . . actually relieved to regurgitate—*this time.*

"What are you talking about?" he says anxiously, with a smidge of frustration, and still completely lost as if he didn't hear, or can't comprehend, or just don't want to believe what just came out of my mouth.

"Comedy, I'm pregnant. Six weeks," I say bravely. "A week after I got here."

"So, what do you want to do?"

"What?" I'm confounded. *What that mean.* "I mean, I'm in school . . . in Sugarland . . . you live here." And have a girlfriend you fail to mention. "How would that work?" *I've never in my life heard the words I love you come out of your mouth.*

"What? So you . . ."

"Looks that way," *by the feedback I'm receiving from you.* I cut him off in disappointed. "It won't work." I justify his reaction. He *doesn't love me.* He loves *that girl . . .* he tells *Her* those word.

"Okay? So what do you want to do? I'm here, whatever you want from me."

He seems genuine. I'm surprised by his calm and supportive appearance.

"Really? I just knew you'd deny me."

"That's cold."

"I mean, I've been here and we hang some . . . and we've sexed just about every time we've seen each other, but lately . . . it has been *me* calling or texting and *you* not responding . . . So, I just *knew* you'd deny me," I casually declare.

As I'm saying these words he steps up to me, places his right hand on my hip and places his left hand to my stomach.

He gazes into my eyes. "Libiya, whatever you want from me." His tone is indifferent.

"Well . . ." I pause in deep thought, ". . . abortion."

Qalbee drops his hand from my stomach and he's silent. We're silent. I take abortion to be Qalbee's initial objective due to his silence—and indifference—and lack of correspondence, which causes me insecurity.

"It's 300 each. My appointment is Friday. I plan to just have Chanelle take me."

I called around earlier just in case Qalbee suggested termination or denied me. I never thought I'd actually need it but his disconnect creates a discouraged feeling in me. I didn't know what to say. I panicked. I didn't know what to do. What I do know is that terminating a pregnancy early when the pregnancy has not yet become a fetus or embryo and is still a simple cell mass is reported by the American Psychological Association to be easier mentally and physically, so *if he's not going to fight this, then it is actually . . . really going to happen.*

"No . . ." Qalbee expresses.

My heart lightens. "What!"

". . . I will. I will take you," he says with indication of relief in his voice and on his face.

I stare up at him . . . hopeless . . . helpless. I'm experiencing several emotions. I'm wounded. "Kay." I respond impassively.

I raise my hand to Qalbee's chest but it doesn't quite make it. I'm too hurt. I walk off.

I DO NOT KNOW how I made it home that night. I lost consciousness somewhere. I remember dropping a few tears as I was starting my truck and the next memory is of me sitting in my truck but in the driveway of my parent's home. I'm thinking I suffered a blackout. Excessive tearing diminishes blood flow from the eyes and to the brain causing lost consciousness. It's a wonder that I made it home safely. I don't know how long I sat in my car, how or when I made it upstairs, or how I got through that awful phone call from Qalbee once I made it to my room.

In addition to my condition, his response to *our* situation, and the decision I made due to him not conforming to the right thing, this dude calls me to tell me that he doesn't get paid until next Tuesday, asked if I would pay his half, and that he'll pay me back later. *Really?* Does he not understand the distress I'm dealing with? So flummoxed I just said *"sure"* and hoped he'd at least thrive to still accompany me to the clinic. I've been so engrossed in my own deep thoughts that I have spurts where I lose consciousness of the world around me. I keep finding myself here and there and wondering how. I've continued to assist my aunt with her home, but I'm worried.

I have fantasized about Qalbee asking me to keep the undeveloped embryo, and asking me to move back and to be his girlfriend. I've contemplated keeping it while I try finishing school there in Sugarland, and losing respect from Rubin.

I'm sure Aunt K knows that there is something up with me by *the* frequent breaks I take—to vomit, or rest, or to keep from toxic fumes. All we have left is to paint and lay fresh carpet, and her place will look like *Home Improvement*.

I finally made my decision without feeling regret or guilt. I've decided to no longer harp on my *"situation"*. I initially chose to abort because Qalbee did not make me feel secure and I was too scared to do this by myself, but now, I'm secure with myself and my decision. My decision is not because he did not ask me not to terminate, or because I want to complete school without dealing with extra financial, mental, and emotional struggles. It's because I desire for my beloved seed to be born to parents that are married. Qalbee and I are not even together *and* we live in different states. My born son will be a product of a father that loves his wife and my daughter will know her father, and be around him. I don't know what kind of father Qalbee would be or if he would even be one.

Since I've known Qalbee he's not been here for me. Sure his mother was ill, but that doesn't change the reality that he has always let me down. He doesn't even have the money to help with this. Is he in debt? How's his credit? What kind of a provider will he be for my child? I know what it feels like to have a father who's never around. Just thinking about my child suffering from having no father hurts me. I don't want him or her to suffer in a home with financial issues too. Sure my parent could assist here and there, but I'm no longer their responsibility. My child is not their responsibility. It has been six days since I informed Qalbee of everything and I only heard from him one time other than that infuriating call that night. How responsible is that?

Tomorrow we will take that 45 minute drive to the clinic, pay respects to the social liberals, and make that trip back. Then I can put this all behind me . . . if only I could black out this whole summer.

Chapter Twenty-Four

AS I WALK UP to the building of obscurity I see my lifeless reflection in the mirror-tint of the double doors. I glance at Qalbee's refection behind me as he carts a tense stare on his face and a bag with my change of clothes in his right hand. I clasp the handle, open the door, take one step in, and chills spread throughout my body. The atmosphere is freezing cold like a morgue. There are big leafy green plants everywhere as if this is a botany lab or as if they're in competition with horticultural cultivators or something. I scan the room and there is a bench that enfolds three of the four walls in a "U" shape. Just above the headrest of the benches are cubicles that border the walls, which have pots filled with Aspidistras, elephant ear plants, and other large leaf plants in them. There are so many plants that no one can rest their heads back because the leaves fall over the borders.

There is a Black couple that sits to the left end of the "U" shaped bench which is right in front of the entrance. They are cuddled up together appearing to be in love—*they will probably regret this choice later in life.* There is a round bench positioned in the middle of the room that resembles a circular solid teak tree bench and a round table in the center of it that a container mixed with other varieties of big leaf plants such as Philodendron and Ficus are potted. There, sits an old Caucasian couple. The man has a scruffy brunette beard, his eyes are blood shot red, and he reeks of alcohol. The women wears a ball cap with the brim low over her eyes as an attempt to hide the black ring around her left eye. Though he is probably the one that gave it to her, she looks relaxed with him—maybe confused . . . scared—high even. The forth wall, which is the open wall, is the footpath that leads to the check-in counter. I make my first step to the right and uncomfortably walk past them. As I approach the counter the glass window slides open. A red head lady hands me a clipboard with papers to fill out and a pen.

"Do you have an appointment or are you a walk-in?"

My voice weak, "I have a 7:30 appointment with Dr. Akili."

"Fill these out. You have two people ahead of you."

I barely get a chance to verbalize a *"thank you"* before she already closes the window. I look up at Qalbee and he takes my hand and leads me to the back. I see a young Caucasian girl, can't be any more than 15, holding a baby that can't be more than six months. I hadn't seen her at first past the round table full of plants and she sits in the far right corner alone. Qalbee sits down not too far from her. As soon as I sit I feel discomfort in my stomach. Seconds later it rumbles. I'm famished. I was informed not to eat or drink six hours before hand but, I actually haven't consumed anything in about ten hours. If I don't count the four pieces of celery in which I vomited twenty minutes after eating them, that will make it out to be twelve hours since I have last eaten.

Yesterday after sweeping out Aunt K's garage I went home. I wanted to sleep in my safe haven before today's crucial event. I needed familiar surroundings. I wanted to be around my own things, smell my candles, feel my comforter . . . hug Mickey. I made it home around five o'clock, took a 45 minute shower, and just let the steaming hot water shower me as I thought about nothing. I later chanted and prayed preparing my mind and heart for today. I ate my four sticks of celery and laid my head on my pillow by seven. By 7:20 pm I was up hurling in my toilet and have had nothing to eat since.

Qalbee and I sat for about fifteen minutes when a tech called the Black couple to the back. Fifteen minutes after that, I was called to the back. The nurse takes my vitals and has me urine in a cup. I'm so shaken with fear that most of the urine drains in the stool and only drops land in the cup. I hand her the cup and present her with an apologetic shrug. She asks me fundamental questions about my health, allergies, and sexual past, and then goes over my anesthetic options. When she steps out to test my urine I read over a few pamphlets. Surprisingly I'm able to retain information with this cloudy, nebulous mind of mine.

I learn that women aged 24 and younger account for about 52 percent of those who obtain an abortion, leaving 48 percent to be 25 years of age and older; and that 54 percent of them used a birth control method during the time they became pregnant. However, unfortunate things like condoms breaking, being used incorrectly, and missed birth control pills neglected to prevent these pregnancies. I'd have guessed that low social economics correlated with abortions as a result of woman not wanting to have to provide for a child long term since they'd be incapable. Conversely, I learned that only 57 percent are at an economic disadvantage compared to the 88 percent which live in metropolitan areas.

After my pre-abortion consultation the nurse escorts me back to the lobby. Shortly after, the tech calls the older couple back. It's not even ten minutes when we all hear ruckus in the back. I hear the nurse saying something about how the lady wasn't supposed to consume anything but since she did they would have to make another appointment. The guy is threatening towards the tech and nurse and minutes later the police escort them out. They were definitely intoxicated, probably on their way to jail. After all the commotion the young girl is called to the back and some guy, maybe my age, finally accompanied her.

Here it is an hour later and the black couple just left. I'm surprised Qalbee is holding my hand and has been since we sat down. This morning he was on time—early even—as if he is Arnold Schwarzenegger and ready to terminate. There was complete silence between the two of us on the entire ride here. He seemed to have had something on his mind. I'm thinking he may have had something he wanted to say because he kept looking over at me, though he never spoke up. Instead, he blasted songs by Kem, Goapele, and other neo-soul music, perhaps seeking to search for his soul.

"Ali . . . Libiya Ali," the nurse calls my name.

I stand, as do Qalbee, but the nurse shook her head.

"You cannot be in there during the procedure but it's only a 15 minute process . . . then we will call for you to come to accompany her in the recovering room."

I look over to Qalbee with sorrow. He kisses me on my forehead, holds me at arm's length, and produces an awkward smirk, but says nothing. I have the urge to hug him but I feel resentful. I don't want to give him the satisfaction. I'm not resentful about this decision, because I am okay with it, but I'm resentful because *HE'S* actually okay with it.

He's never once asked me how I am doing. I manage a smile and follow the nurse through the doors.

I am led to a room to undress down to my bra, and am given a hospital gown to cover. I place my sweats and t-shirt in a plastic sack and my underwear in a separate sealed plastic hazard bag. I signal that I am done and the nurse leads me into the procedure room. Dr. Akili introduces herself and the rest of her team. I try my best to display certainty and show no fear so that I won't give them any basis *not* to carry out this procedure. Dr. Akili asks me to lie on the procedure bed, and immediately places an oxygen mask over my face. The nurse pricks my arm with a needle which she announced to be a sedative to ease my nerves and dull the pain. I'm offered nitrous oxide to self-administer if I feel I need it anytime during the procedure. Dr Akili asks me to bring my legs up onto the end of the bed, and I comply. They began asking me general questions about myself—I assume to get my mind off of the procedure. Dr. Akili dilates my cervix and then inserts a small straw like suction device into my vagina which she announces it to be a cannula. I feel discomfort as I experience my cervix dilating. A loud suctioning noise similar to a hair dryer or vacuum cleaner roars. I begin feeling severe cramping, *far more relentless than menstrual cramps.* It's possibly contraction cramps. I immediately go under but, I can still hear, vaguely. The machine aspiration equipment goes off but I hear Dr. Akili and her team looking over the removed tissue. Though hazy, I make out that they are examining to be sure that they have suctioned out the entire cell mass. Instantly, I hear nothing.

I come to, opening my eyes to a new room; however, it feels very familiar. Qalbee is sitting next to me. He's holding my hand! *It's* the hospital room from my dream so long ago, it's a recovery room. I'm lying under a warm blanket, still in the hospital gown I wore during the procedure. Yet someone has put my change of underwear on me along with the sanitary pad that was packed with them. I slowing begin to recall. I vaguely remember walking myself in here, with the assistance of the nurse, and Qalbee hugging me on the way to the bed.

QALBEE OPENS THE DOOR for me as we walk out the clinic. There is a slight pain in my side causing me to limp so I'm moving very slowly. Qalbee shovels his arm under my shoulder to aid me like I am 95 with bad legs. As we approach the Cutlass Qalbee speeds up to open my door then assists me in. *My, what a gentleman he has become! I should get pregnant and abort more often.* I'm internally sarcastic, possibly from bitterness. *Forgive me.* Qalbee hops in the car seeming to feel some kind of way as it shows in his trembling fingers as he starts the car.

I am starved. What shall I have Chanelle bring me to eat? Na, she's only going to say "that blank need to be getting you something to eat". Not because she's not supportive, but because she loathes Qalbee. *NEXT . . . okay, what shall I request that mother cook? HA!* I laugh inside. She will only say the same thing, but do much more to him. I'd mourn two losses today.

"You are out of it," Qalbee says concerned and saving me from a path of obscurity by capturing me from my reverie.

"I know. I feel high."

"You never been high," he says with the first sight of a fraction of a smirk all day.

I chuckle. "I know. But I am starving. I have the munchies."

He looks away from the road and stares at me authoritatively. "You can't eat for another hour".

"I know." I chuckle some more. I feel nauseous, "Aohw," I grunt. "I'm feeling sick." I look down to the floor and clench the door handle to manage the pain.

"Dr. Akili said to take that antibiotic and with eight ounces of water," Qalbee says, and then holds up the pill bottle.

I snatch it. "Yea, thanks." Instead of opening it I place it in my lap brushing him off. I chuckle at my acrimony towards him. "Keep those eyes on the road. We don't need any more deaths today." I continue with the resentment. *Forgive me.*

His puppy dog eyes look heartbreakingly at me, and then he turns away.

"Where's the water?"

He sulks as he hands me the bottle of water.

"You were scared in there!" I chuckle.

"Not scared," he assertively clarifies.

"Nervous."

"Worried . . ." His grip tightens on the steering wheel as he looks straight ahead. ". . . about you." He looks over at me. ". . . And if I made the right decision."

"Decision?" I'm offended. "You didn't make a decision. You left that all on me". I emit a miniature maniacal chuckle to discredit him. "Pull over, pull over . . ."

Qalbee instantly pulls over to the shoulder.

"I gotta . . ." Before I could speak the words, I feel lumpy chunks burn through my esophagus and taste bitter liquid flooding my taste buds. The smell of my raw, empty stomach fuses the sourness of my vomit as it spouts onto the pavement releasing a stench so pungent I almost hurl again. I continue clinching the door while I lean my nose to the cement to heave any lingering vomit. I look up at Qalbee and he's staring apprehensively at me, though states nothing.

"Ok, my fault," I apologize for him having to witness that. "I don't think I drank enough water."

Qalbee continues to stare at me with both hands strangling the steering wheel.

"Okay, I'm ready to eat."

When I am strapped in and secure in my seatbelt, he pulls off.

"I will stop and get you something."

"No thank you. I'll have Chanelle bring me something." *You have done enough.*

WE ARRIVE AT AUNT K's house. Qalbee gets out, walks around the front of his car, opens my door and aides me out of the car.

"I'm fine. You can go," I say with pride and gratitude.

"Okay, I'll check on you tonight."

"Kay."

I somehow managed to wilt to my aunt's spare room. I did not want to be bothered with anyone. I called Chanelle to bring me some I-Hop but I forgot she does not get off until six. My aunt came home with ET's Barbee Que, so I savaged it and had been asleep until now. I sit pressed against the toilet as I inhale the odor of my vomit. My body doesn't react to these antibiotics very well. The doctor said to still take them because any amount in my system is better than none. I finally manage to place one hand on the commode and the other on the sink and hoist. I reach my flimsy arm to grab the soap. I wash my hands, and pour Listerine in my mouth to sanitize the pong. I begin gargling when I hear my cell phone ring. After 30 seconds I sputter. I lean against the wall, wilt to my bed, and answer.

"Yes," I gruffly greet, then lay my head down.

"Was checking on you."

"Awe thanks, really." *Thanks for nothing.* "I'm fine, just nauseated from the antibiotics. A bit drowsy too." *I wish you were here with me.*

"I was thinking about you and needed to check on you," he conveys with genuineness.

I wish you were here taking care of me instead of calling checking up on me.

"But I'll let you gets some sleep."

Gee, "Thanks." *FOR NOTHING. Of course that's all.*

"I'll check on you tomorrow, later."

"Kay. I love you Qalbee," I hear clicking as I finish my confession.

I hear the dial tone. He's gone. I lay the phone to my heart. *He didn't hear me tell him that I love him.* I'm sad. I close my eyes. Maybe I should have told him that I love him the day I informed him about the pregnancy. Maybe he would have felt secure with my love for him. Maybe he needed to know that I want to spend my life with him, to look out for him, support him, and cater to his every existence. And maybe he would have felt confident enough to convey similar feelings. I cry myself to sleep.

I REPLAY "SAVIN' ME" by Nickleback over and over as I lay in bed curled up in fetal position with my pillow covering my head. Chanelle has come over to console me. She's sitting next to me at the edge of the bed, enraged.

"And you still have not heard from him?"

"Chell, NO!" the sound of my voice vibrates through an open space, the same entrance I'm receiving air from.

"That CREEP!" her tone amplifies. "It's been a week . . . He has some nerve," she protests. But she's not finished, she's on a tangent. "So he gets you pregnant, takes you to get an abortion, don't pay his half, I might add, and don't answer your calls or check on you?" She breathes. "He's a straight BITCH!".

I lift the pillow from my face and I'm actually embracing a smile. "Thank you for caring, Chell." I've been saying the same thing—*in my head*!

Chanelle stands. "How are you so calm about all this?"

I have not thrown up since that last time a week ago, my appetite is beginning to pick back up, and I will be far away from this place in two weeks. I have sat, laid, cried, laid, and cried some more in this room, daily. I'm tired of it. I went by Qalbee's apartment and planned to let the air out his tires, but I couldn't do it. I have reflected on our relationship and I take full responsibility for my own actions in all this. Yes he's wrong in some parts, yes he's a straight female dog in all this but being closed up in these for walls, I had an epiphany. I cannot blame him for something he's always been and have always done. I sit up.

"This dude has never been reliable. I'm the dumb one for even continuously dealing with him. I just should have known."

Chanelle quickly sits beside me and looks into my eyes with unease. "Wrong again. You can't blame yourself for his low down behavior. Please don't," she begs with concern.

Oh. No. Let's not think I have the Battered Woman Syndrome— he hit me "cause he loves me and I deserve to feel pain"—*nothing like that at all*. Please. Trust!

I stand and head for the bathroom. "This is my thing. I have called his phone. I have left messages on his voicemail. I have texted him a few choice of words, and *no* call back." My mother even left him a heart to heart on his voicemail about how they both lost their mother at a young age, that she would take him under her wing, and how he has all opportunity to take responsibility in all this . . . *and this dude STILL never responded?* He's straight cold. I can't tell Chanelle all that or she'd be at his apartment keying his car as we speak.

I begin running bath water for myself.

"He's a straight BITCH!" she says with a vengeance.

Yes he is—even more than you know.

Chanelle walks into the bathroom. "Let's go bust out his car windows!" she says with enthusiasm and motivation.

"You know I can't." I begin brushing my teeth. "It's just not my character." I sputter. "Karma is a mug," I mumble. "But I did leave him a caustic and disparaging poem," I say proudly, heading for my book of poems.

"What? A poem?" She looks at me like I'm useless, like a poem is not enough, like she wants to obliterate his automobile right this second in some way.

"Yes a poem. Busting out windows is too destructive. And it's not just a poem, it's a caustic and disparaging poem," I repeat indignantly. *She doesn't know it, but I had intention to vandalize, damage, and harm but, writing this poem detained me from undergoing cardiac arrest on many angry nights.* I hand her my journal, and then shoo her out the bathroom so that I can undress.

She shakes her head. "My girl is so morally stable."

"Ha," I huff, ". . . morally stable . . . I just had an abortion," I squall. I close the door shutting out Chanelle. I begin undressing when I hear Chanelle yelling through the door.

"Libi, you are the most honest person I know," she expresses. I smile—*here she goes*!

"You show so much compassion towards anyone, *everyone*—family, friends, strangers." Her voice lowers as she continues, "Losers that don't deserve it," she adds and I can hear disappointment in her voice.

I roll my eyes and lie in the tub.

"You always see the good in others, you are truly a good person Libi," she spills. "Don't forget that."

"UM hum," I grumble, blowing her off, feeling a bit pinched about her *"don't deserve it"* comment—*which only means SHE DID NOT HEAR ANYTHING I just said in this past hour . . . LIKE taking responsibility for my own actions OR . . . she just disagrees.* I internally complain feeling unheard.

"Thanks, can you just read?" I huff and my eyes roll given that she's exhausting me. I'm quiet and full of anticipation as she reads, wondering what she thinks.

THE FEELING

This girl has no luck
It commenced when she got hit by a truck
Her body parts were extra crushed
Under the tires her remains were stuck
And their laid her guts

This girl did not learn
It began when she got caught in the fire's burn
Through her pores, her blood runs
Ash black, her flesh turned
And there she lies, cooked, well-done

This girl was a fool
It commenced when she fell into the pool
Her skull hit the bottom stool
Drowning, her corpse turned blue
And there she'll float and mildew

This girl went to the extreme
It began when she fell from the 11-foot building
Her soul so windswept, she's suffocating
Her carcass paralyzed, fragile as a string
And there fractured, laid her dreams

This girl and her sweet-love departs
This is when it all truly starts
She couldn't take them being apart
Her death intense, like the piercing of a dart
It's . . . the feeling of a broken heart

LA July 2002

Chanelle bursts through the door. I quickly slide the curtains just enough to hide my nudity.

Startled, I shout, "Girl!"

"You are sick with it!"

"Yea, that's my other coping mechanism. I left that on his door." When I think back to that night I feel vulnerable, my chin descends to my chest.

"Yea . . ." She too looks down as if she feels my pain, then looks up. ". . . *he's really not calling you back,*" she says matter-of-fact-like, with emphasis. "That poem *screeeams* PSYCHO."

I chuckle at her feedback then look up with a smile! "It was my closure." I can move on.

Heart Failure

Chapter Twenty-Five

October 2002

When I looked into the mirror of those double doors three months ago, I saw darkness. But today I zoom-in on my mind's eye, focusing in on my thoughts, and magnifying in on my feelings that day, and I realize... I'm proud! I made a decision and followed through with it. No matter what disagreements and judgments others have, or what conservatives think or conformists believe, or what the assumptions are of everyone else who has never been in a situation similar to mine, I made a decision, and I'm happy. I deserve no judgments. I'm experienced enough to know that various people have various burdens... empathetic enough to understand that people use various actions for dealing with their various skeletons... and am *cultured enough to appreciate that these people will choose the best procedure that fits each-and-every-last-one of their various situations. So, with that thought, again, I am proud of myself! I look into the eyes of my reflection, and as it stares back at me, I can really see myself. I'm forced to face myself. I see my feelings, my thoughts. As my fingers clinch on the handle of those double doors, I no longer feel doom, I feel optimism! I wasn't depressed about the termination, I was harboring feelings of resentment about Qalbee's actions in all this but he too has to face his skeletons. I am over it. I am over him. I knew what was best for my undeveloped egg, despite Qalbee's lack of fight, and I am satisfied with my choices and with myself. Furthermore, I am confident that I will know when it is the best situation to bring a child into this world. And I'm aware that I may not be the perfect mother, but I know for a fact that I will sacrifice every piece of myself trying to be—my son or daughter will be proud to proclaim me as his or her strong, loving mother.*

I'M HEADED TO MY new apartment. Elaina and I thought it was time, being juniors this year, that we'd try living on our own. We already work so much together with Prada E and talk all day every day, when we're not with our dudes. We figured we can do without living together too. I spend so much time with Rubin that I should have simply moved in with him but his mother and step father are staying with him until their home completes renovation. He's at my place majority of the time. Elaina has been sewing her wild oats, and her traffic and Rubin wasn't getting along. There were no issues between him and the guys. It was merely the safety aspect of me being there that Rubin wasn't trusting. He's protective! Elaina and I are still best buds with no hard feelings, which I hear is hard to come by between roommates. We were lucky enough to have shared two years with little disagreements!

I exit the freeway, when my phone rings.

"Yay'yes!" I playfully answer.

"You almost here?" Rubin asks anxiously

"Yes! I just exited the highway. Why, what's up?"

"Hurry!" He rushes.

"Okay, okay!" I respond with enthusiasm influenced by his excitement.

I pull into the parking lot and Rubin rushes out and climbs in.

"Okay? Where we going!"

"You'll see!"

Rubin points out the directions the whole way. Why we didn't change places, I don't know. I'm thinking he thought it would be more exciting this way, which it is. It's keeping me in suspense. We pull into a shopping facility.

"Turn here. Pull up in here."

I park and it's Kay's Jewelry store! He scampers out the truck, comes around and opens my door, takes my hand, and vivaciously leads me inside.

We stand at the glass booth looking at rings as the retailer stands behind it.

I point. "I like that one!"

Rubin looks at it then looks at me and begins smiling. He grasps the back of my head and locks our foreheads together. Through my peripheral I see the retailer shove the ring in Rubin's hand. Rubin kisses my ring finger, slides the yellow round rose cut diamond on it, and then kneels down. I'm smiling radiantly with excitement!

Nodding my head with a beaming smile I say, "YES!"

Before I know it Rubin's tongue is down my throat, publicly displaying affection in front of the retailer and other customers.

RUBIN DROPS ME OFF at home while he goes broadcasting the news to his mom, and probably to Jason, which is perfect because it gives me time to find a home for the lingering items that weren't privileged enough to when I first moved. Rubin will be happy to come home to an unpacked and organized home, as will I—finally. Given that I'm not here much, I haven't had much time to hang my framed pictures, art canvases, or unpack the box full of kitchen appliances. Accordingly, I plan to have it all done by the time Rubin gets back. Elaina is on the way. She'll probably help me. I told her the news just as Rubin's tires burned the concrete. She should be here any second.

"Damn Libiya, you been in this apartment for almost a month and still have more junk to put up? Father God, lord of lords, and Mary of the book . . ." Elaina complains as she walks into my bedroom with a sealed 15x12x10" economy cardboard box from the living room. She used her key.

"I know," I utter reprehensibly. "Some of these are belongings I had at Rubin's place. My mother always called me a pack rat," I reminisce. "I can't help it, I'm a sentimental person! I keep everything!" I enthusiastically divulge.

"Uh um, you gone have to get rid of some of this stuff."

"I know. I'm such a hoarder." I shake my head.

Elaina glances over at me looking suspicious. I hear a thump rattle from my small red waste basket that sits by the entry door of my room. Elaina has dropped one of my items in the trash.

"HEEYYY!?!"

"So where's the ring?" she asks disregarding my protest.

Because I'm in such high spirit, and because I know that whatever it was most likely needed dumping anyway, I choose my battle and go along with her subject change.

"I don't have it," I say casually as I pull one of the oil paintings out of the box and lay it on the king size sleigh bed Rubin bought for us.

Elaina stops pulling items out of the box from Rubin's house and from the entry door she looks up at me mystified.

I giggle and roll my eyes. "It's in layaway!" I'm still giddy.

"Whuut?!? I never heard of a proposal waiting in layaway," she declares with much sarcasm and a hint of criticism.

"It's better this way," I defend still pulling out canvases. "It gives us time to get other things together."

"Like what?"

I stiffen. "Me getting Qalbee out my system," I confess, while looking at her through my peripheral and placing the last canvas down on the bed with the others, anticipating her reaction.

"Uuuuh, he should have *gotten* out your system when they suctioned *his baby out your stomach*," she utters with no tolerance.

I say nothing.

Elaina looks over at me. Her face turns sad and regretful. "Aw, my bad girl. I didn't mean that." She walks towards me.

I manage a smirk. "Yea, girl you right," I admit.

She squeezes between me and the footboard to sit then prompts me to sit with her. I squeeze between her and a canvas then sit. Elaina wraps her arm around my shoulder and I lay my head on hers.

"No, girl, you and him have a history. No one can say when you should be over someone."

"Yea, you right about that . . ." I raise my head ". . . our history is just that . . . History." I stand because there's no need for getting all sensitive and mushy. My head is healed from him. My thoughts don't reflect back to him nearly as much as they used to.

"Well, I know niggas that don't have *close* to the past you and him have and *still* can't let go."

"Emotions are a complex entity . . . psychophysically influenced, and changes with the wind."

And like my emotions, my thoughts drifts back to three month ago when I returned to Sugarland. I had been back from Edmond a week before I went by Rubin's house. He had got word from Jason, who heard from Bambi whom ultimately got word from Elaina that I was back. He kept calling me trying to reach me, but I just was not in the mood to communicate or look at a dude. Well, towards the end of my funk, I received word that Rubin was beginning to believe that I was utilizing the "weak-male-move" via ignoring his calls and hoping he'd get the picture and go away—the way cowardly guys do females. *That was definitely not the case.*

Actually, by that time, I was beginning to miss Rubin. When I finally did get over my adversity towards guys, I didn't have the moral fiber to face him. Nonetheless, I finally grew brave one night and dropped by his house unexpected, totally not my character. I remember back when Elaina and I were living in the dorms, folks would knock on our door regularly for a variety of different reason— *let's go out, can you assist me with my assignment, what's up with Prada E?* Well, finally we stopped answering because we had our own studying and work to do. We were tired of being divested from our overachieving disciplines. We ended up taping a sign on our door quoting the rap group Outkast, which read: "I'll call before I come.

I won't just pop up over out the blue." And here I was knocking on Rubin's door without being formerly invited.

The moment Rubin opened the door of his posh pad with those boxers hanging off his hips, that cute blanket draped around his bare shoulders like a lonely soul, and that fresh clean cut taper, my love for him rocketed! I wanted to jump in his arms, lie with him, and just forget the world. He embraced me, called me his yellow flower, and stood there inhaling my presence. That night we flipped through the multiple music stations on his plasma screen, listened to some Snow Patrol, and silently cuddled. We've been going everywhere together since: to the grocery store, running errands; several museums, theatrical plays, and Astros games; and he's taken me to meet his family in Louisiana. But, regrettably, today after that kiss in the spotlight of the jewelry store when he wrapped his arms around my stomach, Qalbee's face popped up in my head instantly. It had been the first time since the day I knocked on Rubin's door three months ago.

RUBIN'S MOTHER, MRS. LIPTON, prepared a dinner for me and Rubin, and her and her husband Mr. Lipton, to celebrate the news in one another's company. Mr. and Mrs. Lipton have been married for about ten years. They met when Rubin was eleven then got married two years later. Mr. Lipton served in the Vietnam War for seven years and when he returned home it was hard for him to find a job because employers wanted a psychiatric evaluation proving he was mentally stable before they'd hire him. Since his veteran's insurance took months to take effect and pay those costs, he began fixing on cars for money. As life took course, he desired mechanics as an occupation and made it his trade, which is how he met Mrs. Lipton—Mrs. Toussaint at the time. She took her 1984 Oldsmobile Omega to get some work done on it in the shop he co-owned and they've been an item since. He retired recently and that's what prompted them to renovate their home.

After devouring blackened tilapia, smothered red potatoes, spinach, and zucchini bread with pleasure, we sit at his six chair oval rosewood dining table playing Gin Rummy discussing me and Rubin's plans for now and for when we are married. He's thinking babies and I'm thinking travel though I do want a child with him some day in the future—distant future. Nothing will occur anytime soon due to our finances anyway. He drives for Coca-Cola at night and is thinking about stocking vending machines in the mornings, and I'm still working at TVU law school library with plans on working with the boys and girls club part-time. Now that we're both in school we pretty much are at the bottom of the totem pole with funds. My mother's family invited Rubin and me to come join them for both Thanksgiving and Christmas, but Rubin is hesitant to attend both gatherings because he claims his money isn't what it used to be ever since he stopped the lone-shark thing, and with planning a wedding, he wants to save all that he has. We're trying to decide which holiday is best for us to attend.

"My money is funny. I'm thinking, Thanksgiving."

"You should give yourself time to gather up some money. Maybe you ought to try Christmas," his mother challenges to motivate her only son.

"Nooooope!" Mr. Lipton instigates while shaking his head "Um um. Not Christmas . . . Then ya gone'na have ta get gifs fa folk ya don't know, son. Stick with Thanksgiven . . . and tell nem ta be thankfa ya even driven way ta meet em." His voice is naturally hoarse, raspy, and deep. He has a Louisiana accent and speeds talk like an auctioneer.

Tickled by his suspicions I defend, "Noooo!" Smiling, I continue, "You won't have to get anyone anything. I usually just bring a dish. Maybe your mother's right. Save for another month then go for Christmas."

"Na, Ronald's right. I'd feel obligated to get people gifts. Made-my-mind, Thanksgiving. Plus it snows 'round Christmas there." Rubin settles.

"Yea. That's the thing about December there. It's too cold for me," I agree. "Plus . . . you can meet everyone sooner!" I grow enthusiastic "Then when Christmas comes around, I can try talking you into going then too!" I tease. I'm excited "And you're just going to love my grandfather! Everyone does!"

"Set up!" Mr. Lipton warns, under his breath.

Chapter Twenty-Six

ELAINA AND I ARE at Almeeda Mall searching for Rubin a birthday gift. Elaina only came for the ride but every shoe store we pass she has to stop and rummage around in it, which only sway my focus now that I am in love with stilettos. I've grown out of my tomboy stage and am now arching my eyebrows on the regular. *But not so fast*, I'll still climb a tree! And, I'm still frugal and disciplined, and believe in having my priorities in line and only purchasing what's necessary. I'm thinking a watch, chain, or some cologne for Rubin. The days are moving at the speed of light and the seasons are changing like capitalism. It's unreal that in just a year Rubin and I will both celebrate special milestones: he'll be twenty-five and I'll be a twenty-two year old college graduate! We have a month until spring and it seems like it was just Thanksgiving—which went well by the way.

My grandfather seemed to like Rubin. Grandpa meets no strangers or enemies. He interrogated Rubin and gave him advice about relationships, marriage, and about me in general all in the same breath. He entertained us the entire visit! One particular incident that populates my mind with amusement is when I stood up from my seat and informed Rubin that I was going to the bathroom.

My grandfather said, "Why you have to tell him? Just go." Then he looked back at Rubin, ignored my presence, and continued his rant, "Why they gotta . . . women always gotta tell you what they doin. We don't care, just go do it," he rants then laughs. Rubin sat there cheesing, teeth glistening and eyes bugged making a "yikes face." Rubin wanted to laugh so bad that his eyes grew beady and his eyebrows lifted to his hair line trying to hold in his amusement as he shook his head in agreement. He might as well had followed suit and said "Gone, get outs her an handle yo business gul." *It was all too funny, though!* I just followed suit, shook my head, and went to handle my business!

Later that night, grandpa told me not to come up swollen, meaning, *don't be pregnant the next time you walk up in here.* I wasn't bothered by his comment. The pregnancy feels so distant. It feels like a lifetime ago. When he said it I was actually relieved not to be pregnant, and chuckled, admiring his bluntness. My grandfather is a straight forward honest man, a no nonsense kind of guy. My mother says that's where I get it from, though, she's the same way! When my cousins and I were little kids my grandpa used to go so far as to step on our toes with his boots on if any of us would walk around his house with no socks or shoes on our feet, and would knuckle the top of our heads if we'd disobey. I learned very early to choose my company wisely because it's no fun being penalized just for being an accessory, especially since a lot of the times I would just so happen to be at the wrong place at the wrong time.

Nonetheless, my aunts seemed to like Rubin and my uncles were indifferent. Being there with Rubin and my family made me happy! He and I had such a good time that Rubin was tempted to go up there in December. I think essentially to chat with my grandpa but when Christmas came around, Rubin and I were fine with spending it together at home. Neither of us is big on paganism. I repudiate propaganda that exists solely to fortify government gain. *That's my hippie talk!*

"Spring isn't coming fast enough for me. I need a man," Elaina breaks my reminiscing.

"What you talking 'bout Willis? YOU HAVE THREE!" I shout as I enter Dillard's.

Elaina follows behind. "I know . . . but can I just have one with each of their characteristics" she pouts.

"Ha, it doesn't work that way!" I huff, heading for the jewelry cases.

"No really, Mark has the height and body, but no fuck action. Dre is goal oriented, determined and with money, but no conversation." Elaina stops at the cologne booth.

"Really?" I'm taken aback. "You would think so since he's so knowledgeable . . . Hum?" I ponder as I spray Pour Homme by Lacoste on my inner wrist to test its scent.

"Right! NO!" she says assertively. "And Laurence . . . we can talk all-day-all-night, laugh, hit up sports games, just everything in common, but he's a mother fuckin hustla . . ."

"Ya betta ask somebody," I imitate Snoop Dogg.

We laugh in unison.

". . . Who never has nothing," she adds another complaint.

Realizing the truth in that, I burst out laughing. "Yes, girl, he's always wearing that same busted up orange 1990 polo like it's today's news. No dude. Just go and get a Wally World T-shirt that's up to date and call it a day," I offer my two cent with further giggles.

"You not right . . ." She begins nodding her head quickly, ". . . but you right though," she firmly expresses giggling as well.

We walk up to the jewelry case and I see a chain that I think is perfect for Rubin's personality but it reads *$800*. We move along to the watches but I see none that acquiesces with his personality and with the type of work that he does for a reasonable price.

"So have y'all decided if y'all are going to Edmond to celebrate both your brother and Rubin's birthday together?" Elaina asks as we walk towards the men clothes.

"Well I'm thinking about asking Sebastian to come here since he's been gone to New York for so long . . . and Rubin's mother is supposed to cook. Plus Rubin and I have had enough of Edmond." My tone depresses and I look down in a daze falling into a stupor.

"What girl?" Elaina asks with anticipation and concern on her face and in her voice.

I can't pull anything over on her. The hurt that I feel must have resurrected through my facial expression giving my dejected spirit away.

"Chanelle told me that Qalbee's having a child." I hold up a no-name shirt to my chest and raise my eyebrows questioning if it is a good pick for Rubin, attempting to deflect my humiliation.

"What the . . . whuuut?" She shouts then places her left fist under her chin and looks in the air like the Greek thinking man and begin calculating on her right fingers.

"Yes. Correct. Three months before I would have been due."

I place the shirt on the rack and head back towards the cologne. She follows.

"Ain't that bout uh bitch. I'm sorry girl." She places her right hand on my left shoulder as we walk.

"No, I'm cool. I knew she was living with him. I guess I just didn't think that far. I guess I know why he didn't contest the abortion."

"Ain't that about a bitch?"

"Pretty much." I pick up a black and white zebra print 17 oz bottle of Eau De Toilette Dolce & Gabbana cologne for men. "Well, I think my mother's coming up here."

"Oh, really! Miss Beauty," she state with a certain amount of inspiration.

"I know. I can't wait! You coming right?"

"Sure!"

I HONESTLY HAD NOT sulked over Qalbee since after the incident about eight months ago. It's crazy, well sad, because I never heard from him after that day. Although I never got direct closure from him, my thoughts no longer stream to him anymore. I remember the days when I would think about him all day every day. Then it would only be when something jogged memories of him, which was anything and everything. It slowed down more, and now, it's very little that augments feelings of him. I have not allowed myself to obsess over him. After Rubin's proposal it only took me a week to erase his face out of my head and ever since, my affection has been preoccupied by my love for Rubin.

Rubin and I are in sync. He makes breakfast when he gets home from his night shift and by the time I'm dressed for class we eat together. While I'm in class he's sleeping and by lunch time we meet up at the Dots on highway 45 and share a meal and milk shake. Then he's off to studying while I head to work. Monday through Friday I work at the library from twelve to three then with the Boys and Girls

Club from 3:30 to eight. On Saturday's I'm back at the library from seven to five. Between the two jobs I get a little over 45 hours in. Rubin tried stocking machines in the evenings but it clashed with his new evening classes so he's now in class while I'm home studying and by the time he gets home I have dinner ready for us. He sleeps a bit before his eleven o'clock shift and then our days start all over again.

Prada Extravaganza is on hiatus—Elaina and I are just too busy. It saddens me because Elaina is actually going on hiatus from school as well. Next year we were supposed to walk across the stage together, snap pictures of our success, and gather all the beautiful flowers and other positive reinforcements from family and friends. Something happened with her father and she's going back home to look after him. She's tried to get her credits transferred hoping that being an honors student would make a difference but she has not found a school that will accept all of them—not even half. I'm just happy she was able to pledge before all of this. Public service is her passion. There were 26 girls on her line and she marched out as deuce. Her line strutted from the top of the student center through the lobby to the yard from one end of the campus to the other wearing purple sweat jackets with hoods covering their hair and gold lettering with their line name and number. They created their own probate introduction theme music with their steps and the bystanders watched, hooped, hollered, and followed. Once they made it to the platform the Ace did her thing then Elaina did hers. She took her hood off and performed her solo! Her flowing hair swung as she stomped the yard, slapped her hands, and chanted her words like Angela Davis: with strength, confidence, and without fear! I was so proud of her!

RUBIN'S BIRTHDAY GATHERING TURNED out bigger than we thought. A few of Rubin's friends showed up unexpected, but it was a pleasant surprise for him. Greg, Dominick, Phillip, and Jason are all childhood friends of his. The latter two were gangsters along with him back in their rebellious stage. Rubin claims that they slowed down a lot, though still have a little edge in them. I don't feel comfortable with Phillip coming around but I trust Rubin's word and respect his wishes. Bambi seems just fine with all of them. She was here earlier with Jason. My brother and Rubin's sister, Rubi, seemed to hit it off pretty well though Rubi left early to get some good night's rest preparing for work in the morning. Sebastian, our mother, Elaina, and Rubin's parents are all that's left now, which are the people we initially expected. We are laid back relaxing to some Gap Band at Rubin's dining table, as we always do when there's a group of us here.

"When are you two going to set a date?" my mother impatiently asks. She doesn't like us shacking up.

"They hadn't yet an they ben datin fa two yers?" Mr. Lipton criticizes shaking his head as if we should feel ashamed.

"That's not all they haven't done since they've been dating," Sebastian snickers as he instigates with pride.

I see everyone's face and I'm positive that mine mirrors theirs, with widen eyes and stunned lips, at the fact that he just volunteered our bedroom business—well not so bedroom business, to our parents. I stare with beady eyes and my expression translates *"PAY BACK"* as I focus in on him.

"TWO YEARS," Mr. Lipton's Louisiana accent is as clear as ever before.

"Two years is perfect!" my mother gloats as her face shines proud as does Sebastian's.

"That's even better timing! So when?" Mrs. Lipton resolutely pressures.

"Actually . . ." Rubin looks over to me. ". . . after she has the baby."

Elaina spits out her drink. Faces are astonished by the second shock of the night. I stare at Rubin while he grips my hand and squeezes as it lies on top of the table. He's smiling at me.

"A grandchild!" Mrs. Lipton is overjoyed.

"Aw shit," Mr. Lipton complains.

"Libiya Sophia Ali!" my mother emphasize furiously.

My brother's expression is impassive. Rubin is laughing.

"Mother . . . I'm not pregnant!" I huff as I roll my eyes, disapproving his joke. "He's only teasing." I lift my hand over his and fiercely squeeze as I stare up at him. "We have not set a date."

"Wait 'til I tell your father," mother continues.

"Ma, I'm not pregnant. Really! I promise. I'm serious."

Mrs. Lipton's face drops with disappointment. "No grandchild?" She's cheerless.

"Thank you Jesus, Allah, Buddha, and Muhammad!" Mr. Lipton catches the multi-religious holy ghost.

"Blasphemy!" Mrs. Lipton contempt's his rejoice.

"Not funny Rubin," mother adds breathing heavily.

"How 'bout this spring?" Elaina gleefully suggests.

"New beginnings!" Mrs. Lipton adds.

"You almost killed me Rubin," my mother states recovering her breath. "I could kill you!" Mother smiles. "Spring sounds wonderful!" she add with relief.

"Libi?" Rubin anticipates my approval with angst.

"It's spring now . . . it'll have to be next spring . . . Fall's good," I inquire.

"If you want a gloomy wedding," Elaina comments.

"Why not this spring?" Mrs. Lipton advocates.

"Libiya will be in Edmond," Rubin declares.

"Besides, it's already March . . . that'll leave us only two months to plan. No rush," I cry.

"No rush for sure . . . TWO YEARS," Mr. Lipton chuckles maniacally and shakes his head as if we ought to be ashamed.

"Pops."

"He's right. What's the hold up?" my mother piggy backs.

"You don't have any obligations in Edmond, do you?"

"No."

"Well, it's settled . . . spring!"

Chapter Twenty-Seven

ELAINA, CHANELLE, AND I are getting dressed to go out to some club that premieres tonight. I needed a mini break from the laborious schedule Rubin and I share. I invited Elaina to come along. It's time that she and Chanelle met. They hit it right off real easy. They have plenty in common, but most of all they both have my best interest at heart. Chanelle can get clingy towards me sometimes because it's always been just me and her—like sisters—but I reassured her that she is my sister no matter what occurs or who we meet or become close to. Elaina *is* one of my closest friends whom I trust and love—like a cousin. I believe that everyone has their own individual relationships with each person they come across. A person should be themselves at all times. There is no need for competition or fighting for attention, especially with females. We have to be comfortable in our own skin and be happy with whom we are. Then, we will be genuinely happy for others in their endeavors, relations, and accomplishments.

What I have learned over the years is that what one acquires today, someone else may acquire tomorrow, and what they gain now, you may never. Everyone is on a different path to their self actualization and the key to confidence is to live knowing that no one is better than you and you are better than no one—*better said by Miss Beauty years ago—we live and we learn!* Chanelle is sensible, and agrees, and now while my parent's vacation in Dubai for the month we're having a slumber at their house for a week.

Elaina, Chanelle, and I have discussed so many personal matters throughout this week. We've cried—and hugged—and consoled . . . and we've cried and hugged some more, and consoled. Elaina expressed feelings about her father, his issues, and the resentment she feels about all the work she's put into school and now having to put it on hold thinking he's probably going to die anyway meaning her digression would all be in vain. She feels guilty for feeling this way. She conveyed her efforts in ceasing these feelings, though can't help it.

Chanelle disclosed that she and some of her cousins were molested for years by their older male cousin during family gatherings when she was a little girl. She's told me before that he'd touched her wrong but she had never told the story in such detail previously. Sometimes he'd take them one by one in a back room and fondle their private area, and after he'd finish taking pleasure in one, he'd call for another. Other times he'd fondle them while they were sleeping over to their aunt's house. The specifics were inconceivable to my ears.

We discussed my abortion and my engagement and whether I want children or not. Elaina teases because I pulled off getting out of wedding planning. She thinks it's pitiful that I'm making efforts to stall the wedding. Chanelle thinks everyone is putting too much pressure on me and believes I need time to relax before I rush into marriage.

Nonetheless, she's being self-absorbed and is merely happy that I'm here longer than a weekend. I'm happy to be here!

"We'll make plans soon. I graduate next year then can start a family." I'm untwisting rollers from my hair.

"YOU? A family? You mean you and Rubin right? Cause you and kids, NAW!" Chanelle stuffs a bite of carrot cake in her mouth.

"I can't see you with children," Elaina seconds while shaking her head applying eye shadow.

"Why y'all acting like I'm a horrible person. Tell me what you really think of me!" I tease while smiling. I shake my hands in my hair to loosen my curls.

"No, it's that you're such a community activist and people's advocate . . . where would you fit the time?" Elaina glosses her already plum lips.

"Plus you have never wanted children," Chanelle confess her true thoughts. "I'm just going to be a spectacular aunt and give my nieces and nephews everything," she mocks my words from back in grade school. She spews out some mouthwash, and then applies her pink lipstick.

"Well love changes you! Y'all ready!"

THE LINE IS WRAPPED around the block. We're able to skip because Chanelle has connections. We walk into the huge quad room with four even walls around and four levels. *Azul is beautiful!* It looks like a huge ocean with all the unusual blue waving lights splashing the walls and aquarium like interior decor. When we skipped the line we went up some stairs outside and somehow we ended up already on the third floor. It looks like level one and two are for regulars, three is for customary people, and four is for famous and recognized *Very Important People*. Elaina has on a plum pencil skirt with a violet loose fitting low cut blouse that shows her cleavage—in an elegant manner—with violet accessories. Chanelle wears a short pink flare out dress with a gold belt just under her bust and gold accessories to match. I have on a white mini dress with a flower print made of diamonds that veers from my left thigh to my right side and over my breast, pedals making the crown of my tube top with Jimmy Chew stilettos and diamond accessories.

We walk around the third floor when Chanelle stops to talk to a group of females. She gives us the okay to keep moving and Elaina and I walk to the second floor when she stops at the bar.

"My feet hurt."

Elaina gives me the okay to keep walking, as our goal was to socialize on the bottom floor because by the looks of it from the third floor, it is most crowded. I reach the bottom step and the first familiar face I see is *Chad!* We hug for a long time in silence. With my arms around his neck and being a step above him, still hugging me, Chad lifts me up then places me down onto the leveled floor.

"Mmm, you're as enchanting as ever! Breath taking!" he cajoles.

I blush. I'm so ecstatic to see him. He too cleans up well. He wears a white button down and dark blue denim. His goatee has grown out and he has it trimmed neatly.

"You're hot!" I candidly joke.

"You back for good?"

"One more year"

"You always been too smart for me!"

"You the smart one . . . you just have attention deficit and lose focus."

Suddenly, I feel someone's breath on the back of my neck.

"Craig's in here," Chanelle whispers.

"Hey Chad, it's sooo good seeing you," I emphasize giving him a warm hug and a kiss on the cheek. "I have to run, but please . . . keep in touch," I yell over the music as Chanelle pulls me.

We take a few steps when Craig walks up on Chanelle. He looks at her from head to toe.

"Sup, Baby doll!"

Chanelle gives Craig an awkward smirk. He looks over at me.

"LIBI?" Craig shouts like he's seen a ghost. "Woman . . ." He picks me up and spins me around, ". . . it's good to see you!"

I smile uncomfortably "Hey Craig! Yes, it's been a long time. Looking good," I compliment.

Chanelle looks over at me and her eyes signals for me to go. Craig takes Chanelle's hand and begins talking to her. I notice Qalbee walking towards me to my left. I turn to my right to take cover. Elaina is walking towards me. I'm relieved. The crowd delays my progress and Qalbee catches up with me carrying a huge smile on his face. He reaches for a hug, but I keep walking in the other direction towards Elaina.

I grab Elaina's arm. "Qalbee's in here," I whisper in her ear loud enough for her to hear over the music as I drag her through the crowd.

Her face shocked. "You want to leave?"

"No, I'm fine."

"Well where he at so I can give him a lil piece of Elaina's alter-ego."

"Girl no . . . let's chill."

We find vacant seats on the third floor by the glass walls that look over the lower levels. A real cute muscular light skin dude hits on Elaina, but she turns him down. Two other guys approach her—a handsome Caucasian from Florida and a real cute bald chocolate guy from New York. They exchange numbers. I started to wonder if my sad aura was scaring folks from advancing towards me, but then I realized that my engagement ring was doing its job. I truly wasn't concerned about getting hit on anyway. My heart was down on the bottom level.

Chanelle walks up.

"Ya boy on the dance floor."

"Yeah, drunk as ever." I roll my eyes. "I'm so relieved I didn't go *that* route in my life," I huff. I roll my eyes again while shaking my head.

"He an alcoholic cause he knows he's made wrong choices in his life," Elaina proclaims matter-of-fact.

"He drunk cause that female. Craig say he just there 'cause they have a child together." Chanelle defends in a way that leads me to believe she wants me to consider talking to him, perhaps even forgive him.

"Whatever. He's weak," I gripe, ". . . coping with all his skeletons through self-medicating with the use of alcohol," I criticize under my breath. "Loser," I chuckle continuing to grumble under my breath. I lean in and place my hand on Chanelle's hand that lies in her lap. "I'm all bitter and thangs," I chuckle again. "I'm sorry."

"It's natural to still be angry . . . the whole situation is messed up," Chanelle comforts.

"Let's dance."

"First, let me use the restroom." I withdraw.

I charge into the rest room and weak from pain, I wilt to the floor squatting to my heels. My heart suffers so fatally that my cry is loud in my mind yet no sound comes from my throat. Tears flow so heavy that my vision is as distorted as a window shield in a storm. My insides shrivel and my esophagus roars like thunder finally freeing the agony. My cry is a howling holler and the echo rumbles like a tornado warning. This F5 twister has destroyed my spirit to no return. Never hearing from Qalbee after our involvement and then hearing that he has a child the age that ours would be is more devastating for me then I realized . . . *and seeing him here, tonight, unexpectedly* . . . I howl some more. I hadn't visualized in a long time what I would do when I finally saw him again. Tonight I wasn't prepared to see him. I wasn't prepared for him to appear happy when he saw me. I don't understand my world right now. I must pull it together and do my best to restore my atmosphere. I don't want to be a Debbie downer for the rest of the night.

MY GIRLS AND I danced to the music, ate VIP appetizers, and enjoyed ourselves. Qalbee and I never ran across each other the rest of the night. I did see him more than enough from the balcony, dancing on the dance floor and getting more and more wasted by the hour. I did enjoy the time with my girls, but inside, my heart was still gloomy—aching—crying—and suffering a storm. For months I couldn't fathom why he'd think we were okay, or cool to where he could try hugging me. It had been a year since he had left me hanging to sulk in a fetal position in my bed, going back and forth vomiting in the toilet. And even without receiving an apology, explanation; or showing some concern, I felt bad for walking away from him that night. I'll never know if he was going to communicate any of those sentiments. But, because I was heartbroken—angry—and damaged, I still needed real closure, so I called.

The phone rang four times with no answer. Ricky Smiley's voice hoaxed me with a prank call then requested that I left a message. Smiling at the thought of Qalbee and his comedy, I worked the nerve to leave a message. I nervously apologized and explained how I was hurting and how much I really wanted to talk to him that night, and hug him, and leave with him and be with him, and how sorry I am if I hurt him by walking away from him.

That was three years ago . . . and I still received no response. I know it was his phone number because Chanelle obtained it from Craig that night. Plus, Ricky Smiley is right up Qalbee's sense of humor. I left for Sugarland a couple of days afterwards and continued my life with Rubin.

The night I returned to Sugarland, Rubin and I lied in my bed and he begged for me to *marry him already*. I told him to get the calendar and we both pointed—*April 1st!*

It Won't Go Away   *Samina Najmah*

TIME FLY THROUGH THE FOUR SEASONS

Where does all the beauty in the air come from?
Is it the ocean's waves that sprinkle me;
 or pollen's nutrients energizing the bees;
  or the feeling of the wind's cool breeze;
   or the blue sky's gazing everything quietly?

  Where does all the beauty in the air come from?
   Is it the fresh cut grass after mowing;
    or the walking in the park feeling free;
     or the look of friends enjoying the pool parties;
      or the range of shades the sun change me slowly?

   Where does all the beauty in the air come from?
    Is it the blowing trees I see?
     or the orange, violet, and brown leaves;
      or the rainfall showering heavily;
       or the colorful rainbows gliding so faintly?

    Where does all the beauty in the air come from?
     Is it the dark smoke coming from the chimneys;
      or the red and yellow fires I watch closely;
       or the sound of snow crunching as I take step 3;
        or the children ice-skating with so much glee?

     Where does all the beauty in the air come from?
      Is it from Spring's blooming flowers and trees;
       or Summer's sun shining on everybody;
        or Autumn's colorful leaves
         or Winter's holiday cheering the families

      Where does all the beauty in the air
       come from . . . the four seasons.

Chapter Twenty-Eight

MARCH BEING RUBIN'S BIRTHDAY month, and April being just a month before finals and graduation, having an April 1st wedding didn't happen for us. The day before my graduation I gave Rubin a silver chain that had an imprint of him, his sister, and his father with their last name carved into it. I apologized to him for prolonging our future together and told him I no longer wanted to wait to be Mrs. Toussaint, which was my exertion of a proposal.

The next day I walked across the stage with my black cap and gown on, accepted my degree, shook the president and Dean North's hands, walked down the stairs of the stage then ran into Rubin's arms. We hurriedly took pictures with our parents, family from out of town, and friends, and jumped into Rubin's Aurora. We headed up the highway and in twenty-five minutes we pulled up to Hobby airport. Thoughts of Qalbee emerged given that the last I had been there was to attend his mother's funeral, but, I quickly cleared my thoughts of him and focused back to Rubin. Rubin grabbed our one duffel bag. We scampered out of the car. Rubin took my hand and we ran swifter than a greyhound dog chasing a rabbit for his owner's waged winnings to board our flight. When we arrived at McCarran International Airport there was a cab waiting. Rubin had previously reserved a car when we were on our way to Hobby. The cab drove us to the Wedding Chapel of Las Vegas. After being cold in Rubin's car, the airport, the cab, and in the chapel, the time came where I had to take my graduation robe off. Rubin wasn't allotted the chance to see my dress until I walked down the aisle.

When my mother packed to come to Sugarland for my graduation, she brought some of her old clothes to give me to donate to a previous client that Prada E still associated with. One item was an old black and white 1980's V-style tube top dress with puffed shoulders and a tutu that had a pencil skirt attached underneath. After my attempt of a proposal, I didn't want Rubin and me to be together the night before we said our vows so I sent him home to pack his belonging. My mother and I took the opportunity to rig the dress. We cut the puffed shoulders and pencil skirt off revamping the dress into a V-neck tube top dress—something like a corset top—with a tutu bottom. I put a black and white petticoat on underneath it to give it more fullness. I wanted to dazzle my newlywed husband when I flounced down the aisle. He and I said our vows, kissed, and then went to our hotel and made love. That was eight years ago.

Now here it is 2012 and I'm already divorced. Our marriage lasted five beautiful years. Today I'm happy to be surrounded by friends, family, decorations, cake, and gifts all for the love of our son. It's his sixth birthday. Rubin and I conceived Sebastian the night of our honeymoon. He was born a month early, though still came out weighing eight pounds, twelve and a half ounces—a half ounce from nine pounds! Sebastian was four when my marriage began to go downhill after Rubin lost his job. His male ego kicked in one too many times—first with hiding for weeks that he was unemployed, pretending he's getting up every night to go to work, then making the mistake of telling Jason, because Bambi ended up unknowingly spilling the beans.

Besides him deceiving me for weeks, I now felt unvalued and insecure, unviable because he didn't value me enough to convey vital information to me and insecure because it led me to wonder where he was all those nights. Though later, come to find out his story about being at his sister's throughout the night checked out. Secondly, he quit school to work more hours. But then he was in between jobs—losing interest in the work, having differences with employees, and feeling he should be paid more for his labor.

I had quit working for the Boys and Girls club after having Sebastian. My nutrition hobby became more than just a hobby after baring him. I chose to make a career out of it. I went to part-time with the library then went for my second Bachelor's in nutrition. Money became an issue in many different ways. Rubin didn't like the fact that when little Sebastian needed things I would be the one to buy it. I tried reassuring Rubin and indulging his ego by explaining that since I'm the one that wanted Sebastian to experience baseball, karate, learn Chinese, and advanced science and math that I surly wouldn't expect him to fund it. Though, further into the year he began verbally taking it out on me—and his mother—causing me emotional distress. I don't believe in letting anyone deliberately obstruct my peace. I understand wanting to provide for your family, but if your family is all you have, why take it out on the ones you love?

So I let him go, believing that he'd get it together without me and little Sebastian in his way, which is exactly what happened. Rubin went back to school, finished his last year, received his bachelor's in criminal law, prepared for the LSAT and surpassed it! He is in his first year of law school. He's a great father to our son and friend to me. After I completed my internship and passed the Registered Dietician exam, I applied for a master's program in advertising and utilized earnings from my nutrition license to pay it off. I moved to Atlanta about six months ago because I was accepted to a PhD program at Atlanta Liberal Arts University; however, the program doesn't allow students to work. All of my superfluous schooling feels useless. Since we have no family there I'm having Sebastian's party here in Edmond. Sebastian negotiated to also stay here for the two mouths he's out of school and I agreed—he and Chanelle's daughter are close. Chanelle and Craig had Cecilia about a year after Sebastian was born.

"It's so good to have you back for awhile," Chanelle expresses as she walks into my parent's kitchen. She places her right hand on my shoulder and leans against the counter next to me.

I exhale a gust of air. "I know!" I smile. "There's no place like home," I acclaim as I wash the last dish in the sink from the party.

"I can't believe *you* saying that Ms. ATL!" Chanelle teases.

I chuckle along with her. "Oh, don't get me wrong, I'm sure I'll be ready to go back by the end of the month . . ." I rinse the saucer and put it on the red dish rack. ". . . though, Rubin's happy 'cause we're closer and it's easier for him to come see Sebastian."

"Girl I still can't believe y'all got a divorce." She sounds baffled.

"Yea . . . we *were* in love . . ." I grab a paper towel from the holder hanging above the sink. ". . . we're still friends now, though," I say with satisfaction as I gaze through the blinds of the window above the sink viewing the backyard. "Sometimes love is just not enough." I turn around and lean on the counter next to Chanelle drying my hands. "When you work really hard to please someone for a long time and they just don't make you feel appreciated, what do you do? Leave!" I causally fold my arms. "He appreciates me now that I've been gone for a year." My eyebrows rise to my hairline as I smirk.

"That's what I don't get . . . that man loved your ass like a goddess . . . how does that change? Love is a crazy thing."

"He still loved me like that during the divorce. I deem that he was simply battling with *his own* insecurities and was unable to bestow what he and I had. Nothing personal. I realized that I had to leave in order for him to get-it-together, to focus and overpower his inner disputes."

"Yea," she agrees. "We're still on for tonight?"

She's taking me to a friend's birthday party at a lounge.

EVERYONE CALLED WISHING SEBASTIAN a happy birthday. Big Sebastian called from New York. He and little Sebastian are really close—he always beat Rubi calling, and they live in the same house. To my surprise, Rubi moved with Sebastian during me and Rubin's divorce. They exchanged numbers the night of Rubin's party, began talking long distance to get to know one another, and at some point became an item. Rubin found out during the deceiving nights he hung low over to Rubi's apartment while he was pretending to be at work for weeks. Come to find out, I was the last to know about that too. Nevertheless, they are a beautiful couple. Rubi deserves a good man and Sebastian is literally that by nature. And Sebastian needs a down chick, and Rubi's definitely that. Their loyalty to each other is phenomenal.

I talked to Elaina after everyone left Sebastian's party. We talk once or twice a week. After the matters concerning her father she went back to school and finished her degree. She applied to the police department, went to police academy, and has been an officer for two years now. She's not married, has no children, and likes it that way. She enjoys her single dating life. I wish she was here to enjoy tonight with me and Chanelle.

"Can I get a sprite with a lemon and a cherry?"

The bartender begins preparing my drink while continuing his conversation with other customer's talking about some high speed chase that occurred this evening. I thought of Elaina and told myself that I'd call when I get back to the table to see if she knows about it. She didn't mention anything about it earlier. As the waiter hands me my drink I glance over and see what looks like a figment of my former love, Qalbee, walking away from the bar. The bartender hands me my drink, I tip him, and walk off. As I approach the table Chanelle and I occupy, I look afar, still wondering if it was him.

"I think I saw Qalbee."

"Up in here? I don't believe it. I hear he's at home with his children at all times." Chanelle is certain. "Hold down the fort, I'm goin to the ladies room." She gets up and walks in the distance.

I sit here for a moment, guzzle my entire sprite, and then scope the crowd. There he is! I impulsively walk to him, but as I approach he's much shorter than I remember, but I think *maybe it's my heels*. I tap him on the shoulder and it's not him. The guy stares at me as if I'm an idiot.

"My bad," is all I manage to utter, then I walk towards the restroom in search of Chanelle. *I would think he'd be anywhere I am— I'm being narcissistic, I'm pitiful to believe my luck has changed.* I get closer to the restroom and notice *that fragment again,* standing against the wall by the door of the restroom. I look through my peripheral as I rush past it walking into the restroom. *IT IS HIM! It's really Qalbee.* My heart palpitates rapidly. I become jittery. *Calm down,* I coach. I rush to the mirror and begin fixing my hair and makeup. I apply my pink lip stick and pace out the door. I'm so nervous I sprint past him not knowing what to say; *how do I initiate a conversation?* But this is my chance for redemption after passing him up last time nine years ago. I turn my head looking back at him and his head is down observing his phone. I turn around fabricating a smile through nervousness then walk towards him. Qalbee's head is still down as his eyes look up at me, but then they quickly drop down giving a double take. He looks stunned. Completely and utterly nervous, but gravely happy to see *my heart*, I strive for words.

"My Qalbee . . . long time no see! How have *you* been?" My tone sounds superior and confident, yet, truth be told, I feel the complete opposite.

"Things are okay with me." He stands there reserved and caustic with his response. "What are *you* doing here?" he says with what seems to be bitterness in his voice as he glances up at me then back to his phone as if I'm a nuisance to him.

"Chanelle was invited and I'm accompanying her."

And there goes that smile!

Qalbee slightly chuckles. "No, I meant in the city," though, he still seems annoyed.

"Oh," I slightly chuckle feeling discomfit.

"Some things don't change." He shakes his head still looking away.

"Riiight," I emphasize, implying that he's popped up in my life, yet again, after all these years and still has this compelling effect on me. "I'm here for awhile. What about you?"

His face turns warped. "I live here," he resolutely asserts while looking into my eyes for the first time though his head's still down as if he's looking over sun shades.

"No, I mean, are you with someone or were you invited?" I ask in another way feeling dumb and upset that I'm this tense.

He lowers his phone placing it to the right side of him and for the first time he actually lifts his head, changing his focus from his phone. "Oh . . . my sister was and I tagged along to get out the house." His eyes are piercing.

And for the third first tonight, I have his full attention. I'm happy—relieved! We stare blankly into one another's eyes. We're so in tuned with each other that we don't hear or see Katina and Chanelle walk up—*at least I didn't*—until Chanelle speaks.

"What's up Q!"

Qalbee and I quickly look over to them, Qalbee tilts his chin up gesturing "what's up", and then our eyes are right back at eye contact. Katina hugs me.

"Hey girl!"

I snap out of what seems to be coaxing between Qalbee and me, then return her embrace. "How are you!" I genuinely ask, happy to see her.

"I'm doing so well. I see y'all found each other," Katina instigates as if we we're destined to meet again—*or, it's possible that I'm projecting.*

"Yea," I respond looking at Qalbee, enticed by his stare.

I snap out of it then look at Katina. "Yes girl, it's so great to see you!" I embrace her hands, holding her at arm's length then look her up and down. "I'm happy that things are good for you." I'm speaking about her life in general and how gorgeous she is. I'm sure she knows that's what I am implying.

"Yea girl, I went and got my associates in nursing . . . and am married with three children," she giggles. "Q's the physician assistant," she stresses, teasing him, and exemplifying that she's proud of him.

"You and Qalbee deserve it."

"Thank you!"

"Wanna walk?" Chanelle asks me.

Katina looks at her, then at me, then briefly gives me a bubbly hug. "Well it was great seeing you . . . take care!"

Chanelle and I take a few steps. I look back at Qalbee and Katina. I turn around, and as I do, Chanelle huffs, her shoulders drop, and her eyes roll.

"Here we go," she stops.

I approach Qalbee. "Call me Comedy." I hand him one of my advertising cards. "It was really good to see you!"

CHANELLE AND I ARE in her car on the way to drop me off at my parent's. When I told her that I almost told Qalbee that I love him she told me I needed to get 600 miles away . . . *back to ATL*. I can't believe the feeling hasn't gone away. I was merely thinking that he and I could hang before I leave just to catch up. But I know he's not going to call me. *Why did I give him my number?* I don't even know why I would want to talk to someone that I know wouldn't call me. I guess because I actually believe that even if he did miss me, he would never tell me—*it's the man's ego*. I huff at the thought. I'm not like that. I can't help but be honest with myself. I know I miss him. I should have gotten his number.

We pull up to our destination.

"I'mma regret this," Chanelle declares while handing me a torn piece of napkin.

"What's this?" I'm confused.

"His sister slipped it to me."

"AHHHHHHH!" I scream forcefully inclining in my seat then leaning forward. *It's Qalbee's cell number!* "Should I text or call him?" I'm hyped! "No . . ." I sit back in my seat ". . . I'll wait for him to contact me." I say with poise.

"Why would you do that?" Chanelle criticizes. "You may not even want to talk to him by then."

I stare at the number while Chanelle stares at me.

"How is this boy still in your heart?" she utters like I'm pathetic.

"I don't know?"

"Just text him asking if, and when, he can meet up with you," she sounds impatient.

I look at her dumbfounded, doubting that he'd agree to any of that.

"That boy is your heart . . . might as well catch up!" Chanelle amends by cheerfully approving.

I smile! "Thank you, girl!" Excited I climb out, slam the door, and race inside the house.

Chapter Twenty-Nine

IT IS REALLY LATE but I couldn't help but call Elaina. I'm itching to tell her about my surreal experience. I call just in time to catch her at the beginning of her thirty-minute break. She goes on telling me about how rough her night has been. She and her partner just experienced a high speed chase after finding that the driver had been harboring two victims for twenty years. One is a forty year old girl and the other is her son whom she was pregnant with when she was abducted. *I'm lost for words.*

Elaina said that she got a lead from dispatch after receiving an emergency call from the abductor's neighbor. It was reported that there was an altercation at the house and Elaina and her partner went to check it out thinking it was a normal domestic violence issue. Elaina knocked on the door; and because it was so much commotion coming from inside, her partner checked the back of the house. A man forced the front door open prompting Elaina to quickly scan the scene.

The twenty year old boy's wrist and ankles were tied as he sat beaten unconscious, leaned against the border of the door. The woman, the boy's mother, was cuffed to the knob of a closet located directly from the front door. The abductor briefly looked at Elaina, pushed her so hard that she fell down, and then he ran. By the time Elaina caught composure and pulled her gun out, her partner came running from around the side of the house, and the man was in his car. They jumped in theirs then called the ambulance for the two victims while they followed him. By 11:45 there were over ten police cars participating in the chase and by 12:00, ten helicopters had joined. The Big Three television networks provided live coverage throughout the chase lasting 25 miles. When I called Elaina, she had just left from the police station giving her statement of the incident.

After all of that I don't want to bother Elaina with a simple matter about my love life. Though, I informed her earlier that Chanelle and I were going out and since I'm calling so late, Elaina knows that something has happened. I present her with the logistics and she encourages me to call. She declares that she doesn't see the harm in wanting to catch up, but then she has to return to duty, so I thank her and we hang up. I lie in my bed and watch the clock turn as I contemplate for awhile. I write a poem to procure a decision, but still, no resolution. Finally, I settle to sleep on it.

THIS MORNING IS LOVELY. I make breakfast for Sebastian and me, get him in the tub, then myself, and take him to the park. We play for a couple of hours then I drop him off with my dad at the Rain Forest Café. I head home. Last night feels like a dream to me, but I look over at the torn napkin lying in my cup holder, and I know that last night is as real as my love for my lil Sebastian! I pass the street I saw Qalbee sitting at years ago—*my, the memories it brings.* But what is even more of a coincidence is that a car that looks just like his is sitting at a neighborhood street, blocks down as I drive closer to home. I stare through my window as the car turns the corner. What are the odds? *It's Qalbee! BEWILDERED is what I am—what are the chances!* I honk, feeling existential about life, but Qalbee doesn't look up. I look in my rearview mirror watching his car roll down the street in the opposite direction. A red light stops me. I reach for my phone then for the napkin in the cup holder and text something quick before the light changes. *"I just saw u. R u busy later?"*

Ten minutes and no response. I pull up to my parent's house and my phone whistles.

"Meet me at the same spot from last night. 7:00."

"K," I text back wondering how he knows it's me or if he knows it's me.

EARLIER I FELT LIKE Leona Lewis as I rummaged through my clothes in search for an outfit that said *"you'll regret that I'm the best you never had"* since he has always took me for granted and never fully gave me a real chance. I didn't want to be too jazzy or too dressy like I'm trying too hard, or too plain like the way he knew me when we were kids. So I took a pointer from Katy and threw on my skin tight jeans. I'm fine now—literally—not to toot my own horn! I'll get my teenage dream heart racing when I introduce the grown, sexy, mature me, and he'll want to put his hands *all over* me.

I walk into the lounge, a bit embarrassed, wondering if he thought it was someone else texting him. Humiliation isn't the word that my core would feel. I walk towards the bar where I first saw the fragment of him. *He's not here. Maybe he's in the restroom? I'm on time . . . maybe he's late.* Feeling self-conscious, I wander in the opposite direction from the restroom hoping he doesn't catch me looking for him. I approach the bar venue that connects to the lounge, and I see Qalbee's beautiful waves shine on the other side of the doors. Except for his face—his expression looks as though he's in a dark place. However, it could just be because he's sitting in a dim corner . . . *smoking a cigarette?*

"You smoke?" I walk up, standing nervously at the booth he occupies. "Well obviously." I roll my eyes at my dumb slip of the mouth, still nervous that he may have thought he had texted someone else. Qalbee's *cancer* free hand raises and he gestures for me to have a seat.

"Just never would have guessed that . . ." I mumble as I sit. "Some things *do* change," I persist, looking at the table.

"It's nothing I'm proud of," he exhales and smoke blows in the air like clouds. "Just life and its many challenges the past few years." His head lowers then he dabs the cigarette and ashes sprinkle into his empty Colt 45 bottle. "I really have no excuse . . . How you been?" he asks lifting his head, quickly shifting from pity.

"Things are actually cool! So much stuff . . ." A smile cuddles my face at the thought of my son and all that I have accomplished. ". . . where to begin!"

"You finished school right?"

"Yes . . . triple times," I huff, exhausted by the thought. "I also have a six year old son!" Again, I beam.

"I can't imagine you with a child," he exhales and smoke trails the air.

"Yea, me either. He's my life." I smile again. "You have two sons right?"

"Yea?" His eyes squint, and his eyebrows furrow, appearing puzzled but he's aware of my source.

"Things get around . . . people talk."

"Right . . ." he agrees and I know Chanelle is a thought in both our minds.

"You still with their mother?"

"Na. We were never really together," he declares just as exhausted as I sounded seconds ago.

"What that mean? How does that happen then with 2 children?"

A tall medium build Caucasian girl with long brunette hair walks up to our booth wearing shorts that exposes her butt-cheeks with a slit cut down to the middle of her white t-shirt revealing the bow of her black sheer bra, leaving no fantasy as she pours our glasses full of ice water. Qalbee shakes his head and waves his free hand excusing to order. He and the *hot waiter Babe* looks at me then Qalbee tilts his head offering for me to order. I shake my head excusing to order, as well. I don't feel all that comfortable about him buying me a meal—*though I should*—but I'm too nervous to eat anyway. The waiter Babe politely walks off into the darkness. The room doesn't give off much light to see, though the chaotic LED disco lights periodically shines various colors giving visibility to Qalbee's expressions.

"I'll be honest . . . after my mother died I was in a dark place. I couldn't talk to Katina or Craig—no one. She, my son's mother, worked with me, and was always around. She never let up," he says as if somehow she saved his life. His affect is sinister . . . sad . . . annoyed even—not matching his tone. "So that was that and we conceived our first son."

I roll my eyes. "Right . . . a few months before *our* situation." My tone is bitter, not matching my affect. I'm long past being bitter.

"Libiya, words can't express how *guilty* and *disreputable* I felt," he emphasizes with much passion twisting the cancer stick in the ashtray.

"I'm fine with all of it." I roll my eyes and take a sip of my water. *I need a straw.*

"I didn't want two baby mommas or two children the same age . . ."

"Is that so? Well ain't that about . . ."

"I know, that sounds selfish."

"Sounds?"

"When you told me you were pregnant I wished she wasn't. I knew she wouldn't have an abortion plus she was too far along."

Oh so I'm the cruel, heartless one who would abort? "Um, I hear you . . . calling me heartless? . . . Na, really, I'm fine about it." *I'm so content with life.* "What affected me is that you never called to check on me after that day."

"That's what I wanted to convey to you years ago when I saw you at that club."

I huff, "Well by then I thought *what a loser.*"

Throughout the night Qalbee and I catch up on our trials and failures, tribulations and errors; our successes and proliferations; and families and mutual friends. It's possible that Qalbee ordered way too many beers from waiter Babe because he divulged how *messed up* he was after his mother's death, how he would isolate from everyone, and how he didn't believe he would make it through it all—his mother's death, a female he wasn't in love with carrying his child a year later, then me getting pregnant months afterwards. He expressed regret about the abortion and how it habitually haunts him still, especially when he rides on that highway in that direction or in the vicinity of that clinic.

"I was torn. That's why I worked, worked, worked . . . I didn't want to think, about anything."

The colors of disco reveal the slight tear in the corner of his right eye. I forgave him long ago, well actually after I disregarded him that night at the club. After listening to him tonight, I can understand not wanting two women pregnant at the same time. Though, the principle in me feels that he should have talked to me and faced the consequences of his *messed up* decisions. I get that she was far along, truly, I get it; and him not having parents to confide in, I empathize—he was going through a lot. I get it—but . . .

"Why not choose me?" He's always chosen things over me.

"I was lost, Yaya." His head low. "Believe me, if I could have chosen, it would have been a child with you. I've never been in love with my boys' mother."

"But you ended up with two by her?"

He lights another cancer stick. "Tryna do the right thing," he proclaims nonchalantly, and then takes a puff.

The fact that he allowed himself to grow weak to cigarettes bugs me, so much that I grow annoyed. The smell is so potent that I'm paranoid of inhaling the second hand smoke.

"We tried, but I just never loved her. She's the reason I began smoking. She's not healthy for me."

So you think? I'm even more annoyed, and now I'm turned off that he could try so hard with a rebound that he never loved, and gave so much that he compromised himself—and his health. I internally shake my head and remain quiet.

"All I do is work, pay my mortgage, and take care of my boys. They're my life."

Qalbee pulls out his Android Galaxy 3, I assume to show me pictures, which reduces my displeasure.

"I'm sure you are a great father, loving, spoiling, and disciplining them." I smile.

Qalbee places his left hand on my right, leans over the table, and then shows me a picture of his boys.

"Xavier and Everick!"

Xavier wears yellow scrub pants and a white doctor coat with the rubber earpiece of a stethoscope in his ears and the chest piece to Everick's heart, smiling his father's charismatic smile. Everick has on a zombie costume with artificial blood sprinkled on his face and down his costume.

"Oh my, Xavier looks so much like you. I mean really, he has *your face*!" I shout with enthusiasm. I'm tickled! "And Everick, he is just adorable." I look up into Qalbee's cheerless eyes. "I'm so proud of you . . . *this* is what I knew was in you way back when. You've grown all-up on me!" I tease.

Half-naked brunette waiter Babe offers us a desert menu.

Qalbee receives it. "Thank you, give us a minute."

She walks off.

"Where's *your* son?"

"He's at my parents'. We are here temporarily. I was accepted into a PhD program in ATL. His father and I were married, but over the years we grew apart." I begin feeling uncomfortable going into too much detail in this setting, so I make it short.

"He didn't handle the obstacles of life very well and would take it out on me." I look up at Qalbee then sip my water. *Dang I forgot to ask for a straw.*

Qalbee's eyes are smoldering as if he's irately concerned. "You?" he questions looking over imaginary shades like the other night while he twists the second cancer stick in the ash tray.

"Oh no," I shake my head as my eyebrows furrow, offended that he'd think that. But, then again, how would he know? I guess I'm more affronted that he'd think I'd accept someone beating me.

"Rubin's much too genuine for that," I defend as I lean back in my seat. "He would just show insecurities," I stress, waving all five fingers of my right hand to obstruct any further obscene thoughts, as I chuckle.

Qalbee places a stick of red gum in his mouth then places a few dollars on the table. I take heed that it's about that time to go. I begin scooting out of my seat as Qalbee stands by my side waiting on me.

"PhD in psychology huh?" He smiles with admiration, leaving no room that I'm practically stepping on his toes and tasting the Big Red gum he's chewing as I stand. "Most things *don't* change!" He shakes his head. "You've always been weird! Psych . . . that's all you!"

I giggle. "What? Weird?" I blush, and our closeness exhilarates me. We exit the bar and then the lounge.

"*That's why* you never gave me any real play." I burst out into laughter then push his chest with an open palm. "You are so right . . . I was so weird!" I admit as I look into the sky. "I still am . . . just not as much," I chuckle.

We reach my two toned, brick red and white, Toyota FJ Cruiser with rack lights on the roof—for me and Sebastian's camping trips. It's a divorce gift to myself. Qalbee pins me against it by being so close up on me.

"You have plans tomorrow night?" he humbly asks.

Though I fear his rejection, I nervously and courageously dare, "Only with you!"

Chapter Thirty

MY HEART TOOK ME to poetry night at an independently owned eatery called Poultry and Pastry where anyone can put their name on the list to express. It was perfect because I had just memorized the poem I wrote the other night called "Surreal". I was number eleven on the list and when the host announced me I delivered like never before! The best part is that Qalbee listened closely and stared intimately, knowing "Surreal" was about him! Qalbee has changed a lot—some for the better, but some . . . well, not for the worse, but his spirit isn't so happy like when we were kids. He's rather cynical. Nonetheless, we're hanging like we've never missed a beat, like the summer we first met! His work schedule keeps us apart in the days and he being on-call sometimes keep us apart during the nights, but just as soon as he gets off he calls me and we meet up. On the nights we're not able to see each other we talk until he falls asleep. I never do.

I'm too amped up and thrilled we're even back talking and hanging again.

On the weekends we haven't gone out to eat or to a movie, we've been getting out of the city! Last weekend he and I went to Atlanta to spend time in my domain, which was huge to me because Qalbee has a fear of heights. The flight was great, well at least for me! I loved being Qalbee's comforter. Later, I tried talking him into going to Six Flags over Atlanta but I realized that too much exposure to heights in one weekend might be a more traumatic and a less efficient method for decreasing his acrophobia. It's possible that we may not have made it on our flight back to Edmond—which wouldn't have been a problem for me. It simply would have been *heaven extended*! However, he did take me to see Mike Epps' comedy show at the Fox Theater. He was hilarious—Qalbee's type of hilarious. And we went to a Braves baseball game that Saturday. I was excited.

Who would have thought my Heart would wine and dine me during adulthood! Qalbee's been taking me out on the town to places he knows is sentimental to me. He burned a music CD for me full of songs that reminds him of me. I ached to listen to it but waited until our drive to Sugarland—no more planes. The first song is "Tired of You" by Foo Fighters, then OutKast's "Prototype" and then my favorite, "Come Close" by Common featuring Mary J. Blige. Qalbee playfully sung the song to me, though with much passion. I could feel the sincerity in his voice and see the love in his eyes. I was overcome by the entire 15 song CD, however, we replayed Isley Brothers' "For the Love of You" repeatedly. I could have burst.

We checked in, showered, changed clothes, and went to a club downtown. We walked in but the bouncer turned Qalbee around because he had on Nike boots. We were both heated because there were so many fellas in the club with tennis shoes, Timberlands, and other non-dressy shoes. Qalbee and I had to drive back to the hotel so that he could change shoes. After all that driving neither of us was feeling the club. We rode around the city, talked about life some more, stopped at Frenchy's Chicken on the south side and then parlayed back at the room.

All the time Qalbee and I have been spending together this past month, he hasn't once tried anything sexual with me. He says he has me on a pedestal and that I'm different than all the other women in this lifetime! He's been catering to my every need—*like the tables have turned*. He's even cooked for me and catered it to me at my Aunt K's house one day, and brought plates over for her and my mother. He's starting to grow on my mother but she still doesn't trust him after the indignity he showed years ago. She believes that if he was really sorry then he'd pay back that money—her money. My aunt despises him. The rest of the family has no problems with him. They enjoy him! Tonight we're hanging out at my cousin's house. They're having a casino party.

Speaking of my Heart! I hear him knock at the door so I rush to put on my green earrings. I have on my black and white Geometric-links pattern peplum top, with black skinny leg pants, my green Jessica Simpson open toe high heels and a yellow jacket to bring out the colors.

I open the door. Qalbee has on blue True Religion jeans and a green and white striped Lacoste shirt. I smile then lean in to hug him; he pecks me on my check.

"Come on in!"

Qalbee sits on the sofa and I head for the downstairs bathroom. I hear little feet trailing from the stairs to the living room and I know that it's Sebastian.

"Thank you," I hear Qalbee utter.

"My name is Sebastian. What's yours?"

"Q."

"Nice to meet you."

"The pleasure is all mine!"

I rush into the living room. "Sebastian, quit harassing people!"

"He's great. He's not bothering me . . . so mannerable and pleasant!" Qalbee commends in amazement.

"And hyper . . . like me," I say as I look at Sebastian and grab his head into a hug.

"Get to bed. You can read your pawpaw a bedtime story." I bend down and kiss him on his cheek in the corner of his lips.

Sebastian extends his right hand to Qalbee then Qalbee reaches out to him and they shake hands. When I see Qalbee's impressed expression I know that Sebastian must have squeezed his hand tightly.

"Take great care of my mother or you'll have to answer to me."

Qalbee chuckles "I'll keep that in mind . . ." Qalbee looks at me with a smile ". . . though know she's in good hands."

"Goodnight Mister."

I rub his baby Mohawk then pat him on his butt.

"Mom," he complains as he runs out the room.

"Goodnight young fella," Qalbee shouts in a whisper.

THE PARTY WAS GREAT! Qalbee seemed to enjoy himself. All night we found excuses to touch each other, rather it be me handing him a drink or making his plate; him blatantly holding my hand between games; or me sitting in his lap as he amused my family with jokes. Besides blackjack, 7-Card Stud, and Texas Hold'em and other pokers games, there were various drinking games, great music, and delicious food. I can't say that we were the last to leave—we wanted our own personal time together so we left early plus neither of us could be out too late tonight. I have a birthday party to get Sebastian to tomorrow by noon; and Qalbee . . . well he never went into details on why he had to get home early tonight. It concerns me because it makes me feel that he's hiding something—like he doesn't trust me and I'm a bit annoyed because he's brought me here to Briton Memorial Park as if he doesn't realize that it brings back horrible memories for me.

We park then he looks at me, apprehension is in his eyes. He tilts his head to the left encouraging me to get out as he opens the door of his black 4-door family sedan. He pulls out a small black bag from underneath his seat. *Now he has me curious.* I climb out of the Dodge Charger and we walk towards the park.

"I can't change the past, but I want you to know that I take full responsibility for my actions in all of it."

He stops walking causing me to stop. He opens the bag, reaches in, and hands me a small gold box. I look with astonishment and then pull the lid up.

"Wow, it's beautiful!" *It's a gold star necklace!* He knows I love stars!

"It didn't cost me $300," Qalbee admits, and then reaches into the bag again. He hand me a Nike Journal made of suede.

"Wow, thanks!" I rub the soft texture. "Qalbee . . ."

"It's not the cash that I owe you but I know you don't care about the money, so I wanted you to have something nice to remember me by." His voice is hoarse as it lowers, "The birthdays and graduations and parties I missed." He sighs then looks away, and our eyes no longer connect. He dreams into the distance seeming to get lost in thought.

"Qalbee?" I whisper out of concern.

He reaches in the bag. "I've already downloaded the songs that's on the CD I made you."

My chin falls to the floor . . . *I know he hates that I use my phone to listen to music, but a 32 gigabyte iPad mini? This alone cost $400.* The corners of my lips extend to my ears!

"What!" I jump in his arms catching him off guard almost knocking him down. He wraps his arms firmly around my waist as my arms hug his neck tightly. I stick my tongue down his throat massaging his uvula and I tasting the strawberry cake he ate earlier tonight. He follows along, deeply kissing me. I feel a smile imprint his face. *I am still in love with this man.* I get my fix then release. All of a sudden the thought of Qalbee omitting information earlier invades my mind.

"There's something you're not telling me," I discern.

Qalbee looks at me with horror as if I know what he did last night. "What?"

"I mean, you don't owe me any explanations, we *did* just meet all over again and all." I'm passive although, his better judgment, third eye, or whatever might want to kick in any second now and be honest because I don't have time for nonsense, those days are over.

"She lives with me."

"Who?" But I snap out of my denial real quick. I know who he's talking about. I begin wheezing. "You've got to be kidding me." I've never had asthma in my life. This man is going to kill me. "So y'all ARE together." I feel my face hit the floor, although, really I'm only feeling the pain of humiliation. I look down and away from Qalbee's eyes, shameful that I continue to allow myself to be hoodwinked by his deceit. My body weakens. I place my right hand on my thigh and lean over to catch my breath. I want to cry but I hold back my tears. I'm angry.

"Nooo. She threatens to take my kids to Detroit . . . so I let her stay with me," he seems frustrated.

I'm so mortified that I impulsively shove the items into Qalbee's chest knocking the life out of his lungs. *Wait—hold up . . . he owes me those things . . . I wanted that iPad and necklace . . . and that journal—all my pain and suffering over the years,* I protest within. Qalbee's wheezing cough struggles to grasp air after my blow, and it knocks me out of my internal tirade. I storm off.

"Trust me. We are not together. I was actually engaged to another woman and Kali ran her off. I despise the bitch," he elucidates, trailing after me.

I stop and turn around. "Wow! That was disrespectful. Y'all *are* something or why . . ." I pulse. I *dare not* ask any questions that will entertain this madness. I sulk. "She wouldn't be living in your house, Qalbee." I shake my head with disappointment. I quickly turn away and resume towards the Charger griping under my breath, "This is why I've never been invited to your home. I knew there was something shaky about this whole thing."

"She needed help with bills . . . it was easier for her to move in . . . she's only there because of my boys. I couldn't leave their mother out!" He desperately cries.

I look back at him, sigh, and roll my eyes. "I don't care about all of that. You didn't tell me any of this."

I'm thankful to reach the car after what seemed to be a lifetime of torture. He presses the alarm on his key chain and the doors unlock. "I didn't want to start something from nothing when you're leaving soon anyway."

"Ain't that bout a . . ." *AAAHHHH,* I scream inside. *Huhhh,* I sigh. Why can't I just get it out and curse this . . . dude out already. Why won't this feeling go away? I rigidly heave the car door open.

Qalbee places his left palm against the back door and leans into the entryway. "Do you think I'd be out here, late like this, regularly, spending all my spare time with you . . . or that she'd even let me out?"

"Let you out . . ." I'm insulted ". . . never mind, I won't even go there. I don't know, but you know what . . . like I said, I'm nobody. You don't owe me an explanation." I slam the door almost smashing him with it.

The ride home is as quiet as the world was before the Big Bang. All I thought about is how I wish this feeling would go away. We pull up to my parent's house and he parrots me getting out of the car—I open the door, he opens the door; I hastily climb out, he hastily climbs, I slam the door, he slams the door. I head for the front door of the house and he grasps my wrist causing me to jerk around into him. His body's so near that I can smell the scent of Bar B Que emanate from his shirt beyond the party.

"Yaya, being with you these last six weeks has been the most fun and entertainment I've experienced in years. I haven't been this happy in a long time."

I stare impassively into his eyes although I can't help but be flattered.

"I don't know what I'm going to do when you leave me. I'll be right back to the same old depressing regiment. You've been nothing but sunshine. You have always been my sunshine."

"Comedy," I giggle in the middle of him spilling his guts, "you've really grown up on me!"

He appears humiliated. I don't know if it's because he's being vulnerable and transparent, or if it's because I've interrupted him during his revelation.

"I never thought I'd hear you say anything like that . . . and to me at that. Man, what's the story?" I concede, asking for the plain and simple truth.

"I swear to you, it's only so that she won't take my boys."

I'm relieved. I feel somewhat embarrassed after getting so upset. I rub my index finger across his lips then hug my palm to his check.

"You've given me some of you then you left me none of you. The day you entered my life, you entered my heart and since that day, my heart has never been complete. It beats only for you."

Qalbee's eyes appear glossy—maybe from the glare of the porch light though I sense that it is emotionally stimulated. He kisses me with passion like death no longer resides within him and that life is worth living. I trust that it is love.

Chapter Thirty-One

QALBEE TOLD ME THAT he didn't want me to leave without us making a commitment and I agreed to that—though only if he promised, and came through on his promise, that he will treat Sebastian and me as priorities for the rest of eternity like we are his immediate family. Since then, he's taken me, Sebastian, and his boys out to the movie theater to see *Thunderstruck* starring Kevin Durant, to Heffner Lake so that the boys could play at the park there, and today we're all at Dave & Buster's. I'm concerned about how our relationship will work with me living so far away but Qalbee encouraged me not to worry. He will make up for everything and make a way.

Dave & Buster's is exhilarating! The boys are shooting hoops, rocking Guitar Hero, and slicing fruit as ninjas, simply enjoying themselves. Qalbee and I are taking pleasure in watching the smiles on their faces and the excitement in their spirits as they connect naturally with one another. After three hours of fun, everyone, including me and

Qalbee, are worn out. We head to get some ice cream cones then call it a day. Qalbee drops Sebastian and me off at home and the boys give dap and knuckles through the car window while Qalbee and I hug. We don't kiss because we want to respect the children. After conversing briefly in the driveway, Qalbee and the boys drive off. Sebastian is staying the night with Cecilia so he and I climb in my truck and I take him to Chanelle and Craig's house. Chanelle comes out to the driveway and Sebastian runs into her house. I sit exhaustedly in my truck while we chat momentarily through the window then I pull off. I feel vibration from my clutch and hear the train echo on my phone. I swipe to answer.

"Hello?"

"Hello this is Kali, the mother of Q's children."

"Okay?" more like *so what,* I respond sardonically.

"I just wanted you to know that we live together," she volunteers this information with attitude.

"I know. He told me. He tells me everything."

"Well did he tell you that we're trying to make it work? That's why he gave me your number," her tone is condescending.

"Well instead of calling me, maybe you could use this time and your energy to work it out with him. Good luck to you." I'm impassive.

"You were around my kids. Stay away from me and my family, bitch."

I hear a dial tone.

I'm instantly enraged at Qalbee because I shouldn't have to be subjected to this, but I know I can't be livid with him because I'm the one that agreed to this, believing in our love. I press the talk button on my steering wheel, state *"blue tooth audio"* then *"Love is Wicked" by Brick and Lace". I* scream every lyric through to the top of my lungs wanting the feelings I have for him to go away. As I shout to the song, I rationalize, *I can be heated that she has my number. I'm furious but I don't want to call him. I don't want him to think that I can't handle this. I know I'd go off like a mad-woman if I called him now. I just need time.*

When I make it home I shower, put on loose clothes, and light a white candle to repel negativity. I seek peace, truth, and protection—protection because I might have to hurt someone if put in the wrong predicament, and I just may need an attorney akin to Johnnie Cochran Jr. on my side. I pull out my journal and wrathfully vent.

Still upset after 30 minutes of writing, I go downstairs to my mother's hall closet and search for another candle—orange—pink—black—TURQUOISE! My mother loves candles. She lights a candle everyday and has every since I can remember. She believes that it cures her from every obstacle she experiences in life, and by the lovely life she lives, I believe in its abilities. Plus, I love the fresh, fruity, and perfume spells. I enjoy the whisper of light that sits above as it aesthetically charms my parietal lobe. I pull out the black and turquoise candles and march up the stairs. *I'll give this black one to Qalbee to augment some strength in him because he's always putting everyone, BUT ME, before himself.* I'm learning that he's actually just a push over. The turquoise one is for me so that I can dispel evil influences and *evoke that peace* the white candle hesitated to do. I have one more week here and I don't want to spend it dealing with drama.

I guess I needed to give the white candle time because with it and the turquoise one burning, I fell right to sleep. This morning I'm feeling optimistic and relaxed, and at the same time, energetic. I stretch my arms, slip on my gray Rylan nit Uggs, reach for my Juicy Couture robe that hangs on the bedpost then race down to the kitchen.

As I eat a bowl of cereal, I scan through my Facebook with my iPhone. I notice some disturbing things then log out and decide that I don't want to talk to anyone for the rest of the day. *I'll only answer my phone if Chanelle calls, merely because she has my child but, I won't accept any other calls today.* Sebastian and I leave in a week and I have two months of clothes and other baggage to pack, so the plan is to get that done today. I have my iPad singing through my portable speakers and my serene candles burning in each room as I wash, pack, and clean all morning. I take a lunch break and prepare myself a turkey sub sandwich, take pleasure in eating it and then I continue my concentrated preparations. I pick out a week's worth of clothes for both Sebastian and I and one set of toiletries for us to share then pack the rest of everything else. As a result of a prolific day, I lay pooped in my bed.

I hear the bell to the front door chime, waking me up out of my catnap. I already know who it is so I trot down the spiral stairs plush with pearl white carpet, past the red leather top table for eight in the dining area, through the contemporary festooned living room, between the Elite black 60" inch Flat Panel HDTV and black and white leather Zuri Comodo sectional, to the main door, and open it.

"Oh," I express sardonically as I roll my eyes. "Come in." I release the door and he has to catch it. "Anyone following you?" I'm sardonic. My attitude is impassable "You might not want to come in if so."

"What are you talking about? Why haven't I heard from you all day?"

I lead him upstairs to my room. He sits on my bed and I reach for the black candle that I pulled out for him last night.

"Nothing. No reason . . . just the fact that *your baby mamma* called harassing me last night."

Qalbee's beautiful brown face turns shameful grey. "Oh?" He looks down placing his right hand on his waves, rubbing down, over his face appearing to recollect. "So that's why she asked to use my phone. She told me her phone battery was out." He appears disappointed—upset—perhaps regretful. He reaches for his phone on his hip, takes it off its clip, and begins sliding through it. "I noticed that your number was deleted earlier today."

Just as I'm about to hand him the candle, a picture of Qalbee, Kali, and their sons appear.

"Wow." I shake my head. "See Comedy, I can't do this. I need more honesty, and less drama."

"Babe, she must have done all this last night."

"Yea, like the family pic she has up on Facebook like y'all together? I saw it earlier. You and her standing together in each other's arm is her profile and y'all with the kids is her cover photo. That's not cool."

He turns fuming red. "I had no idea." He hops up.

"I love you, God knows I love you . . . too much, but fix that or it's goodbye . . . and for real this time Comedy." I hand him the black candle.

He looks at the candle as if it's a weapon of mass destruction. By his dazed eyes and askance expression I know he's skeptic of what it *symbolizes* but he accepts anyway. *Qalbee and I have known each other for so long that we've had many conversations, and I'm certain he knows that it's a meaning to why I'm giving him this particular candle—though I'm sure his skepticism is by him not remembering what it* represents.

"I love you Yaya, only you."

He kisses me and I reciprocate. He hugs me, squeezing me tight, and I return the love. We stand here hugging intimately, feeling the rapid blood flowing feverishly through each other's embrace as our hearts beat with desire, desire to make this work, to monogamously commit, to wake up next to one another each and every day and connect intimately with devotion, and desire to share the rest of our lives together forever. I've never heard those words come out of Qalbee's mouth. I've waited thirteen years for those words to roll off his tongue, enter my ears, and cure my heart. Extremely engrossed emotionally, I'm caught in the moment and I take Qalbee's hands in mine, pull him on the bed, and I lie flat on my back. Qalbee engages by lying on top of me.

He whispers softly, "I love you Yaya."

Qalbee raises my cropped t-shirt over my head, reaches around and unfastens my bra, then pulls off his shirt. In unison we take our shoes and socks off then pull our pants and underwear down. Qalbee urgently begins seducing my body with his soft, moist, tongue descending from my neck down to my stomach while gently rubbing my breast. He sucks my clitoris enthusiastically as if it's a cherry seed with surplus meat. He suctions it between the roof of his mouth and the tastes buds of his tongue, savoring the flavor. Then Qalbee licks in a circular motion soothing my clitoris, and obliquely soothing the tension of my boiling blood flow. Unexpectedly, he slips his soft, wet tongue inside then licks frenziedly around savoring the smell—taste—texture—and moment while concomitantly producing secretion. I feel my sealed eyelids rapidly blink from the incalculable sensation. I moan.

Qalbee eases his tongue out then turns me on my stomach. He satisfies my inner craving by penetrating his elongated penis deep inside. My entire nervous system stimulates as his penis maneuvers profoundly with purpose triggering every sense in my body. I tremble out of control and experience aching so excruciating that I rethink my views of the electric chair—*vibration with pain isn't so bad.* I've missed Qalbee's smile, face, swag, jokes, voice of rapture, and musk for so long, and yearned for his touch since we met all over again, that his physical contact feels so jubilant that I immediately climax. *But, I wasn't ready . . . I haven't pleased Qalbee,* I whine. I urgently roll over, laying him on his back and me on him. His penis stands vertically upright, pointing to the ceiling and I sit on it. I take both his hands into mine, hold them down on the sheets above his head, restraining him then begin thrusting back and forth. The freak I never knew was in me uncontrollably rides him, driving around and around and up and down. I feel no release from him so I raucously propel. Over-stimulated again, I gush. I cry out a squealing whimper and my stamina begins failing me. Qalbee gently rests his hands on my butt, bringing me to a halt. His touch is delicate, his expression is fragile, and his passion has weakened. He had ejaculated but I was so gone by his touch that I was too numb to realize it. He sighs.

Qalbee gathers himself, as do I, then we get dressed. Qalbee reaches for the black candle then rests his right palm on my chest feeling my heart beat. He stares purposefully into my eyes and I sense that he's grateful for our time together. I tear up from being marveled by how intense our relationship has always been. I question *why the feeling won't go away even after all life's obstructions over the years and wonder if we'll work out this time* . . . but then I remember.

"Contact me when she's out your house."

I shower when Qalbee leaves and as water rinses my face I realize that I don't want him to wait until she moves out, I want him to *make her leave—we'll figure out away to see the boys often enough.* I step out of the shower, lotion my body and as I put on my Victoria Pink pajamas, I hear the chime of the doorbell. *I take it back and this is my chance to tell him*! Knowing it's Qalbee at the door, I briskly run down the stairs, past the dining area, through the living room between the flat screen HDTV and sectional, to the main door, and jerk it open. A five foot ten Caucasian female with long brunette hair and a butch stature stands at the door.

"Hi Libi, I'm Kali."

"I know who you are and you're going too far knockin on my door. You might not wanna knock on my door ever again in your life," I threaten. "Go harass yo baby daddy. He's not here." I come across as calm as possible, yet, I'm livid.

As I'm slamming the door she slides her foot in the crack.

"I'm not here to start any mess. I was hoping you could help me." She peeks her head through the crack.

"Help you . . . are you serious?" I open the crack slightly further.

"Q disrespects me. He walks around that house ignoring me."

"And, what can I do for you?" I'm aloof.

"He seems to listen to you. For some reason, he cares about what you think," she attempts to affront. "Woman to woman I was hoping you wouldn't disrespect our home together and stop calling him and stop having him out so late, for our kids' sake," she huffs as she grows frustrated exhibiting an attitude.

"He's a grown man. He will do as he pleases. Since I've known Qalbee, he has done what he pleases." *That's for sure.*

"I just thought you'd understand having a child and all. You wouldn't want to break up a happy home." She patronizes.

"It's time for you to go."

I slam the door inadvertently smashing her finger. Before I can lock it she shoves the door open almost hitting me in the face. I close my fist into an American Sign Language 'S', reach back, and punch her in her face. I hear a fracturing noise. I see shock enter Kali's face as she rests both hands on her nose protecting it. I slam the door and lock it as if I just threw out the trash. I head for the kitchen, take a bowl from the cabinet, enter the freezer, scoop a hand full of ice, and then trot upstairs to my room. I call Chanelle to see if she can have Sebastian here early tomorrow morning and things are according to plan. I slide through my iPad, search for the perfect song to dream to, immerse my knuckles into the bowl of ice then lay down for the count as I listen to "Tell Him" by Lauryn Hill.

SEBASTIAN IS IN THE back seat of my truck while Chanelle and I say our goodbyes in my parent's driveway.

"I'm proud of you for finally, after *all* these years, standing up to your heart and using your brain. If it is meant, then it will be."

"I concur." I give her a hug, "I love you girl, and I will call you when we make it."

I pull out of my parent's drive way and attempt to prepare my mind for this twelve hour drive. I can't help but think about the audacity of *that girl* . . . coming to my home—my parent's home at that. I'm not even upset at Qalbee for not being able to control his mutt. I'm actually in a better place knowing that he actually does listen to me and care about what I think. Last night when we made love, I saw that the feelings he has for me won't go away either. I now know that Qalbee actually loves me! But I will not contact him ever again. He must make this right. He must get her out of his home and he must choose me this time. He will have to find me or I will go on with my life as I did before. *Though, my heart will need time heal before I can search for a new heart because life without Comedy, is impossible to bare.* It angers me that he left me with this anticipation—*knowing he's failed me every time . . . leaving me with major doubt in our success.* Though . . . if it was meant, it would have been.

Qalbee

2012

I SPEED THROUGH EVERY green light and bang the steering wheel at the red ones as if drumming to the beat of "When I Was Your Man" by Bruno Mars, is going to change the light any faster. Subconsciously, I know I need to release this aggression before I make it home. *This Bitch done went through my phone, erased Sunshine's number, and done put pictures of us up on Facebook like we an item*, I irately grumble. I pull up to my house and negativity fills the atmosphere. In from the garage, into the kitchen, I slam the door. Heavy footsteps tread in my direction.

"Don't bring your problems home that you have with that home wreckin bitch," Kali yells with attitude coming from the living room.

I get so close up in her face that my nose touches the top of her forehead as I yell, "DON'T YOU EVER SPEAK OR EVEN UTTER *ANYTHING* ABOUT HER AGAIN!"

"WHAT ARE YOU GONNA DO Q . . . what, hit me?" her expression is snide and superior. "YO MOMMA . . ."

I grab Kali by her waist and lift her, obstructing her abuse from going any further. I carry her outside to the yard, pace back inside, and lock the door. As I check and lock every door and window of the house I hear her banging on the front door but I ignore it and begin searching for her keychain. I find them inside of her tennis shoe that lies in front of the bedroom door. I slide my house key and garage key off then throw her chain out the bedroom window into the front yard. I race to the garage and I can hear her on the other side of the metal garage door as she drives off. I gather all the boxes I have, head back inside, and begin boxing up her belongings.

THE SOUND OF BANGING at the front door wakes me from my nightmare. I peek through the blinds and it's Kali and her uncle. *Huh*, I sigh then lethargically slide out of bed. Last night I lit the black candle Yaya gave me and packed up all of Kali and the boys' things, which took me all night. Then I made Yaya another CD and wrote her a note expressing my love for her. *I'm ready to live my life with the woman I love—I want to make her my wife.*

I take my time brushing . . . gargling . . . and rinsing my mouth as Kali and her uncle bangs at the door. Then I spew out. I slide on what Yaya has me calling *swishes*, put on my blue work T-shirt, head for the living room, and open the door.

"Good . . . Thank God . . ." I express with relief. "You can help get this shit out my house," I utter to Uncle Marvin never acknowledging Kali and then I turn back into the house.

Uncle Marvin follows behind me daring not to speak a word.

"What about our boys? They're in Marv's truck," Kali speaks, sounding worried and desperate.

I bend down to get a box. "Take them to Detroit. I'm a damn good father . . . they know it, you know it, and I know it. You will no longer control and manipulate me by using my boys."

I look up at Kali for the first time and both of her eyes are swollen up like tics and are purplish black underneath. Her nose is covered with gauze bandages and it's bruised all around. Abruptly, Yaya's face comes to mind and it troubles me. I intentionally plunge Kali's box onto the floor.

"What did you do?" I accuse. "What happened Kali?" I'm outraged.

Uncle Marvin walks between us carrying a box out the door. I follow behind him, though speed past him to get to my boys. I take both of them into my arms, hug them tight, and tell them how much I love them and how nothing but death could keep me from them. I hold them in my arms for approximately 10 more minutes as Uncle Marvin continues to carry boxes out. I squeeze then kiss my boys, give Everick a high five and Xavier knuckles, then rush back inside. I grab the CD and note, my wallet and keys, and jump into my Charger. I start it up, state "blue tooth audio . . ." "Hey You, Get off My Mountain" by the Dramatics", reverse from the garage, gear in drive, press on gas, and speed up the street to my destiny.

I knock on Libiya's parent's front door and Miss Beauty answers.

"She's already gone."

Epilogue

EVERY SINCE I PULLED out of Libiya's parents' driveway twelve hours ago I have been in such a dream state thinking about how much time has passed since Libiya and I first met, and the first kiss . . . then there was the whole thing about *me being her first. I've always loved her,* I'm passionate about that . . . and now, here I am on the break of tears worried that I may lose her. I call, but there's no answer so I leave a message, *"I kicked Kali out . . . the boys are my life but you are my heart, and I can't have a life with no heartbeat and I can't go another day without you in it. I'll fly to Timbuktu if I had to, because I need you—it's that thing called love."*

My fingers twitch as I grip the steering wheel and my body trembles with concern as I cruise down US Interstate-20 East headed to Atlanta, Georgia in search for my Sunshine. I view my speedometer to check my speed because I've been going 90 miles per-hour practically the entire way. I'm good on gas because I exited 49

Fulton Industrial Blvd 10 miles back. To my right I see my exit—56A McDaniel St.

I pull up to the 4-way intersection and to my surprise I see Yaya's FJ Cruiser. I'm in the middle lane but I need to get into the right lane. I fan the lady in the white car on the right of me signaling to let me over—she gives me the go ahead. I press my gas, gear over in front of her, and see a diesel truck coming towards me full speed—we collide. I feel soreness in my nose from the airbag though more crucial, is the pain from my broken neck. I hear nothing . . . and smell nothing . . . I dimly see Yaya running towards me as I sit, leaned into the airbag unable to move. I read her lips, *'Qalbee, I love you, please stay with me . . . don't go away . . .* 'I see nothing . . . I feel nothing.

Qalbee
The Feeling

July 2002

 I ride up the road awfully angry at myself for being the sap that I am. On impulse I hit the steering wheel accidentally swerving into the passing lane. Horns beep from the lingering twelve o'clock traffic and middle fingers fly up like birds. Tears rush my cheeks and it's difficult to see as if there is a storm taking place. I wipe my eyes to see, but snot persists, oozing down my lip. I finally pull up to my apartment, though, don't want to go in. I hate that bitch. I sit in my 1998 Cutlass Supreme, my prized possession, and stare at the apartment number 225 in deep regret. After a half hour I lackadaisically climb out of my car, reluctantly stroll to the door, use my key, and grudgingly walk in. *This bitch smells me walking in this door*, I irritably complain as she walks into the living room.

"Hey honey," Kali attempts to flatter me while trying to kiss me on my cheek.

I wave my elbow in the air shrugging her away from me. "Sup," I respond, irritated, as I walk into the kitchen.

"What's up with you, and the funky attitude?" Kali presses as she follows right behind me.

"Just not today . . . not right now." My aggravation has heightened. I grab a bottle of water from the refrigerator.

"If your mother were alive she wouldn't approve of how you treat me being 3 months pregnant with your child," she instigates.

Kali knows I hate when she tries verbally abusing me by bringing up my mother. Suddenly I shove her by impulse, getting her out of my personal space.

Her snide face is now confounded.

"I didn't ask for none of this." I throw up my hands and I wanna holla—feeling like Marvin Gaye as a result of her always giving me the blues. I head for the stairs.

I shower with Yaya on my mind. I'd normally listen to Nas or JayZ as I wash up except, constant thoughts of Yaya is all my mind can mull over. I hated seeing her like that . . . delicate and defenseless . . . though she's so innately sovereign and collected, I knew she'd come out strong. Nonetheless, I still hate I put her sanguine spirit through this. I pray that this doesn't fracture her vivacious buoyancy—she's the one sunshine that keeps me smiling and laughing. I just couldn't have her settle for my troubled life.

I replay "Into the Ocean" by Blue October over and over as I lay in bed curled up in fetal position with my pillow covering my head. It's working to keep Kali out of my face but not so much for this massive migraine. My stomach is nauseated and my head's on fire. I've been lying in the position since this afternoon and by the looks of the street lights that illuminate my room through the bedroom window, it's late. I roll over, reach under my bed, feel for the bottle, open it, and take a 20 milligram capsule of Prozac. It scratches slowly down my throat, prompting me to deliberately salivate to aid it down.

When my mother died last year I had no one and my sister was just as damaged as me. We had no place to live until Craig and I finally found this apartment then Katina moved in with grandma. Craig was always working and Yaya was gone, getting on with her life. My life was on shaky grounds, concurrently affecting my job. I'd be late repeatedly, call in and miss days constantly and just simply did not care to convey anything to my supervisor . . . I didn't care about anything. Consequently, my supervisor caught on and referred me to a psychiatrist. *Why did he do that?* It only generated thoughts of Yaya and how I didn't have her in proximity to hold and talk to. I visited the psychiatrist once; got the one prescription filled, and shelved it. I hadn't taken one until Kali got pregnant . . . then when Yaya told me she was and now, after this dreadful day. I grab my phone from under my pillow, search through contacts, and press 'Sunshine'.

"Yes."

She sounds gruffly. *I feel bad.*

"Was checking on you." *I can't get the vision of you in the clinic out my mind—I hated seeing you like that.*

"Awe thanks, really . . . I'm fine . . . just nauseated from the antibiotics. A bit drowsy too."

Her voice is warm, *she's so strong. I feel even worse. I wish I were there with you* "I was thinking about you and needed to check on you," *but hearing your voice makes me face my mistakes and how much of a sap*

I am . . . and my guilt. "But I'll let you get some sleep." I recoil, not wanting to shed any obscurity.

"Thanks."

"I'll check on you tomorrow, later." So perturbed, I quickly press end. I lay the phone to my heart and close my eyes. *It's all so painful.*